WINGED REAPER

REAPER'S ASCENSION BOOK TWO

SHELLEY RUSSELL NOLAN

For Fluffybutt and Fleabite

I hovered over the twisted body of my latest client, streetlights in the large roundabout shining down on the accident scene. So young, he looked to be barely out of his teens, face oddly serene despite the carnage surrounding him. He lay on the verge of the highway leading west out of Easton. Skid marks decorated the road, motorcycle wreckage strewn for metres in all directions. No sign of another vehicle.

This late at night, it could be hours before he was discovered.

I sighed, wishing I could help him. In astral form there was nothing I could do, and even once I returned to my body, I couldn't risk exposure by notifying the authorities. In the past week I'd had more than my fair share of contact with the police, and any more would bring with it a scrutiny I couldn't afford if I was to keep my identity as a reaper secret. Nevertheless, part of me longed to call Sam, Detective Lockwood, and tell him the truth.

I shook my head, hair flowing around me as I forced thoughts of Sam and his steady hazel gaze out of my head and focused on the task at hand. I clutched the necklace that had turned me into a living reaper and called forth my client's soul. It sprang free, eager to continue on its journey, full of light and hope. A sense of contentment and goodwill swept over me as I stored the soul in my necklace, extinguishing its light. Immediately, the familiar draw of my physical body pulled me back to Chris's penthouse.

Chris Bradbury was a former reaper, would-be lover, and the man I'd sacrificed my mother's soul for.

Jonathon Grimm, the Grim Reaper, had warned me what would happen if I didn't turn Chris's soul over to him. He had promised to torture my mother's soul for an eternity if I defied him, and I had done it anyway. I'd had no choice. I couldn't give in to Grimm's demands, no matter how much I wanted to set my mother free. Too much was at stake. But that didn't make it hurt any less.

Grief choked me as I floated through the ceiling of the penthouse. My body lay on the queen sized bed in the spare room I'd been using for the last couple of days. My arms were crossed over my chest, fingertips brushing the necklace that bound me to the Underworld. I slipped into my body and waited for my senses to awaken, tears dampening my cheeks.

A crash followed by shouting met my ears and my heart rate sped up. I forced sluggish muscles to work, wrenching myself into a sitting position and throwing my legs over the side of the bed. I lurched to my feet and stumbled towards the door. Each step woke me up that little bit more and by the time I reached the hallway I was running, breath coming in gasps.

I burst into the living room.

Chris stood with his back to the wall, one of the dining room chairs held up in front of him as Professor Michael Killian thrust a knife at his chest. With one arm in a sling, Chris was still able to counter the Tr'lirian's every move. Tall and with well-built frames, they were evenly matched, neither able to gain the upper hand. Killian lunged forward and Chris again swung the chair to block him. Then Killian disappeared.

I gasped. He must have slipped into the astral plane. Unlike

Chris, I couldn't see into it when in physical form. His eyes narrowed as he tracked the professor's movements, then he pivoted at the hips and swung the chair around a scant second before Killian reappeared and thrust the knife at his chest.

I grabbed the first thing I could find, an empty glass off the dining table, and threw it at Killian. It hit his shoulder and he spun around to face me. Nostrils flaring, dark blue eyes locked on mine, he stalked towards me.

I clutched my necklace with one hand, and held the other out in front of me. 'Drop the knife or I swear I'll reap your soul.' The necklace warmed beneath my hand as it sensed my intent.

Eyes narrowed, he stopped and let the knife drop to the floor. Behind him, Chris put down the chair and scooped up the knife. Then he moved to my side.

'Are you okay?' Chris leaned in close, blue eyes concerned.

I shook my head. 'What the hell is going on here?'

'Killian's pissed we didn't let Grimm kill us and came back to do the job himself.'

My eyes widened. Killian's clan leader, Cade, had planned on using us to free his ancient enemy from Hell, or Demania as they called it, so he could kill him once and for all.

That was where Chris and I came in.

My necklace was the key that would open the doorway between the Underworld and Demania, while Chris was the bait to lure Almorthanos into the open. Unfortunately, we both had to be dead to play our parts.

'You're crazy if you think we're going to let you kill us so you can get Almorthanos out of Demania.'

Killian smoothed down his dark brown hair and straightened his suit as he frowned at me. 'I did not condemn myself to a mortal existence just to have you little brats ruin everything.'

I shook my head. 'And you have no problem with killing innocent people just to get your way?'

'Innocent.' He snorted. 'Please. You both have blood on your hands.'

I flinched, the truth of his words hitting me like a slap across the face.

'You can't blame Tyler for reaping the souls of wraiths who were trying to kill her,' said Chris, 'or for her half-brother. She did what she had to, to save lives.'

Andrew had been a serial killer, murdering women who looked like me. He'd shot Chris in the arm and shoulder and I'd been struggling with him, desperate to stop him from killing more people, when the gun he'd been holding went off. I may not have pulled the trigger, but guilt at his death still haunted me.

Killian's full lips formed a sneer. 'That may be so, but what about you? How many lives have you destroyed? Not including hers.' He pointed at me.

Chris stepped forward. 'You don't know what you're talking about.'

'I know exactly what I am talking about, but I see Tyler is unaware of the role you played in your previous life.' Killian smirked at me. 'Tell me, Tyler, was it worth it? Sacrificing your mother's soul for the man responsible for her death?'

'That's enough.' Chris grabbed Killian's arm, knife aimed at his throat, and ushered him to the front door. 'You're leaving.'

A cold shiver swept over me as I scurried after them. 'What are you talking about? My mother died in a car accident.'

Killian looked over his shoulder at me as Chris pushed him outside. 'Ask him what really happened the day your mother died.'

Chris slammed the door shut, locking it with a snap. Then he grabbed the chair he'd used as a shield and carried it to the dining table, slotting it in its place. He put down the knife and picked up the glass I'd thrown at Killian.

'I need a drink. Want one?' He disappeared into the kitchen without waiting for my answer.

I followed him. 'What was he talking about? What do you know about my mother's accident?' She'd died in a car crash when I was a baby, and Grimm had kept her soul to use against me twenty-five years later.

Chris kept his back to me as he poured a large measure of scotch into his glass. 'Forget him. He was just trying to cause trouble. He's pissed he gave up his wings for nothing. His big sacrifice is worthless if he can't get Almorthanos out of Demania.'

While I didn't doubt Killian was annoyed his plan had failed, the way Chris was avoiding my eyes set my pulse racing. 'Look at me.'

His broad shoulders stiffened as he slowly turned, glass at his lips, eyes shadowed.

'Tell me the truth. What did he mean?' I wiped sweaty palms on my jeans before crossing my arms in front of me.

'Tyler, please, you don't want to know this.'

'If you won't tell me, I am out of here.' I backed up, letting him know I meant what I said.

He set the glass on the bench and walked over to me, putting a hand on my shoulder. I pulled away, chilled by his bleak expression.

He sighed. 'Why don't we sit down?'

'No. Tell me now.'

He gave another sigh. 'I was walking home from the pub. My licence had been suspended six months earlier for drunk driving. I'd had too much to drink and could barely stand, let alone walk a straight line. I ended up in the middle of the road and your mother had to swerve to avoid hitting me. That's when she lost control of her car.'

I shook my head, nausea bubbling in the pit of my stomach. 'Andrew said it was me, my crying that caused the accident.'

'He was just a kid. I doubt he even saw me, and I was long gone before anyone else turned up.'

I covered my mouth with both hands, stifling the scream threatening to erupt.

'Tyler, I am so sorry. I never meant for it to happen. I was going to turn myself in to the police when I realised someone had died, but never got the chance.' He gave a rueful shrug. 'I got my licence back the next day and, after too many celebratory drinks at a mate's place, I lost control on a sharp bend and slammed into a lamppost. Then I wound up as Grimm's newest recruit.'

I pulled my hands away from my mouth, letting them hang at my sides. 'How long have you known it was my mother you killed?'

'I recognised your name from the news reports. I wanted to tell you, but there was so much going on; hiding from Grimm and being Lockwood's number one suspect. It never seemed like the right time.' He grabbed my hand and held tight. 'I tried to make it right. Told you I would give my life to free Grace, was willing to hand myself over to Grimm to save her soul, but you wouldn't let me.'

I tugged on my hand but he refused to release it.

'I meant it then, and I mean it now. It we can't find any other way to free her I will turn myself over to Grimm. I'll do it right now if that's what you want, just please stop looking at me like that.'

I closed my eyes, conscious of the heat of him, of the strength in his large hand. I retched, sickened to think of his hands touching me. Thank God I'd never given in to his attempts to get me into bed. Bad enough I'd let him kiss me, hold me.

He let me go and I stumbled to the sink, barely making it in time to empty my stomach. He reached over me to turn on the tap and I cupped my hands to bring water to my lips, desperate to wash away the taste of bile and betrayal. I gulped down water and then rested my head on the cool granite bench top. Chris rubbed my back and I pulled away.

'Don't touch me.' I wiped a dripping hand across my mouth, eyes wide.

'Tyler, tell me, how can I make this right?'

I held back a scream. Nothing could make this right. I had sacrificed my mother's soul for him, for the man who had killed her.

I raced to my room, grabbed my bag and threw my belongings into it. I zipped it up and headed for the door.

Chris blocked my way. 'Can we please talk about this?'

'There is nothing to talk about.' I brushed my long fringe out of my eyes and glared at him. 'You lied to me, you knew who I was all along, and you never said anything. How could you do that to me?'

'I was wrong, I see that, but I was so scared of losing you.'

I shook my head. 'You never had me to lose. And you never will. I don't want to see you ever again.' I pushed past him and strode to the front door, refusing to look back as I wrenched it open. Tears blinded me as I stabbed the call button for the elevator.

Inside, with the doors safely shut, I wiped my eyes with the back of one hand. The elevator doors opened and I hurried through the foyer. In the visitor car park, I located my Corolla and tossed my bag on the passenger seat. I drove all the way home, trying to block out the last image I had of my mother, being dragged back to the Underworld, terror in her eyes.

There had to be another way to free her soul from Grimm.

I just had to find it.

CHAPTER 2

$\mathcal{I}$ pulled into the driveway of my flat and got out of the car. I was almost at the front door when a figure stepped into view, shrouded by shadows.

I dropped my bag, ready to run. No one with good intentions would be waiting on my doorstep after midnight on a Thursday.

Then…

'What the hell?' I took a step forward.

'Hello, Tyler. My name is Emily, and I'm really sorry to just show up like this, with no warning, but I think I might be your cousin.'

I opened my mouth, too shocked to form words. She looked just like me. Same heart-shaped face, caramel skin and long black hair, though she had a blunt fringe. Even the curve of her mouth mirrored mine and her brown eyes, currently filled with hope, were eerily familiar. We could have been identical twins, let alone cousins.

I swallowed heavily. The uncanny resemblance meant she had to be a descendant of Malia, Almorthanos's sister, like me. 'Wow, yeah, from the looks of us, you could be right, Emily.'

Her face lit up and she bounced on the balls of her feet.

'Oh my God, I am so excited to meet you. I have been waiting here for hours, wondering what I would say to you and what you would say to me and if you would believe me or not, and here you are, and you do, and this is the most exciting thing to ever happen to me.' She clapped both hands to her cheeks.

I laughed. I couldn't help myself. With the week I'd had, and the night I'd just endured, it was a change to be around someone who was genuinely pleased to see me.

'How did you find me?'

'I saw your picture on the news and it blew me away. I thought I was looking at a picture of myself, but the reporter said you were Tyler Morgan, from Easton, and that your half-brother was a serial killer who killed your best friend and tried to kill you too, and I was like, whoa, that is so scary.'

I stiffened and her face fell. 'I'm so sorry, I'm such an idiot. You lived it, so you don't need to hear some stranger talking about it, even though we are cousins and...'

I put up a hand and she thankfully stopped talking. I took a deep breath and let it out slowly. I would have to get used to the notoriety that came with being in the news. 'Why don't we go inside, and you can tell me why you think we're cousins.'

She nodded and moved aside so I could unlock the door. I switched on the living room light as she scooped up a suitcase and followed me inside.

She set her suitcase by the door before taking a seat on the couch, crossing her legs at the ankles and holding her clasped hands between her knees. She looked like a chastened schoolgirl, even though I guessed she was close to my age.

I sat beside her. 'So, Emily, where did you come from and how did you figure out we were cousins?'

'Well, to be honest, at first I thought we were twins, because we look so much alike, but the reporter said you were twenty-five and I'm only twenty-three, so that ruled that out. But then I started to wonder if maybe one of us, or even both of us, had been adopted, and we were sisters at least. So I went to my parents, sure they had been lying to me all my life. And they had, but not the way I'd been thinking. It was my father who'd been adopted.' She gulped in air.

'Dad said Grandma and Grandad Wilson adopted him when he was five. Of course, I wanted to know why no one ever told me, though it explained why I didn't look anything like my cousins on the Wilson side. Not that I look like the cousins on my mother's side either. I've always been the odd one out, until now.' She gave me a quick grin.

'My mother was adopted,' I said, voice quiet. It hurt to talk about her so soon after Chris's revelation. 'She died when I was a baby.'

'Which is great. Not that she's dead. I mean that she was adopted too, because it means you are most definitely probably my cousin because my dad said he had a baby sister who was adopted into a different family. But he didn't know who took her, and never tried to find out. Which I thought was weird, I mean, if you were adopted and knew you had a biological sister somewhere, wouldn't you want to find her? But he said the Wilsons were his family and he didn't need another one.'

Emily grimaced. 'From what Dad didn't say, I think he has bad memories from before Grandma and Grandad adopted him, but I still think it's weird he never tried to find his sister. And it's really sad the adoption people let them get split up. You and I could have grown up together instead of only just finding out about each other.'

I let Emily's words wash over me. It was surreal, looking at her, listening to her fill the silence that had enveloped the flat since Sarah's death. She yawned, and I was helpless to stop myself from copying her as the late hour and little sleep hit me.

Emily giggled. 'That was cool, that we did that, like in sequence.'

Eyes watering, I nodded. 'Very cool, but I'm going to have to call it a night.'

Her eyes dropped. 'Of course. I'll get out of your way, and let you get some sleep.' She stood and fished a mobile phone out of her jeans pocket. 'I'll just call a taxi and get them to take me to a motel.' She hesitated; eyes hopeful. 'Can I come back and see you tomorrow, I mean today, after you wake up?'

'You don't have to go, you can stay here if you want,' I said, the words slipping out before I could stop them.

Her eyes lit up. 'Really? You don't mind?'

The sheer delight on her face made me feel better about my impromptu invitation. Maybe it would be good for me to not be alone on my first night back in the flat.

'Can't have my new cousin staying in a motel when I have an empty bed. Only... it was Sarah's room.' My bottom lip wobbled as I said her name and Emily scooted over and put her hand on my shoulder.

'It must be so hard for you, to lose your best friend like that. I can go to a motel if that would be easier on you, or I can sleep on the couch, whatever suits you best.'

'I don't want you to leave, or sleep on the couch. It will be good to have someone else in the flat with me.' I stood up and headed down the hallway, grabbing clean sheets out of the linen cupboard outside the bathroom, Emily at my heels. 'All Sarah's stuff is still in here,' I said as I opened the door. 'I haven't had a chance to pack it up. I guess I'll do it tomorrow, after her funeral.'

I let out a slow breath, not looking forward to saying goodbye to Sarah forever, taking little comfort from knowing I carried her soul around with me in my necklace. After Andrew had killed Sarah, Grimm had got to her, turning her against me, telling her it was my fault she was dead. He'd taught her how to become a wraith, reanimating her dead body, and sending her back to the flat to try to kill me. I'd had to reap her soul for the second time, ending her chance at rebirth, to stop him using her.

'I'll help you pack up her things, and I'd like to come to the funeral with you, too, if that's okay.'

Grateful for the distraction from my depressing train of thought, I gave Emily a watery smile. 'Thank you, but you don't have to. You didn't even know Sarah.'

'But I know you, now. Besides, we're family and that's what family is for.'

I found it hard to reconcile her idea of family with the one I'd grown up with. My father looked down on me because I'd been born a girl, and my stepmother, Rhonda, blamed me for my elder half-brother turning out to be a serial killer. Not exactly the kind of family who stuck together. I had no idea if Denise, Andrew's mother, blamed me for what he'd done, but I guess I'd be finding out soon enough. Andrew was being laid to rest on Monday.

At least, I hoped he was laid to rest. I wouldn't put it past Grimm to turn Andrew into a wraith and send him after me, although he'd need a recently dead body to stomp about in.

Emily helped me change the sheets on Sarah's bed, chatting to me the whole time, but I hardly heard a word she said. I was too busy picturing a stranger's dead body chasing me, with Andrew's soul doing the driving. The image followed me as I said good-night and sought my own bed, sure sleep would be long in coming, despite how tired I was.

Nightmares were an occupational hazard since I became a reaper, and I had a horrible feeling matters were going to get even worse in the days to come.

The sheets were tangled around my legs when I woke. I fumbled into a sitting position before switching off my alarm. Nine o'clock. The last time I'd checked, before finally falling asleep, it had been four in the morning. The urge to hit the snooze button and crawl under the covers was strong, but Sarah's funeral started in two hours and I needed every minute of it to steel myself for facing her family.

It had been hard enough the day after she'd been murdered, knowing her distraught parents thought we'd still been best friends. They'd had no idea I'd caught her in bed with my now ex-boyfriend, Logan.

I stumbled out of my room and entered the bathroom. Splashing cold water on my face, I gazed into the mirror, expecting to see my reddened and puffy eyes.

My mother stared back at me.

Was I dreaming?

I pinched myself on the forearm, blinking to clear my vision.

Mum was still there, peering out at me, mouthing words I couldn't hear. I put my hand on the mirror and her image moved closer, becoming sharper. A whisper of sound teased my ears, then became words that brought back the guilt and horror of finding out I'd sacrificed her soul for the man who'd killed her.

'Help me, Tyler, please, help me.'

'Mum… I'm so sorry.' Tears poured down my face. Her hand came up and she placed it against mine, the cold glass cutting me off from her touch.

'I don't have long, so you must listen carefully. You weakened Grimm, making it possible for me to contact you, but it won't take him long to recover. You must get me out of here before that happens. The things he'll do to me…' Her voice cracked. 'I can't take any more. It hurts so much.' She shuddered and covered her face with her hands.

I shook my head. 'I don't know how.'

'There must be a way. That reaper Grimm was searching for got away. Ask him how he did it. It's my only hope. Please, Tyler, before it's too late.'

I opened my mouth, about to tell her how Chris had gained his second chance at life, but didn't speak. I couldn't take the chance that Grimm would find out and use it to free Almorthanos. Besides, duplicating Chris's resurrection required the death of a person related to the soul. There had to be a way to free Mum that wouldn't need anyone else to die.

'I'll do what I can, I promise.'

'Hurry, Tyler,' she said, her shape blurring, 'there isn't much time.' She disappeared. I kept my hand on the mirror, sobbing, willing her to return.

'Are you okay, Tyler? Is there anything I can do?' Emily asked through the closed door.

I scrubbed my eyes and took a deep breath before I answered. 'I'll be okay, thanks. I just need a minute.'

'All right, but I'm here if you need me.'

I avoided looking at the mirror as I composed myself before exiting the bathroom. I walked into the kitchen, not sure if I was ready to face Emily but in desperate need of coffee.

I froze when I spotted her. She was wearing the same pyjamas as me, making me feel as if I'd entered one of those crazy mirror exhibitions at the show where you saw endless reflections of yourself.

Emily laughed, and I blinked to clear my head.

'I guess here's all the proof we need,' she said. 'We must be related. No DNA test required.'

I frowned. 'Do you want to do a DNA test?'

She shook her head. 'We're family, I'm one hundred percent sure of it. I don't need a stupid test to prove we're cousins.'

Her mouth dropped open and her eyes went wide. 'But if that's what you need, to be sure, I'll do it. I don't want to do anything that will make you unhappy, or have you send me away, even though I am terrified of needles.' She shuddered but lifted her chin, eyes determined. 'I'll let them jab me a hundred times if that's what you want.'

'Wouldn't want to turn you into a pin cushion. Besides, I don't need a DNA test to tell me we're related either.' If by some bizarre coincidence my mum wasn't the baby sister her dad had mentioned, her resemblance to Malia still meant we must be related in some way. I thought about mentioning that both of us were dead ringers for my mum as well, and my smile dipped. Okay, not ready to go there.

I turned away and busied myself by filling the kettle and setting it to boil. 'Coffee?'

'Yes, please.'

I made us both a cup of coffee, stirring two heaped teaspoons of sugar into mine. I took a fortifying sip, welcoming both the shot of caffeine and the sugar burst as I surveyed the meagre contents of the fridge and pantry. It had been over a week since Sarah and I had gone shopping for groceries and I'd been lucky the milk for our coffee had still been in date.

'How does toast sound?' I pulled a loaf of bread out of the

freezer and pried four slices out of the packet, laying them on a tea towel to defrost.

Emily put her mug on the table. 'Let me make breakfast. I love to cook and, I hope you don't mind, I checked out what was in the fridge earlier and you have everything I need to make omelettes. They are my breakfast specialty and you won't regret it.'

I opened my mouth to say no, appetite non-existent, but the pleading look on her face had me nodding instead. 'An omelette sounds great.'

In no time at all Emily served me a plate with a light and fluffy omelette and she'd even managed to make the toast look fancy, with trimmed edges and cut into triangles.

'Hmm. This is delicious.' I took another bite, washing it down with the fresh coffee she placed at my elbow.

Emily sat across from me and talked non-stop, telling me about her family and starting out as a veterinarian. While she talked, I ate and sipped and before I knew it my plate was empty and my second cup of coffee gone.

Emily stood and collected my dirty dishes, carrying them over to the sink.

'You cooked, I'll clean up,' I said.

'No, I'll take care of it. I'm the one that made the mess. Getting to stay here with you, help you out, is more than I hoped for by showing up unannounced on your doorstep.'

'As you said, that's what family is for.'

She jumped forward and hugged me, the squelch of the wet cloth connecting with my back making me wince and her jump back.

'Oh my God, I'm sorry. I'll wash it for you, or give you mine if you want, after I wash them of course.'

'Emily, chill out,' I said with a smile. She grinned back at me, still looking sheepish. 'It's fine. I needed to get dressed anyway.'

She nodded, keeping silent, and I left her to her dishes and headed for my room. The smile on my face died as I contemplated what I would wear to say goodbye to Sarah. We'd been friends since kindergarten, had been inseparable until last week. It didn't seem possible that she was gone forever.

After selecting a black skirt and a dark purple blouse, Sarah's favourite colour, I headed into the bathroom to apply my makeup. Mum didn't appear, and I was both disappointed and relieved. Guilt over not saving her warred with not wanting to be reminded of how badly I'd failed. But I pushed that aside to concentrate on hiding the dark circles under my eyes.

I was straightening a slight wave out of my hair when Emily joined me in the bathroom and placed a small makeup bag on the bench.

I blinked to dispel tears before they ruined all my hard work. Sarah and I had often shared the bathroom. But with Emily chattering on constantly, appearing to speak about whatever popped into her head, it was hard not to stay in the present. I was thankful for her sudden arrival in my life. With her at my side Sarah's funeral would be that little bit more bearable, I hoped.

CHAPTER 4

I wiped my hands on my skirt and looked around the crematorium's car park. Connor's car was two bays down and Dad's 4WD was on the other side of it.

'Are you ready for this?'

I managed a nod for Emily. A smile was beyond me. Then I made my way to the spacious chapel with large glass doors along both sides. A small crowd lingered in the front entrance, while others were waiting inside the chapel. A couple of the reporters from the *Easton Chronicle* were already seated, as well as Anne Porteous, my and Sarah's boss in the front office.

Greg Curtis, the sports reporter, gave me a wave. He sat next to Moira Rutherford, who would have the unenviable task of reporting on the funeral. News was news, no matter who it happened to.

I didn't recognise many of the people gathered, although I had met a lot of Sarah's relatives over the years. Her parents sat in the front row on the left, but I wasn't ready to approach them. First, I had to face my own family.

Dad, sweat darkening his blond hair and his large belly barely contained by his old sports jacket, stood beside wife number

18

three, Rhonda. Her face, as she watched us walk over, was anything but inviting. Connor, on the other hand, wore a huge grin.

'This is Emily Wilson, my new cousin. Emily, this is my father, my stepmother Rhonda, and my half-brother Connor.'

Emily smiled and held out her hand. 'Lovely to meet you all. I can't tell you how happy I was to find out I had a cousin.'

Dad sniffed and turned his back on us. Rhonda, long brown hair slicked back in a bun, crossed her arms in front of her chest and frowned down her nose at Emily. Connor stepped forward, ignoring Emily's outstretched hand, and enveloped her in a hug.

'Welcome to the family, Cuz,' he said as he lifted Emily off her toes.

Emily, cheeks flushed, laughed as he set her back on her feet. 'Thank you, Connor. I just wish I was meeting you all on a happier day.'

'Any day is happy when there's a pretty girl around,' he said, blue eyes twinkling, looking particularly handsome in his stylish suit and tie.

I elbowed him in the side. 'She's our cousin. Behave.' The deepening flush in Emily's cheeks from Connor's flirting had me frowning even more than Rhonda.

'Actually, I don't think we are related,' said Emily. 'Not technically. Tyler's mum was my aunt, so that makes us cousins. But you have a different mum, so we wouldn't be cousins, unless you can have a step-cousin.'

'I hardly think this is the time or the place to be concerning ourselves with who is related to whom,' said Rhonda in frosty tones.

Emily's face fell. 'Of course, I'm so sorry. I didn't mean to offend anyone.'

I glared at Rhonda, while patting Emily's shoulder. 'You didn't, Emily. It's fine.'

Connor grinned. 'Of course it's fine. Cousin or not, this family could do with some fresh blood.'

'Connor.' Rhonda grabbed his arm. 'It's time we took a seat.' She pulled him along with her and Dad as they entered the chapel.

I gave Emily another pat. 'Sorry. My family isn't exactly user friendly.'

She braved a smile. 'That's okay. I guess springing a new cousin on them at a funeral wasn't the best idea. Maybe I should wait in the car.'

'No way.' I took a deep breath. 'Honestly, this is going to be hard for me, saying goodbye to Sarah. I really appreciate you being here, for support.'

'Of course.' It was her turn to give me a pat. 'We do this together.'

I gave a nod, tears blurring my vision. We started to walk into the chapel but someone took hold of my arm and pulled me to one side. I looked up and met Chris's eyes. Dressed in a smart blue suit, the white sling on his left arm replaced with a more stylish black number, he looked impossibly handsome. Not that I cared.

'Tyler, we need to talk.'

I glared at him. 'I'm not interested in anything you have to say.' I tugged my arm free and walked back to Emily, ushering her into the chapel ahead of me. Most of the seats had been taken but the last row on the right was empty.

'Oh my God,' she said in a whisper as we sat down. 'That was Chris Bradbury. He is even more gorgeous in person than he is on television, and in the magazines. And that deep voice. Wow, talk about sexy. I can't believe you know him.'

I leaned in close and hissed in her ear. 'Shush. Now is not the time.'

'Sorry,' she whispered back, giving me a sheepish grin.

Someone sat down on the other side of me and I tensed, sure it would be Chris. I twisted around to tell him to get lost, and heaved a sigh of relief when I met Sam's hazel gaze. He gave me a nod and then looked over at Emily, eyebrows raised.

The undertaker requested that everyone stand and I gave Sam a shrug. I'd have to explain Emily's arrival later. Now I had to watch as Sarah's coffin was carried down the aisle, a photo of her beaming face nestled between two large arrangements of purple and white flowers on the top.

Tears streamed down my face and I swayed as grief over losing my best friend hit me all over again. Sam slid an arm around my back, holding me steady until it was time to sit down. He covered my left hand with his, thumb forming soothing circles on my wrist.

At the first words, describing Sarah and her zest for life, I leaned into Sam's side. The warmth of the body pressed into mine was the only thing keeping me from sobbing uncontrollably as Sarah's father delivered the eulogy for his only child. The grief etched on his face, the broken words, and the heartbreaking pauses as he sought to control his crying so he could finish his speech; it was all too much.

I closed my eyes and rested my head on Sam's shoulder, blocking everything out as I focused on the feel of his suit beneath my cheek and the way his shoulder rose and fell with each breath he took.

Sam nudged me some time later and helped me stand as Sarah's sobbing parents were led down the aisle. He continued to hold my hand as we waited for the front rows of mourners to exit the chapel and congregate in the front entrance. We were the last to walk out. I reluctantly released Sam's hand as I made my way over to where Sarah's parents stood accepting the condolences of those who had come to witness their daughter's farewell.

I eased myself through a gap in the crowd and Sarah's mother spotted me. Her face, already pale, went sheer white. She shook her head, mouth open but no sound emerging. She tugged on her husband's arm and he leaned in closer to her, concern on his face. She pointed at me and when he looked up I could read anger in his gaze before he took his wife's arm and they both turned their backs on me.

My breath caught in my throat and my body flushed with heat. I tried to move forward, but a hand on my arm pulled me back. Connor turned me around to face him, his expression grim.

'I wouldn't if I were you. Mum and I tried to give our condolences a minute ago and some big guy stepped in and told us we weren't welcome. Being related to Andrew makes us persona non grata.' He shrugged. 'Can't blame them, I guess.'

I backed away, avoiding the gazes of those around me as I made my way out of the crowd and sought Emily. She stood in the middle of the grassed area to the left of the chapel, face lifted to the sky, eyes closed.

She opened them when Connor and I approached, and her brow creased. 'You okay?'

I gave a sharp nod, the only response I could manage right then, and cast my eyes over the crematorium grounds as Emily and Connor made small talk.

The chapel rested on a small hill and the slopes leading down to the road were dotted with headstones marking the final resting place for Easton's dead. Ornaments, faded photographs and vases filled with flowers nestled around many of the headstones.

'Hey, Tyler,' said Connor, 'I saw you giving Bradbury the cold shoulder. Does that mean I can tell Logan you're single again? He's still keen to give it another try.'

I spun around. 'You have got to be kidding me. How could you think I would want anything to do with him, ever? The guy cheated on me.'

'Come on, he's a mate. So he made a mistake. All he wants is a chance to make it up to you.'

I glared at Connor, ready to tell him in no uncertain terms just what I thought of his mate, but Rhonda appeared and cut me off.

'Connor, we're leaving. Are you coming?'

'Nah, I think I'll keep the girls company. Get to know my new cousin.'

'She's not your cousin. She's nothing to you.'

Emily flushed and hung her head while my eyes went wide. Looking at Rhonda, the contempt in her eyes made me shiver and a shadowy image of Grimm appeared in my head. Why would I connect Rhonda to Grimm? A memory niggled at me, but it slipped away when Connor spoke.

'What's your problem, Mum? There's no need to be rude.'

Rhonda screwed up her mouth, and then heaved out a sigh as she smoothed down the skirt of her linen sheath dress. 'Look, your father and I have something we need to discuss with you. You can get to know Tyler's cousin another time.'

Connor shrugged. 'Fine. I guess I'll catch up with you later, Emily.' He nodded his head in my direction and walked off with Rhonda.

Emily still stood with her head down and I touched her lightly on the shoulder. 'Don't take it personally. Rhonda's not the nicest person at the best of times, and she's never been a fan of mine. Watching Connor flirt with you will probably give her nightmares for weeks.' Again the shadowy image of Grimm appeared, probably triggered by my mention of nightmares.

'But she's your stepmother.'

'Yeah, with an emphasis on the "step" part,' I said, with a tight smile. 'Come on, let's get out of here.' I took her arm and we walked towards the car park.

'Tyler, can I talk to you?'

I stopped and waited for Sam to stride over to us. I could see

Chris in the background, watching, and shifted position so Sam blocked my view.

Sam gave me a smile and then looked at Emily, eyebrows raised.

'This is my cousin, Emily,' I said, 'on my mother's side. She's staying with me for a while. Emily, this is Detective Sam Lockwood.'

'Nice to meet you, Emily.' He held out his hand, a warm smile on his face.

'It's nice to meet you, Detective Lockwood,' said Emily, pumping his hand. 'Wow, a detective. That must be so exciting. Catching bad guys and all that, though I guess it isn't all like it is on TV.'

'Not quite. There's more paperwork, for starters, and fewer gadgets,' Sam said, his smile widening. 'Can I have my hand back now?'

'Oh, I am so sorry.' Emily dropped his hand, a blush pinking her cheeks. She looked from me to Sam and back again. 'I'll go and wait by the car.' She fled before I had a chance to say anything.

Sam shifted his feet and ran a hand over his close-cropped brown hair. He cleared his throat, but I jumped in before he could speak.

'Thank you for your support in there.' I inclined my head towards the chapel. 'I don't think I would have got through it without you and Emily. She's been great.'

'I thought you didn't know anyone from your mother's family?'

'I didn't. Emily saw me on the news and tracked me down after finding out her dad was my mum's brother.'

His brow furrowed. 'Normally I'd warn you to be careful of any relative coming out of the woodwork, especially after you've been in the news. But from the look of her, there's no doubt she's the real deal. Still, I think you should be careful. With what you've been through, you might want to take it slowly with your new cousin.'

I hunched my shoulders. 'I better go. I have to pack up Sarah's things and deliver them to her parents. Emily is going to help me.'

Sam stepped closer, taking hold of my arm. 'I saw what happened with the Abbots. Don't take it personally. They're hurting and looking for someone to blame.'

Hard not to take it personally when two people who'd meant so much to me turned their backs on me, but I didn't say anything. They were right. I was as much to blame for Sarah's death as Andrew was.

'I also saw you with Bradbury. I take it the two of you are no longer together.'

I shot a glance at Sam, leaning towards him when I saw his hopeful expression. I caught myself, pulling my arm free, taking a step back. 'I can't do this. Not here, not now.' I fled to the car, gulping in air as I unlocked the door and slipped into my seat.

Emily climbed into the passenger seat, face red. 'I am so embarrassed, but I just got so excited to be meeting a real life detective. I swear I was not trying to hit on your boyfriend. Please don't hate me.'

'Of course I don't hate you. And Sam's not my boyfriend.'

'Really? I just thought, with you guys holding hands and you snuggling into him during the service, that he must have been your boyfriend.'

'No, no. He's a friend, kind of, and I wasn't snuggling. It was, I was… upset, and he was comforting me. That's all.'

'If you say so, but he definitely wasn't sending out a friend vibe. To me, it looked as if he was really into you. And Chris Bradbury did not look happy to see you talking to him.' She gave a sigh. 'I can't believe you got to go out with him.'

'We weren't going out, Chris and I, we just got thrown together during the murder investigation. That's kind of what happened with Sam, too,' I said, as I started the engine and backed out of the car park.

'You are so lucky to have two hot guys crushing on you. I read these romance novels, where the main character has two guys fighting over her, and it always seems so exciting.'

'Yeah, well, my life is not a romance novel.' It was more of a horror story.

Emily nodded and for the rest of the drive home, I listened as she talked about anything and everything. She kept talking as we boxed Sarah's belongings up. Then we packed them into the back of Sarah's VW. Emily drove my car while I drove the VW to Mr and Mrs Abbot's house, parking it in the driveway. I put the keys in an envelope and left them in the letterbox. Cowardly, maybe, but I thought they would prefer it that way to having me hand them over in person.

Though all I wanted to do was go home and hide under the bed, pretend that last week had been nothing but a bad dream, I stopped in at the supermarket and bought enough groceries to last the next few days. Halfway to the flat, my necklace went cold. I kept driving, unable to pull over and enter the astral plane with Emily in the car. I struggled not to react when the cold grew more intense.

'Are you okay? You've gone pale.'

I gave Emily a tight smile. 'I'm okay, just a bad headache. Think I'll have a lie down when we get home, and try to stop it from turning into a migraine.'

'You poor thing. I get bad headaches too, they're not fun. My dad does as well, so it must be a family trait, like black hair and brown eyes.'

By the time we reached the flat the skin under my necklace felt frostbitten. I must have looked pretty bad, as Emily took the keys off me, unlocked the front door and practically pushed me towards my bedroom.

'Go, lie down and get better. I'll put the groceries away.'

I didn't argue, heading straight to my room. I locked the door and lay on the bed. When I took astral form, I sighed with relief at leaving the stinging sensation behind, wishing this day was over already.

CHAPTER 5

I floated through the ceiling of a low block brick home and found a man and a woman sprawled on the lounge room floor, heads bloodied and battered. A man in a bright yellow high-visibility work shirt and dark blue pants was tugging on one end of a large leather couch. A baseball bat, blood congealing on the thickest end, was tucked under one arm.

His face was mottled, body rotting from the inside out.

Before I had time to process the presence of a wraith, I heard what sounded like a small child crying. The wraith pulled on the couch, wrenching one corner out from the wall, and stumbled backwards, dropping the bat as he lurched around in an effort to regain his balance. He scooped up the bat and hefted it over his shoulder.

A small boy huddled behind the couch. He tried to scramble over the top, ducking down when the wraith swung the bat at his head.

The bat hit the wall with a crunch, leaving blood splatters over the fading wallpaper. The wraith lurched around the exposed end of the couch and lifted the bat high.

'No.' I surged towards the wraith; hand outstretched ready to reap his soul. He spun and swung the bat at me.

I experienced a weird shivering sensation as it passed through my astral body. He swung it again and again, faster and faster, unable to do any damage but using the wind it created to keep me back. I darted to the side, making another attempt to get to him, to touch him, so I could take his soul.

I caught a glimpse of black just before a dark reaper barrelled into me. The force of its attack shoved me backwards even as it flipped over and came at me again. I dived to the left to avoid its charge. On the other side of the room, the wraith continued his attempts to get to the boy. I had to stop him, but with the dark reaper in the way I was running out of time.

I had to do something.

I roared, sending a huge psychic blast into the dark reaper, but even though the black cloud comprising its astral form thinned, it didn't stop it from ramming me and forcing me even farther away from the wraith and the little boy.

Anger towards the dark reaper and the wraith filled me as the necklace chained around my throat started to vibrate, its heartbeat resonating throughout my body. I focused on it, acting on instinct, drawing in aether, the psychic energy that coursed through every living thing. It swirled inside me, clean and powerful, and a bright light flared when I hurled it at the reaper.

The reaper shattered into thousands of pieces, glass like black shards spraying around the room. Though stunned by what I'd just done, I pulled myself together and faced the wraith.

'Run.' Psychic energy amplified my voice and the wraith staggered. But I wasn't talking to him. I risked a glance over my shoulder. The little boy was still behind the couch, curled into a ball.

I didn't want to risk shooting out another beam of aether as I had no idea if it would hurt the boy. But I could use a psychic blast. While my last attempt had sailed harmlessly through the dark reaper, it would work on the wraith's physical body. I focused on my intent, draining as much of my energy as I dared and sending it out in one concentrated burst. It hit the wraith in the abdomen and he reeled, arms windmilling as he sought to keep his balance.

'Run.'

At my second shout, the boy's head flung up, eyes wide, and he looked straight at me.

'Go.' I sent another blast of energy into the wraith, speeding up the decomposition process and forcing it away from the couch. He fell to his knees and crumbled to the floor; his body unable to rise.

As the boy darted out from behind the couch and made for the front door, the wraith detached from his host body and floated towards the man he had murdered.

I flew through the air, getting between them, blocking the wraith when he made an attempt to get to the woman. No way was I letting him get hold of another body.

I heard the front door of the house open and then slam shut.

The boy was free.

The wraith, now in a malevolent black astral form, came straight at me and I prepared to do to him what I had done to his friend. At the last second he twisted in mid-air and shot up and through the roof.

I wanted to follow the boy, to ensure he was okay, but as I hadn't reaped the souls of my two clients I was tethered. I had to hope he'd be okay until I could go and check on him. I reaped the souls of the man and woman, but I didn't place them in my necklace. Instead, one in each hand, I went in search of the boy.

I floated through the front door and was relieved to see him across the road, clasped in the arms of a young woman with red hair. His face was pressed into her shoulder and she was patting his back. A man stood next to them, eyes roaming the street while he talked on a mobile phone. I drifted closer and the light of the two souls I held got brighter.

The little boy turned his head and looked at me. His eyes filled with wonder when he saw the souls, and their light expanded to touch him. He snuggled back into the arms of the woman holding him and closed his eyes, tense little body relaxing.

I placed the two souls into my necklace and got the feeling they were content.

I was anything but.

As my astral body headed for home, I worried over what I had witnessed. The wraith had killed the two people whose souls I now carried in my necklace and tried to kill the boy as well. But why?

I arrived home and reconnected with my body, shaking as I pulled myself into a sitting position. I stumbled into the hall, thoughts racing as I reached the kitchen and switched the kettle on. I needed coffee, strong and sweet.

I'd only ever had contact with two wraiths, both of them sent to kill me by Grimm. Was he behind this latest attack? Was this his sick way of replacing the energy I'd taken from him when I'd broken the chain of souls anchoring him to the physical world? As horrible as it was, that was the only explanation that made sense.

I poured boiling water into my cup and opened the fridge in search of milk. When I closed the fridge, a yellow Post-it note fell off.

I picked it up and read the short note.

Hey Tyler,

Connor is showing me around town. Hope you don't mind. Call if you need me.

Emily.

Her mobile phone number was written neatly underneath.

I poured milk into my cup, stirred my coffee and took a sip, not sure if I liked the idea of Emily spending time with Connor. But I wasn't my cousin's keeper.

I sat at the kitchen table, the silence of the flat wrapping around me. Now would have been a good time to have Emily chattering on, distracting me from my dark thoughts. As it was, the scene I'd witnessed at the reaping played over and over in my head. I needed to know what was going on, but the only person I could talk to about this stuff was Chris and I was not going there.

The urge to talk, to discuss it with someone who knew what I was talking about and who might have valuable insights to share, was a tantalising thought. But the only other person I knew who was part of the dark world I'd been dragged into was Killian, who wanted me dead. I had no one else to talk to.

Unless…

I bolted into the bathroom, desperately hoping Mum would appear and would be able to answer all my questions. The mirror remained empty of anything but my reflection. I trudged back to the lounge room and flopped on the couch.

What was I going to do now?

My mobile phone rang and I pulled it out of my handbag. The caller ID read "Sam".

Should I answer it? Maybe hearing his voice would lift my spirits?

I hit the talk button and held the phone up to my ear. 'Hello?'

'Hey.'

I sighed, relaxing back into the couch, eyes closed. 'Hey.'

'Tough day?'

'You could say that.'

'Want to grab something to eat?'

I held my breath, wanting to say yes, not sure if it was a good idea. I had valid reasons for not getting involved with a homicide detective.

'It's just dinner, nothing else. You've got to eat, so why not do it with me? Or do you and your cousin have plans?'

'Emily's out with Connor. I don't know where they are or when they'll get back.'

'Even more reason to have dinner with me. You shouldn't be alone, not tonight.'

'Okay,' I said, surprising myself. But he was right. I did need to eat. I'd skipped too many meals as it was in the last week, and I'd need to keep my strength up to be ready to face Grimm when he came for me.

'Great. I'll pick you up in half an hour.' Sam disconnected and I stared at my phone.

Half an hour to get ready?

Seriously?

$\mathcal{I}$ climbed into Sam's car. It wasn't the unmarked one, but a sleek gold BMW. Immaculate inside, with leather upholstery and all the gadgets a tech whiz could wish for, it still had the new car smell.

'This is not what I pictured you owning,' I said with a smile.

'What did you think I'd drive?'

'A big 4WD, or a utility; something you could go off road in and get dirty.'

'I haven't got time to go off road, unless it's for work.'

'But you have time for cruising around in a BMW?'

'I got it on loan from the impound yard while my work car is at the panel beaters.'

'What happened?'

'A suspect in a homicide tried to make a break for it and rammed his motorcycle into the side of my car,' he said as if it were as commonplace as putting the bin out.

'Oh my God. You weren't hurt were you?' The thought of turning up to reap and finding Sam was to be my next client scared the hell out of me. It could happen. He was a homicide detective. He came into contact with bad people all the time.

Sam flicked a glance my way, an amused set to his mouth, hazel eyes twinkling. 'Do I look injured to you?'

Fantastic is what he looked like. My heart hadn't stopped racing from my first sight of him. I'd opened the front door at his knock and admired the way he filled out his dark blue jeans and long sleeved shirt. It was the first time I'd seen him dressed in anything other than a suit, and the casual look was a winner. I especially enjoyed walking behind him as he'd led the way to the car. He'd opened the door for me, making sure I was properly seated before shutting the door and moving around to the driver's side.

Now, as he applied the clutch and the brake, I could see his leg muscles tensing beneath the denim. He exuded an air of strength that made me feel safe and excited at the same time. I drew a shaky breath into my lungs, tearing my eyes away from his legs.

'You okay?'

I forced myself to smile and gave a nod. This was just dinner out with a friend. Not a date. I couldn't allow myself to forget that. I did not need any other complications in my life. Trying to keep Sam from finding out I was a reaper would be a major headache.

The car came to a stop and I looked out the windscreen. We were in the car park of a steakhouse. The caricature of a bucking bull adorning the saloon style wooden doors was also painted on the side of the building, along with a sign promising the best steak in town. A neon flashing bull stood next to the front doors, advertising a mechanical bull, waiting for adventurous diners.

Sam turned off the engine but made no move to exit the car, so I remained in my seat as well. He turned to face me and for once the confident and considering gaze was missing. His brow was furrowed as he looked at the flashing bull and then back to the black lace dress I was wearing.

'Guess I should have worn jeans,' I said with a wry smile. 'I didn't know where we were going, so I wasn't sure what to wear.'

'I can take you somewhere else if you like, but they really do have the best steak in town.'

'Can't wait to try it then.' I unclipped my seat belt and opened the door. By the time I manoeuvred my way out of the car, careful not to let my thigh-skimming hem rise too high, Sam was at my side. He locked the car and placed his hand at my waist, steering me towards the veranda that encircled half of the steakhouse.

With the warmth of his hand burning through the thin material of my dress, I had to keep reminding myself this was not a date. He leaned forward to open the door for me, the clean, male scent of him tantalising, making it harder to keep my distance.

That distance was tested even further when the wait staff ushered us to a table for two nestled in a corner, away from the noise and colour that centred on the mechanical bull. I had my back to the rest of the room, with nothing to distract myself from the man seated across from me. His knees brushed mine under the table as he took hold of my right hand.

'I'll just ask this once, and then I won't bring it up again. How are you holding up?'

I sniffed back automatic tears and his grip on my hand tightened.

'By a thread, I think. With everything that's happened in the past week, today was the worst. Saying goodbye to Sarah, knowing her parents hate me.' I shook my head. 'Honestly, it was easier to deal with Andrew trying to kill me.'

'It's tough. Believe me, I know. But the worst thing to do is shut yourself away and dwell on the bad things. You need to get back out in the world, and have some fun.'

I managed a smile. 'You don't expect me to have a go on the bull, do you?' I nodded over at the crowd of people whooping and yelling as someone tried their luck.

Sam's even white teeth flashed as he grinned at me. 'I think that would be too much fun, especially in a dress. You look beautiful, by the way. I like your hair down, although it would be nice if you stopped using it to hide from me.'

I gave him a rueful smile, caught ducking my head and hiding behind my long fringe. I lifted my chin and tucked my hair behind my ears. 'Better?'

'Much better. Nice to see some colour in your cheeks, too,' he said in response to the blush sweeping over them at his intent stare.

A pretty young woman appeared beside the table. 'Hi guys, I'm Maddie and I'll be your waitress for this evening. Can I get you any drinks?'

I tugged my hand out of Sam's, grateful for the interruption, and smiled at the waitress. 'Can I get a glass of white wine, please? And some water.'

'Sure. And what would you like?' She turned to Sam; pen poised over her order pad.

I glanced around the room as Sam gave his order. Maddie handed us a menu each before heading to the bar. We spent a few moments in comfortable silence as we perused the menus. Every kind of steak imaginable was on offer. I decided on a fillet mignon with vegetables and mushroom sauce on the side.

When Maddie returned with our drinks I placed my order and listened as Sam ordered an entrée platter and a large prime rib.

'Hungry?'

'Starving, and I figured you'd help me with the platter. Trust me, when it hits the table you won't be able to help yourself. But while we wait for it, you can tell me about this new cousin of yours.'

I told him about coming home and finding Emily on my doorstep, voice catching as I thought about the reason I'd fled Chris's penthouse. If Sam noticed my hesitation, he didn't mention it, and I soon got caught up in my tale. His entrée arrived and Sam urged me to try one of the spicy chicken wings.

It was delicious, and he didn't have to try hard to persuade me to taste some of the other selections on the platter.

Before I knew it, the platter was gone, I was on my second glass of wine, while Sam still nursed his first beer, and our main meals were placed in front of us. We both tucked into our food, and the conversation slowed as we ate. The noise in the rest of the steakhouse had risen as the patrons congregating around the bull continued to drink.

'Is that safe? I'd have thought getting on a mechanical bull while drunk would be against occupational health and safety.'

Sam pointed at a dispenser on the wall near the front bar. 'That thing spits out single use breathalyser units. They're not terribly accurate, but the manager insists anyone who wants to ride the bull gets tested first. Anyone over the legal driving limit can't ride. Those that pass are made to sign an indemnity form, waiving their right to sue if they get injured. Doubt it would stand up in court, but it is enough to get them a licence to sell bull rides to idiots looking for a thrill.'

'You've never had a go?'

'That's not the kind of adventure I'm interested in,' he said, with an easy smile.

'Of course, bull riding would be tame in comparison with catching bad guys. So, what kind of adventure does get your heart pumping?'

His smile vanished to be replaced with an ardent look that set my heart racing. 'Sitting here with you and trying to pretend I don't want this to be more than a night out to cheer up a friend.'

'I...' I shook my head, willing my heart beat to calm down, fighting the urge to leap across the table and into his arms. 'I can't go there, Sam. My life is so far from normal I can't even begin to think about dating.'

'Fair enough. I get that your experiences with men haven't been so great lately. I don't know what went wrong with you and Bradbury, and I don't want to know. But it's clear he hurt you even more than that Miller guy did, and I want to throttle him for that.'

My bottom lip wobbled at the compassion in his hazel eyes. 'What, no, *I told you so?*'

'Tyler, no. I just wanted to let you know I'm not going anywhere. When you're ready, I hope you'll give us a chance.'

I wished it were that simple. If I was just suffering from a broken heart, what better place to heal from it than in the arms of a man who truly cared about me? In all of this he had remained the same; a pillar of strength and honesty, and it was his honesty that forbade a relationship between us.

At the thought of disappointing him, watching as suspicion and secrets eroded his care for me, my heart really did break.

I pushed back my chair and stood. 'I have to go to the bathroom.'

I spun around, nearly colliding with the waitress collecting plates from the patrons sitting at the next table. I murmured an apology and fled to the toilets, gazing at my haunted reflection in the mirror, wanting to smash it to pieces so I could no longer see the guilt and desperation building in my eyes.

A toilet flushed and a young woman emerged from one of the cubicles. She stood at the sink next to me and washed her hands. In the mirror, I could see her frown as she took in my frozen posture and the horror-filled grimace on my face.

'Are you okay?'

I couldn't tear my eyes away from her reflection, from the death's head blotting out her features.

She was going to die.

CHAPTER 7

I bolted out of the bathroom and scanned the restaurant, looking for the threat. Instead, I caught the reflections of more death's heads. They were in the mirrored pictures lining the walls, and the glass that lined the back wall in the bar, their owners oblivious to descending doom.

So many of them.

How was this possible?

The saloon doors in the entrance slammed open and a crowd of people surged inside, lurching, staggering, mottled faces on all of them. Two brandished knives, one held a cricket bat, the other two were unarmed but just as deadly as they launched themselves at the first person they came across.

Screams and shouts of shock rang out as the rest of the patrons realised what was happening. Some leaped to the rescue of those already under attack, but most of them surged towards the back of the steakhouse, desperate to get away from the horror that threatened them.

I struggled against the tide of panicked people, trying to force my way through. If I could get to the wraiths I'd be able to reap their souls. I had to get to them before they killed someone.

Too late.

My necklace emitted a burst of cold so sharp it drove me to my knees. I struggled to stand, but the crush of people around me made it impossible. I fought to centre myself while legs jostled me from every direction. The cold in my necklace increased. I held back a moan.

Someone landed on top of me, pushing me flat to the floor, arms out in front of me. The weight on my back increased. I struggled to get my hand underneath me, to reach my necklace. Only in astral form did I have a hope of getting near the wraiths now.

My fingertips grazed a wing. I dug my nails in. I was sucked out of my body, hovering above the chaos. People were crammed into the area behind the mechanical bull, some holding bar stools and chairs in front of them. Others brandished steak knives. The wraith with the cricket bat swung at them, but a tall man in a cowboy hat blocked him with a bar stool. Another wraith was throwing anything she could get a hold of at the beleaguered patrons.

That lot were okay for now so I searched the rest of the room. Sam was wrestling with a wraith, trying to get his assailant to drop a knife. I wanted to rush to his aid but our young waitress, Maddie, was trapped by the other knife-wielding wraith. Crouched behind the front counter, she held a stack of menus above her head to fend off the wraith's attempts to stab her. He was twice her size and she wouldn't be able to hold him off much longer.

I moved to help her, but was pulled up short. I still hadn't collected the soul of whoever had died, the need to reap tethering me in place. I scanned the room, searching the scattered chairs and tables for my client. It wasn't the large woman pinning my body to the floor. She struggled to her feet; her eyes wild as she dived under a table.

I spun back around and spotted a man sprawled on the

ground in front of the long wooden bar. A woman kneeled beside him, performing CPR. I flitted over to them and reaped the dead man's soul, holding it in my hand as I launched myself at the wraith trying to kill Maddie.

He never saw me coming. I had my hand wrapped around his neck, calling forth his soul, before he could react. His body crumpled to the ground and I waited to be hit with the penalty for an illegitimate reaping, but nothing happened.

I didn't stop to wonder why. I still had four more wraiths to deal with. And they had company. Two dark reapers floated throughout the main room, waiting for someone to die so they could pounce on the soul.

I focused on my necklace, trying to form a beam of aether as I had only hours earlier so I could take them out.

My necklace's heartbeat remained dormant. Dammit. Why wasn't it working?

I'd been furious when I'd done it the first time. Maybe anger was the trigger. But though I was angry, fear for the people fighting for their lives throughout the steakhouse overwhelmed it. It was up to me to save them.

Screams came from the kitchen.

I pushed my astral form through the wall, arriving just as my necklace warned me I had another soul to reap. I had to take it before either of the dark reapers did.

A man with an apron wrapped around his middle was being held up by two young girls in waitress uniforms. A knife protruded from his chest. Three young men, also wearing the steakhouse logo on their shirts, held large pot lids up as shields. On the other side of the kitchen the wraith was plucking knives from a knife block and throwing them at the teenagers. He saw me and took off through the swinging door that led back into the restaurant, a knife still gripped in his hand.

I reaped the soul of the chef and went after the wraith.

He had the knife raised, ready to stab it into Sam's unprotected back, both dark reapers hovering above him. Sam's attention was still on the wraith in front of him. He had no idea about the threat behind him and I was too far away to get to him in time.

'Sam, behind you.' I put everything into my shout, my astral form sagging to the ground as I used up a considerable amount of psychic energy, desperate to make myself heard.

Sam spun around, dodging the blade aimed at him and kicking out with one leg. The wraith went down, knife falling from his hand. Sam threw himself backwards as the first wraith tried to take advantage of the distraction. He swung his knife at Sam, narrowly missing him.

I reaped the wraith's soul and the empty body collapsed to the ground. I turned to take care of the other wraith. He took one look at me and pulled out of the body before I could move. Twin thuds sounded as the wraiths over by the mechanical bull did the same and a collective gasp swept through the steakhouse as the survivors realised their nightmare was over.

I put the souls I had taken into my necklace and was swept into my body, shuddering as the penalty for reaping two illegitimate souls hit.

CHAPTER 8

J rolled into a ball, riding the wave of ecstasy that swept over me. Intense pleasure wiped out thought and left me a quivering mess. Seconds later agony took its place as fire lashed my body over and over again.

I could hear Sam's voice, but couldn't understand the words, or feel his hands on me as he tried to roll me over. Unable to move or respond, my muscles had constricted, holding me in place while every nerve ending I possessed screamed. After what felt like an eternity of torment, the pain ended abruptly, leaving me shaking and twitching, nerves taking a stuttering step towards life.

'Tyler, can you hear me?' Sam's concerned voice, panic beneath the husky surface, broke through the memory of pain.

I groaned and unwound my limbs, blinking blearily into Sam's worried eyes.

'Hey,' I said, voice croaky. I struggled to sit up, but his hands on my shoulders pressed me back down.

'Lie still, I need to find out where you're hurt.' He gently probed my body, searching for injuries.

I brushed his hands aside. 'It's okay. I'm okay. I just need a drink of water.'

This time he let me rise, hazel eyes cautious as he scanned my face. 'You can't be okay. I was right here, Tyler. You were in agony.'

'Someone fell on me. I'm just winded, that's all.'

'Winded?'

I nodded, dropping my eyes as he continued to stare at me. He helped me to my feet and I looked around the ransacked steak-house. Bodies littered the floor, not just the ones the wraiths had hijacked. Apart from the man whose soul I had reaped, there were three more bodies; four with the chef in the kitchen.

Three souls had been taken by the dark reapers. So many innocent people dead. Madness. Sheer madness.

Sam gripped my shoulders and turned me around to face him. With one hand he tipped up my chin. 'Look at me.'

I fought to keep my gaze steady.

'I heard you, you warned me, and I swear your voice came from behind me. But you were over here. How is that possible?'

I met his searching eyes, cursing the need to lie to him. 'It wasn't me, couldn't have been. As you said, I was over here.'

'And the people who did this...' He pointed at the bodies. 'I'm guessing you don't know anything about them, right?'

'How could I?'

Outside, sirens blared, and a small army of uniformed police officers and paramedics swarmed inside the steakhouse. Sam did not take his eyes off mine.

'They look like Sarah did, after her miraculous return from the dead. Same as the drug addict from the service station last week, and a man who killed his ex-wife and her new husband earlier today.'

'I don't know what to tell you, Sam.' The truth felt like lies on my lips, but what else could I say?

I certainly couldn't tell him I suspected Grimm needed souls to rebuild his power and in his Grim Reaper guise he fed on the souls of people who died violent deaths.

'I can't stay here.' I pulled away from Sam. 'Please, I have to go.'

Sam shook his head. 'This is a crime scene. No one can go until they've given their statement.'

I gave a short nod, begrudging the time it would take to be processed. Sam called one of his officers over and I was led to where the rest of the survivors had been herded. As I waited for my turn to make a statement, the anger I'd found so hard to call on during the attack built inside me. I would make Grimm pay for all the deaths his minions were responsible for. I gripped my necklace tightly, wishing he was in front of me now so I could blast him to smithereens.

The cold beneath my fingers registered a scant second before I was pulled into the astral plane, called to reap, my empty body falling to the ground.

I held on to my anger, sure I was being taken to another wraith attack, ready to strike the moment I arrived at the reaping. The necklace's heartbeat thrummed through my body, reassuring me that this time I would be able to deliver another annihilating blow against one of Grimm's minions.

Instead of an attack, I came to a stop and hovered over the top of a pedestrian crossing, staring down in dismay as two paramedics worked frantically to save the life of a teenage girl. Blood pooled beneath her head, the stain spreading across a white crossing marker. A young man was being held back by a police officer, tears streaming down his cheeks.

Over at the kerb rested a car with the driver's side door open. A second police officer stood beside it, talking to an elderly gentleman. The old man wrung his hands, body shaking as he looked from the girl on the ground and back to the police officer with him. 'She's going to be all right, isn't she? I wasn't going that fast, and I swear, I didn't see her. She came out of nowhere.'

The police officer's face was grave. I could tell he knew the situation was not going to have a happy ending, for anyone involved.

I wished it could be different. I wished that instead of being called to reap a young life I would get to prevent it happening. Why couldn't I have arrived just before the accident occurred and been able to stop the girl from stepping onto the crossing?

I slipped between the paramedics, anger ebbing as I determined to do whatever I could to ease her passing. Her breath came in slow, painful gasps, eyes unfocused, limbs jerking as the paramedics continued their futile efforts.

I placed a hand on her cheek and her gaze sharpened. Her eyes met mine and I gave her a watery smile as I shifted my hand to the hollow above her collarbone. She let out one last soft breath, eyes closing, lashes brushing pale cheeks, and I called her soul to me.

The golden light of her soul illuminated the astral plane. I placed it in my necklace and readied myself to return to the steakhouse, sure there would be questions asked about my sudden collapse.

But the pull of my physical body took me in the opposite direction and I tensed, fearing what I would find when I arrived at my unknown destination.

CHAPTER 9

reconnected with my body as they were wheeling me into Easton Base Hospital's emergency department. A mask covered half my face and I couldn't move my arms. I lifted my head and peered at the straps holding me down, and the cannula inserted into my left arm.

A paramedic patted my arm. 'It's okay. You're at the hospital. You're going to be fine.'

I stared up at her, surprised to recognise her as the same woman who had taken care of me after I'd been kidnapped by Andrew.

My head bounced as she wheeled the ambulance trolley over a ridge in the floor.

'I can't stay here.' At my muffled protest, she simply patted my arm once more and wheeled me around a corner. A man in hospital scrubs stepped forward and she rattled off my details to him while handing him a chart.

'Please, I have to get out of here.' They continued to talk over top of me, the mask making my words indistinct.

Now it was the nurse's turn to pat my arm. 'Won't be long

now and we'll get you settled in a bed. Just need the doctor to have a look at you first.'

I shook my head, but that made me dizzy so I settled with rocking my body from side to side.

The paramedic pressed down on my shoulders to still my motion. 'Tyler, you need to calm down. Everything is going to be okay.'

'No, I need the mask off.'

She slipped the mask off my face and I spoke in a rush. 'Please, I can't stay here. You have to untie me.'

'You're not going anywhere until a doctor has treated you.'

'I don't want to be treated. I want to leave.'

'Not happening. You collapsed. You need to stay here where we can monitor you and find out why.'

'No, I have to go now.' I couldn't stay in hospital while Grimm might have his wraiths killing innocent people. I had to stop him.

'Look, even if a doctor was willing to release you, I doubt they'd sign the discharge papers unless there was a responsible adult here to take care of you.'

My mind raced. Sam was out, and so were Dad and Rhonda. I also couldn't involve Connor or Emily in this. That left one person.

'Call Chris Bradbury. He'll come and get me; I know he will.'

The male nurse snorted. 'Sure, and I'll give George Clooney a ring while I'm at it.'

'Do it,' said the paramedic. 'She's his girlfriend.'

'What?' He stared down at me, surprise on his narrow face.

The paramedic pulled him aside and in a low murmur explained about the first time she'd treated me. Moments later, the nurse returned.

'If we call Mr Bradbury, and ask him to come to the hospital, will you promise to behave and let us treat you?'

I nodded and he produced pen and paper. I gave him Chris's

mobile number and closed my eyes, waiting for the man who'd betrayed me to arrive.

I'd been examined by a doctor and he was lecturing me on the perils of leaving the hospital when Chris barged into the examination room. His blue eyes were wild, hair mussed. He brushed past the doctor and took my hand.

'Are you okay? They wouldn't tell me anything over the phone, except that you were here and were asking for me.'

'I'm fine. Just a bit shaken up,' I said, pulling my hand free. Just because I'd called him to bail me out didn't mean I'd forgiven him.

'Miss Morgan has suffered a lapse of consciousness, and a possible concussion. I would like her to stay overnight so I can run tests to determine if there is an underlying issue causing her to pass out. I would also like to make arrangements for a counsellor to speak with her. After what she witnessed—'

Chris's eyes narrowed. 'You were at the steakhouse? Social media is going crazy with witnesses reporting they were attacked by zombies. Wraiths?'

I nodded, throat closing over as memories swamped me. I pushed them aside and met Chris's eyes. 'I have to get out of here, but they won't release me without a minder.'

'Why call me?'

'There was no one else.'

'Mr Bradbury,' said the doctor, barging in between us and peering belligerently up at Chris. 'I hope you're not planning on assisting Miss Morgan in this foolhardy plan. She needs to remain here at the hospital, for further tests.'

'I can provide Tyler with everything she needs. I will see to it that she has the best possible care, but we are leaving now.' Chris took my arm and assisted me down from the examination table.

I stood smoothing my dress while the doctor insisted I sign a waiver stating I had left the hospital against his advice. Once that was done, with Chris's hand at my elbow, I walked out of the emergency room and into the car park.

Chris didn't speak until I was seated next to him in the back of a black limousine. 'So, where am I taking you?'

'To see Killian. We need to find out how to stop more wraith attacks, and I'm hoping he has some answers to give me.'

'Is that wise? The doctor said you could be concussed. Why don't I take you back to the penthouse, and get my doctor to come and check you out?'

'There's nothing wrong with me. I was called to reap, that's all, and couldn't get away. But that doesn't matter. Five wraiths just attacked a restaurant full of people. If I hadn't been there to stop them, more innocent lives would have been lost.'

Chris stared at me in silence for a moment and then pressed a button on the arm rest and gave the limo driver the address for the motel he had booked Killian into two days earlier.

After that, he twisted around and lifted one eyebrow. 'Do you think these attacks are aimed at you?'

'If the wraiths were after me, why attack other people? I weakened Grimm, and now I think he has his wraiths out there gathering more souls for him to use.'

'What makes you think Killian can help?'

'I'm stretching, I admit, but where else can we go?'

Soon we were standing in front of the motel's reception desk. The young man on duty gave Chris a wink, before dashing both our hopes.

'Professor Killian checked out this afternoon and I'm afraid he didn't leave a forwarding address.' His smile widened as he eyed Chris.

'Mr Bradbury,' he said in almost a purr, 'if you give me your number, I'll be sure to let you know if he returns at any time.'

'Thank you,' said Chris, an easy-going smile on his handsome face, 'but that won't be necessary.' He took hold of my arm and we left the motel.

I pulled my arm free as we neared the limo parked at the kerb. Shoulders slumped, I gave a sigh and rubbed my eyes. I stumbled and would have fallen if Chris hadn't grabbed me around the waist.

'That's it. I'm taking you back to the penthouse.'

'No.' I pushed him away. 'I am not going back to your place.'

'Look at you. You're so tired you can barely stand. You need to rest.'

'Take me back to my flat then. I'll sleep better in my own bed.'

He opened his mouth to say something, but I cut him off. 'I have my cousin to look after me. I'll be fine.' He still didn't look happy so I said, 'I'll call you in the morning, and we can work out what to do next.'

Much as I hated having anything more to do with Chris, he was the only person I could discuss any of this with. I slipped into the back of the limo, closed my eyes and relaxed back in the luxurious leather seat. We were almost at the flat when I groaned.

'What's wrong?'

'I don't have my keys. My handbag must still be at the steakhouse.'

'Somehow, I don't think you'll have a problem getting your things back.' Chris pointed out the window. We were pulling up out front of the flat and there was no mistaking the police car parked in the driveway. I got out of the limo and immediately a young police officer climbed out of the patrol car and approached me.

'Miss Morgan?' She slid a sideways glance at Chris and then returned her attention to me.

'Yes.'

She held out my handbag. 'Detective Lockwood asked me to give this to you with his apologies. He'll be tied up at the scene for some time, but he will contact you tomorrow. I tried to find you at the hospital but was told you'd discharged yourself.'

I took my handbag, conscious of Chris's heavy gaze. 'Thank you. I'm sorry I kept you waiting so long.'

A smile creased her lips for a second before they firmed into a line. 'Just doing my job.' She gave a nod and then marched to her car. I stood to the side of the driveway as she backed out and then faced Chris.

'Thank you for bringing me home. You can go now.'

'Tyler…' He took a step towards me.

I backed up, a hand in front of me. 'We are not friends. I'll work with you to stop Grimm, but that's as far as it goes.'

Chris stared at me for a long moment before he turned around and went back to the limo. I entered the flat and pulled my phone out of my handbag. It showed two text messages, one missed call and a voice message from Emily. She and Connor had returned to the flat, and he'd taken her to the wine bar for dinner when they couldn't contact me. She promised to be home by ten o'clock, and hoped I was doing okay.

I checked the time. Half-past nine. The temptation to go straight to bed, curl up under the covers and pretend this had all been a bad dream was strong. But first I needed a shower to wash away the scent of death I felt sure clung to my pores.

Minutes later, drained yet clean, I slipped into my pyjamas, opened the bathroom door to let steam out, and stood in front of the mirror to brush my hair. When my mother's reflection appeared instead of mine I lost it, bursting into tears.

'Tyler, sweetheart, what's wrong?'

'Wraiths are killing people. I think it's to get Grimm more souls and I don't know how to stop him.'

She nodded. 'He's getting stronger, but he still needs more souls before he can take corporeal form again. I overheard him ordering his reapers to collect as many souls as they can. You have to get me out of here before he is back to full strength. He'll torture me, and then he'll come for you.'

'I don't know how.'

'You must. If that other reaper did it, then so can I. You just have to find a new body for me and we can be together again. I never got a chance to be a mother to you.' Her voice broke. 'Please, Tyler, free me so that I can be with you again.'

'It's not that easy.'

'I'm not asking you to kill someone for me. People die all the time. Next time you reap a woman's soul, after ending her suffering you could put my soul into her body.'

'Mum, I...'

'All I want is to be with you, to hold you in my arms. You were just a baby when I died. We have so much lost time to make up for. Find me a body, so I can live again.'

I shook my head and closed my eyes, feeling hemmed in on all sides. 'You have to be related to the body for it to work.' The second I spoke, I regretted it. Hoping I hadn't just made another monumental mistake, I opened my eyes.

Mum wore a thoughtful expression. 'So that's how he did it.'

'Promise me you will keep this to yourself. If Grimm finds out how to get Almorthanos a new body we would be in big trouble, and imagine if other reapers were to go around killing their relatives just to get a second chance at life.' It would only work for those with Tr'lirian heritage, but I thought it best not to mention that. The fewer people who knew Chris was half Tr'lirian the better.

'Of course, I won't tell a soul. But tell me, how did he know it would work?'

'It was an accident. Chris had no idea he was related to the person whose soul he was called to reap until after it happened.'

'But it did work. So that means there is hope for me.'

'I'd give you my body, in a heartbeat, but then Grimm would be able to use me to free Almorthanos and we can't let that happen.'

Mum frowned, tapping her finger against her lips. 'I don't

want you to sacrifice yourself for me. But if you could find someone else, another female relative—'

'There isn't anyone.' I bit at my bottom lip. 'And even if there was, would you really want someone else to die just so you could take over their body?'

'Of course I would never want that. I'm just saying it is a possibility. But if you don't find another way to free me from the Underworld soon, it will be too late. Grimm is getting stronger with every soul his reapers bring him. Soon he'll be even more powerful than before.'

'Do you think I don't know that?' I threw my hands in the air, sick of coming up against the same road block.

Emily stuck her head inside the bathroom. 'Tyler, are you okay? I heard shouting.'

I glanced at the mirror, but fortunately, Mum had vanished. I wouldn't have to explain to Emily why my dead mother was talking to me from the mirror.

I turned back to Emily. 'I was just talking to myself. Guess I was louder than I thought. I didn't even hear you come home.'

'I kind of sneaked in. If you were asleep, I didn't want to wake you. And if you were busy with the handsome detective, I didn't want to interrupt. I was so happy when I read your note. He seems nice, a real gentleman, and I thought a night out could be just what you needed to put a smile back on your face.'

She frowned. 'You don't look as if you had a good night. You look even more exhausted than this afternoon.'

'I'm tired, that's all. I was just about to go to bed.' I didn't want to get into an explanation of what had happened at the steak-house. I kept sneaking glances at the mirror, hoping Mum hadn't caught sight of Emily before she'd disappeared. I wasn't ready to tell her I had a cousin until I'd found another way of getting her out of the Underworld.

'Let's go into the lounge,' I said, 'and you can tell me about sight-seeing with Connor, and your night out.'

Emily gave a happy sigh and allowed me to usher her into the lounge. She sank down on the couch, a dreamy expression on her face. 'Your brother is great. He's so funny. He had me laughing the whole time.'

Uh oh. 'Connor is a big flirt. I wouldn't take him seriously.'

She blushed. 'I didn't mean it like that. He was just a lot of fun to be around. I mean, I know he's had some bad stuff happen to him too, but he seems to have put that behind him. I admire him for that, but I don't want you to think I have a thing for your brother.' She put her hands on her cheek. 'Oh my God, this is so embarrassing.'

'No, it's fine. I just wanted to warn you not to get caught up in his whole Mr Nice Guy routine. You've only known him a day and I don't want you to get hurt, that's all. But I am glad you had a good time.'

'Thanks, but he's not who I came here to see. You're my family, and I want to get to know you better.'

'There's plenty of time for that. Right now, I really do need to go to bed or I'm going to fall asleep on the couch.'

'I'm tired too. Must have been all that walking Connor and I did this afternoon.'

I pretended not to notice when she once again blushed on mentioning my half-brother's name. Having Emily fall under Connor's spell could lead to disaster.

CHAPTER 10

*D*ead bodies lay everywhere, most with souls missing, while dark reapers swirled in the astral plane above them. Wraiths lurched between the dead and as I hovered in the air one slid out of a body with a face mottled so badly the features were unrecognisable. A gun lay discarded next to the decaying corpse.

The wraith worked its way into another motionless body and forced it to sit up, a grotesque grin forming on the dead man's face as the first sign of mottling appeared.

The call to reap had come as a painful shock, ripping me out of a deep sleep with a blast of cold from my necklace so intense I was sure the skin under the necklace would never defrost. Now I understood why the call had been so strong.

The dead had blood leaking out of what I guessed were bullet holes. Wraiths continued to take over the bodies of the fallen, reanimating them, shuffling forward to form a line that stretched across the hall. On the other side of the line huddled the survivors of the initial massacre, a disco ball sending patterns of light across their terrified faces. There were no doors or windows at this end of the hall; nowhere for them to hide or escape.

Blue and pink streamers hung around the hall and balloons bobbed about on the floor. A large banner wished Amy and Jack a happy 18th Birthday.

Sprawled on the floor in front of the line of wraiths were two bodies with bullet holes between their eyes. He wore a sparkling gold hat, and for her it was a silver crown studded with pink stones.

I floated over to them, my backs to their family and friends, and faced the silent wraiths. A dozen sets of empty eyes stared back at me.

What were they waiting for?

As a group they took a step forward, some of them grabbing hold of their neighbours to steady themselves as they forced the body they had stolen to move.

I lowered myself to the floor and placed a hand on first Amy's and then Jack's throats. Tears fell down my cheeks, and I gave a start when they hardened, and shattered on the floor around me. Normally my tears were as diaphanous as my astral form, dancing around me like iridescent butterflies. I pushed my surprise aside as the twins' souls answered my call. I placed Amy's in my necklace, but kept Jack's out so I wouldn't be dragged back to my body.

The wraiths lunged forward, and I rushed towards the one closest to me. I ripped out his soul and moved on to the next one.

I could hear yelling, screams of pain and people cursing as the other wraiths attacked the partygoers, but I didn't break off my own attack.

Two, three, four wraiths fell, their souls stuffed into my necklace after each reaping. Now it was hard to separate the wraiths from their victims, as they had forced their way into the press of people. The wraiths trampled over the bodies of the fallen, showing no reaction to the blows from those they were trying to kill.

Pounding on the front doors from outside didn't appear to faze them, but it did buoy up the spirits of the remaining survivors. They rallied, creating a circle with the youngest in the middle, hiding under the present table, and the strongest on the outside. They fought with whatever they had, fists, belts, high heels, desperate to ward off the nightmares stalking them. Gifts for the unlucky twins flew through the air and slammed into the wraiths.

I harried the wraiths from behind, but could not get close enough to reap any of their souls. Two dark reapers had left their bodies when the residual psychic energy had been used up and kept darting at me from either side. One of them snatched Jack's soul out of my hand.

I harnessed my anger and clasped my necklace, focusing on its heartbeat, drawing in aether. I filled myself with it, astral body quivering as I sought to contain it. Light flared all around me as I pointed at the reaper and released a concentrated burst of energy. It hit her in the middle and she shrieked, an ear piercing scream of agony, before she exploded into thousands of shards of black glass. Jack's soul floated back to my hand and I turned around to face the rest of the wraiths, my astral form still glowing.

They broke off their attack on the survivors and stepped towards me just as the front doors of the hall burst open at my back. I ignored the newcomers, my hand still gripping my necklace. I called forth another burst of energy, bracing myself against the intense vibration in my body. I fired at the biggest wraith, squinting at the blinding light that accompanied it. His body hit the ground even as more dark glass exploded out of it to strike the wraiths on either side, shredding dead flesh.

The light emitted by my astral body faded and I struggled to keep myself in the air as I raised my hand a third time.

The bodies the wraiths had inhabited collapsed as they fled, their dark astral forms passing through the roof of the hall, roaring in anger over being forced to retreat.

I lowered my hand and sank to the floor, barely able to move as I brought Jack's soul closer to my necklace. I cast my eyes over the hall one last time.

Police with guns drawn spread themselves around the hall, checking the bodies of those they came across, while others hurried to help the living.

Sam kneeled beside the body of the wraith I had just killed, inspecting the gaping hole below his neck where the soul had exploded outwards. He used a pair of tweezers to pick up a shard of black glass and put it in an evidence bag. He spotted the remnants of my tears and rummaged among them, finding a teardrop that hadn't broken. He stared at it for a long moment before placing it in another evidence bag.

I sighed as I said his name, and his head swung around.

He looked over at where I was, brow furrowed. His eyes scanned the hall, and I held my breath lest I make another noise and betray my presence. Slowly, the weight of my diaphanous arm impossibly heavy, I placed Jack's soul in my necklace and allowed the call of my body to carry me home.

Shapes floated in the air around me and I tensed, sure they had to be dark reapers come to punish me for killing their own. But these shapes were colourless, virtually invisible as they followed me back to the flat and I sensed no menace from them. They came to a halt when I reached the flat, watching as I slipped through the roof.

I landed in my body and gasped as pure ecstasy enveloped me, setting my body on fire. I writhed on the bed, moaning as intense pleasure robbed me of thought. I shuddered as again and again my body found release; my dignity shredded.

Then came the pain. It slammed into my body and I couldn't move, couldn't cry out as it blasted my spirit into pieces.

The last thought I had, before oblivion came to claim me, was that this must be what it felt like for my mother when Grimm tortured her. I welcomed the dark, cheeks wet with tears, and didn't resist as it pulled me under.

CHAPTER 11

*S*unlight crept through a crack in the curtains. I rolled over and groaned.

My body throbbed, remnants of the penalty for reaping the souls of the wraiths lingering in the muscles and nerve endings. I struggled into a sitting position, out of breath and dishevelled.

This was more than pain. It was a deep seated weariness that had me questioning my ability to think, let alone to walk. Not that I wanted to think. I didn't want to contemplate the extra souls added to the number I would need to reap before I no longer had to be a reaper.

The deaths of the ones I had killed by channelling aether through my necklace shouldn't have added to my soul count. But, as effective as it was, the toll it took on me meant I could only use it as a last resort. I needed to come up with another way to stop them that didn't wipe me out or require me to be a reaper for the rest of eternity.

I dragged myself out of bed, stumbled down the hallway and entered the kitchen. The flat was quiet as I put the kettle on and spooned coffee and sugar into my mug. I was rummaging in the fridge for the milk when Emily appeared.

'Morning,' I said in a mumble, sprightly conversation beyond me.

Emily didn't respond. She sat at the table, hands held in front of her face, seemingly inspecting her nails. I shrugged and carried my mug over to the table and sat opposite her. I wanted food to go with my coffee but didn't feel like standing to make something. Maybe Emily would like to use some of our new groceries to whip up another delicious omelette?

I brushed aside my fringe to peer hopefully at her and she stopped staring at her nails to give me a quizzical look. 'What?'

'Nothing.' I sighed and took a sip of my coffee, relishing the caffeine and sugar hit to my sluggish system. I gulped down half the cup and forced myself to get up to fill a bowl with cereal and milk. On auto pilot, I grabbed a banana, peeled it, and then chopped it into slices before adding it to the bowl.

Emily raised her left eyebrow at me as I sat back down in front of her. 'Where is my food?'

I frowned, but pushed my bowl across the table to her and got up to make myself another bowl. She did make me breakfast the day before, so I guess it was only fair that I should return the favour.

When I returned to the table her face screwed up and her eyes narrowed. 'Surely you have something better to eat than this?'

'Sorry, but unlike you I can't whip up a feast with four ingredients or less. Cooking really isn't my thing.' I spooned cereal into my mouth.

'What is your "thing" then?'

I shook my head. 'My brain hasn't woken up yet so I'll have to get back to you on that one.' I puffed out a laugh. 'Right now I just want another ten hours' sleep and a bucket load of caffeine.'

'There is no time for sleep. I want you to take me to visit your family.'

'Seriously? After the reception Dad and Rhonda gave you yesterday I'd have thought they'd be the last people you wanted to see.' I peered at her and she dropped her gaze. Ah, maybe it wasn't Dad and Rhonda she was hoping to see. 'I doubt Connor would be there, not on a Saturday morning.'

'Connor?' Her forehead wrinkled. 'Oh, your brother.' She shook her head. 'I want to speak to your stepmother, and your father, of course. We're family, and it's important to me that I establish a closer relationship with your loved ones.'

Loved ones wasn't a term I would use to describe Dad and Rhonda, and I doubted Emily's friendly overtures would be well received, but if that was what she wanted…

'Sure, I'll take you over there. Just let me finish my breakfast and fortify myself with another cup of coffee.'

Emily pushed her untouched food across the table, slopping milk over the side of the bowl, and stood up. 'I'll get dressed.'

My eyebrows lifted as she sashayed down the hall. Instead of going into her room she went into mine, and I heard my wardrobe door being opened. I gulped down the last of my breakfast, washed it down with cold coffee, and strode to my room.

My eyes bulged. She stood in front of my wardrobe, completely naked, the white dress from the void held up in front of her body. She smiled at me. 'You don't mind if I wear this, do you?' Without waiting for an answer, she slipped it over her head.

I blinked several times as she bent down and rummaged through my collection of shoes. She tossed those she didn't want on the floor behind her and finally settled on a pair of silver stilettos.

'Perfect.' She sat on my bed to put the shoes on and then stood up. 'You'd better hurry up and get dressed, Tyler. I'll wait for you outside.'

I hurried into the hall after her, mouth hanging open. She wobbled for the first few steps, a hand on the wall steadying her. She soon got the hang of the heels and made her way confidently down the hall, hips swaying from side to side.

'Emily, are you feeling okay?'

She opened the front door and threw a sly smile over her shoulder at me. 'I've never felt more alive.' She walked outside, closing the door behind her.

I stared at the door, blinking rapidly. What had happened to my bubbly, effervescent cousin? She was acting like a completely different person. Eyes wide, I gripped the door.

What if she *was* a different person?

I ran back to my bedroom and pulled on a pair of denim shorts and a shirt. I stumbled on the pile of shoes Emily had left on the floor and slipped on a pair of flats. I bolted into the bathroom and splashed water on my face. I peered into the mirror, staring into haunted eyes with dark shadows underneath, hoping my mother would appear and dispel the horrible thought that hammered its way into my head.

She didn't appear and I swallowed heavily, willing my cereal and coffee to stay in my stomach. I struggled not to panic; to think about it rationally. If Mum had somehow managed to get her soul into Emily's body, I doubted she'd be acting like a femme fatale. And Mum wouldn't kill someone, just to get a second chance at life. So the horrible direction my thoughts had taken me had to be wrong.

I looked at the reflection of my necklace, still not used to its new shape. The black winged skull had morphed into a white winged woman's head after I'd bonded with it and used it to blast Grimm. Now that I thought about it, that hadn't been the only change. Before, whenever Mum's soul had been near, the necklace had sent tiny shocks into my body. That hadn't happened the two times she'd appeared in my mirror.

I dragged a brush through my hair and brushed my teeth, hands shaking. No, this was crazy. What I was thinking was crazy.

A sick feeling in my stomach, I grabbed my bag and keys and rushed out the door. Emily stood beside the car, running her hands up and down the sides of her body as she admired her reflection in the window. She turned as I approached.

'About time you showed up.'

I shook my head. 'Are you sure about this?' I waved a hand at the dress, the silk making it abundantly clear she wasn't wearing underwear, clinging to the hope this was all a stunt to get Connor's attention. 'If you want to convince Rhonda you're daughter-in-law material this might not be the best way to go about it.'

'She should be so lucky as to have me marry her son, but I have other plans for him.' She gave a throaty laugh. 'Don't worry, Tyler, I know exactly how to handle your stepmother.'

I gulped down my nerves as I got into my car, and waited for Emily to slide into the passenger seat. She did so with a surprising amount of hesitation, watching while I buckled my seatbelt before she did the same. But once she was secure, she tapped her fingernails on the dash.

'Hurry up and get this thing moving.'

I switched on the ignition, watching out of the corner of my eye as she gripped the dash with one hand and the armrest with the other. She sat up straight, eyes closed, as I backed out of the driveway, almost as if she was afraid of being in a car.

Oh my God.

'Mum?'

She opened her eyes and glared at me. 'Did you just call me Mum?'

I stared at her, unable to speak.

She gave a harsh laugh. 'Don't be ridiculous, Tyler. I'm not your mother.'

'But you're not Emily, are you?'

She just smirked at me; eyebrows raised.

I sucked in a breath, both relieved and horrified. 'Who are you? What have you done with Emily's soul? I want her back, now.'

'That's not the way it works. You ever want to see your little cousin again, take me to your stepmother.'

A hard knot in my stomach, I did as ordered. I didn't speak the entire way, and neither did the stranger wearing Emily's body. Whoever sat beside me had to be a relative of mine as well, but who was she? Or he?

And where was my mother's soul? Grimm must have tortured her to make her reveal the secret to getting a new body.

I gulped down tears. Emily was dead, her body taken over, and I hadn't been there to save her. It was like Sarah all over again, but this time Emily had every right to blame me for her death. If I'd kept my mouth shut, Grimm would never have come after her.

I pulled into the driveway and parked behind Rhonda's car. I turned off the engine while the person beside me fumbled at the seatbelt and the door handle. She awkwardly got out of the car and smoothed the dress down over her hips. I climbed out and followed her to the front door, convinced by the sway in her walk that she was a woman, one who revelled in her sexuality.

It was painful, and monstrous, to see my sweet and bubbly cousin's body being used this way. I wanted to rip out the impostor's soul, smash it into thousands of pieces, but first I had to find out what she had done with Emily's soul. Maybe if I could find it, I could return her to her body before this woman had a chance to do any damage.

She rapped on the front door and stood back, hands on her hips.

Rhonda opened the door and cast a disgruntled glare at me. 'What do you two want?'

'Is that any way to greet an old friend, Rallani?'

Rhonda's tanned face went pale and she sagged, gripping the door for support. The woman in Emily's body pushed past her and entered the house. Rhonda stared after her and then pulled herself up straight, her eyes meeting mine with a snap.

'You stupid bitch. What have you done?'

I took a step back, stunned by the hatred in Rhonda's eyes. She shot another glare at me and stormed inside. I followed a moment later, even more confused than before.

I stepped into the lounge and found Rhonda and the stranger facing each other. Rhonda had her arms crossed in front of her and looked guilty. The stranger was smirking, chin lifted, clearly amused by Rhonda's discomfort.

'I'll deal with you in a moment,' the stranger said to Rhonda. She sashayed over to me and grabbed my necklace, tugging on it. A loud crack came from my necklace and a burst of energy shot out of it. The air crackled, like the aftermath of a lightning strike, and she snatched her hand back.

Pain etched on her face, she cradled her hand against her chest. 'What have you done to my necklace?'

'Your necklace?'

'Oh for God's sake. You don't even know who she is, do you?' Rhonda threw her hands in the air.

'There is no God. You know that better than most, Rallani. Or do you prefer Rhonda these days.'

I stared at the pair of them. 'Will one of you please tell me what the hell is going on?'

Rhonda glared at me. 'She's Malia.'

CHAPTER 12

I sank onto the couch, staring up at the woman who had stolen Emily's body.

Malia. The Tr'lirian whose actions sparked a war among her own kind and whose remains hung around my neck.

She smirked at me. 'I should probably thank you for providing me with this new body, and the knowledge of how to get into it. Without you and your little cousin, I would have remained trapped in the Underworld with Grimm.'

'I don't understand.'

'Of course not, you thought you were talking to your mother. Poor Grace, begging to be freed, imploring her beloved daughter to come up with a way for her to escape Grimm's evil clutches.' Malia wore a cruel smile. 'Grimm never had your mother's soul. It was me all along.'

I shook my head, hands gripping the cushion beneath me. 'That's not possible.'

'Did you really think your mother would be able to contact you from the Underworld without Grimm's help?' She stalked across the lounge and glared at me, hands on her hips.

'I want that necklace. It's part of me, and I didn't spend my last miserable years on Earth filling it with power so you could use it to defy me. Give it back.' She reached out to grab it again, and this time the shockwave sent her reeling. She landed on her butt and scrambled to her feet, face red, hands curled into fists.

'What have you done to my necklace? It responded to me in the Underworld. I felt it. But ever since it turned white I've felt nothing. What did you do?'

I stood up. 'I guess it decided it didn't like you anymore.' I stepped towards her, one hand on my necklace, the other reaching for Malia. 'But it likes me and I can send you back to the Underworld anytime I want.'

Nostrils flaring, she did not back away. 'If you reap my soul your cousin's body will die and there'll be nothing for her to come back to.'

I glared at her, wanting so badly to reap her soul. But I wouldn't do it. Not while there was still a chance of saving Emily.

Malia smirked when I let go of my necklace and she pointed at it. 'I will get that back, as soon as I work out what you did to make it turn against me. But that can wait until it's time to free my brother. First, we need to find him a new body.' She licked her lips and faced Rhonda. 'That's where you come in. Well, your son, actually.'

Rhonda went pale and it was her turn to take a seat. She stared up at Malia, eyes wide. 'No. Not Connor. Please don't take my son.'

I grabbed Malia's arm and spun her around to face me. 'Are you crazy? There's no way I'm letting you put Almorthanos's soul in Connor's body. Besides, the body has to be related for it to work.'

Malia patted my cheek. 'Don't worry, dear, everything will work out fine.'

I jerked my head back, stung by her motherly tone. 'Don't touch me.'

Malia ignored my anger. She looked over at Rhonda. 'Are you going to tell her or will I?'

She didn't wait for Rhonda to respond. She tossed back her hair and sneered at me. 'Your half-brother has more Tr'lirian in him than you do. Rallani is a full blooded Tr'lirian, as well as being my cousin. So Connor's body is perfectly suitable for housing my brother's soul.'

I shook my head. 'No, that's not possible. Rhonda, tell me she's lying. Tell me you're not a Tr'lirian.'

Rhonda's nostrils flared as she got to her feet. She didn't look at me, too busy towering over Malia. 'We may be cousins but I have given enough to Almorthanos's cause. You cannot have Connor.'

'You will do as you are told, Rallani. You failed us once and were punished for it. We will not be so lenient if you defy us now.'

'Lenient,' Rhonda scoffed. 'You forced me to marry a man I detested. Connor is the only good thing to come out of this marriage and I won't lose him.'

'Hold on, are you saying they made you marry my dad?'

Rhonda gave me a sharp nod.

Malia smirked. 'Rallani was supposed to watch over Grace Morgan, and befriend her. But your mother died before we recovered my necklace. So Rallani was ordered to keep an even closer eye on you, and the best way for her to do that was from your father's bed.'

My eyes sought Rhonda's, and a dark memory fell into place. 'Last week, after Andrew kidnapped us, you said something about Grimm.'

Rhonda glared at me. 'I told you I'd save Grimm the trouble of killing you if you put Connor in danger again. And here we are.'

'I thought it was a bad dream.'

'This is worse than a bad dream. Do you realise what you've done? Do you?'

'I didn't ask for any of this.'

Malia laughed. 'Don't worry. Your pain will be short-lived. As soon as we have Connor, you will die and Almorthanos will be reborn.'

'You are not taking Connor.' I sidestepped Rhonda and glared at Malia.

'Until we get what we want, more people will die. Grimm's wraiths are everywhere. Every town. Every city. People will suffer the most gruesome of deaths, deaths you could prevent if you and Connor hand yourselves over to us. Two lives, in exchange for thousands.'

'No, there must be another way, another body you could have. Not my Connor.' Rhonda kneeled in front of Malia, tears streaming down her face. 'Please, Malia. I have done everything you ever asked of me. I gave up my wings and my immortality, and chained myself to a man I hated. Don't take my son.'

'Ah, Rallani,' said Malia, tapping Rhonda on the forehead, 'if you truly had done everything I asked of you, Grace would still be alive and your precious son would not exist.'

Rhonda scrambled to her feet, desperation in her eyes. She picked up the lamp table from beside Dad's recliner and advanced on Malia. 'I won't let you kill my son.'

I scooted in front of Malia, 'Rhonda, no. Don't hurt her.'

'Are you crazy? She wants to kill Connor, and you. Why would you protect her?'

'I'm not protecting Malia. I'm protecting Emily. That's her body.'

'Then get Malia out of it. Reap her soul. Kill her. You have to do something.'

'I can't reap Malia's soul. Emily's body will die if I do, and we'll be no closer to saving Connor.'

Rhonda lowered the table. 'Promise me you won't let them have Connor.'

I nodded. 'I swear I won't let them have him.' Malia and Grimm had already taken too much from me. I would save Connor, if it was the last thing I ever did.

'How touching, and so very futile. There is no other way. You and your brother are going to die.'

I heard the sneer in Malia's voice as I turned around to face her, fists clenched. 'I may not be able to kill you, and I may not know all the things my necklace is capable of, but I'm a fast learner. You'd be surprised by what I can do with this.' I tapped the necklace and took a step towards her. 'I could rip your soul right out of Emily's body and shatter it into thousands of pieces.'

She laughed; a derisive cackle that sent chills down my spine. 'I just heard you tell Rallani that you won't hurt me, too scared your precious cousin's body would be irreparably damaged.'

'I can always change my mind, especially if I lose all hope of getting Emily back.'

'You would not dare.'

'Try me.' I took a step towards her, making sure every ounce of hatred I bore her showed on my face. 'If you want to keep your soul intact, you need to work with me.'

Malia's eyes narrowed. 'What do you want?'

I swallowed down my hope, not wanting her to see how desperate I was. 'I want to see Emily. I need to know her soul is safe, that Grimm isn't torturing her or using her to increase his power.'

Malia's tilted her head back, nostrils flaring. 'Impossible. If we let you near her you'll try to kick me out of her body and put her soul back in.'

'All I have is your word she's safe. If you don't give me proof of life, then that means she's gone forever and there's no point letting her body live. You have twenty-four hours to show her to me or I'll find you and kill you, for good this time.' I put a hand on my necklace to emphasise the threat.

Malia took a step back. 'Fine. I will arrange for you to see Emily.'

'While you're doing that, you can tell Grimm his wraiths are not to take another life.'

She shook her head. 'I have no control over Grimm, and nothing I say will stop him from replenishing his supply of souls. You weakened him, threatened his control of the Underworld, and he is determined never to be made a fool of again.' She smirked at me. 'Any deaths at the hands of his wraiths are on your head, not mine.'

Stomach clenching at the truth of her words, I grasped at straws. 'Isn't Almorthanos his master? Get your brother to order Grimm to stop killing people.'

'It doesn't work that way. You want Almorthanos to rein Grimm in, let him out of Demania. Otherwise, this negotiation is over.' Malia looked over at Rhonda. 'I want you to contact Talaom. He is needed to assist my re-entry to this world. It has changed greatly in the centuries I've been locked in the Under-world and I need to gather our forces. Almorthanos is keen to meet Cade in battle once more.'

Rhonda snatched up the phone and punched in a series of numbers. Mouth set in a grimace, she rattled off a string of words in a language I'd never heard before. Her expression soured even further as she listened to the response.

She hung up the phone and glared at Malia. 'He'll be here in five minutes. You can wait for him outside. I don't want you in my house a second longer.'

'Ah, Rallani, this anger you bear concerns me. Surely the rebirth of the Davilian Clan is worth the life of your son. Once Almorthanos has defeated Cade's forces, we can return to Angellin and live as gods again. You are still young enough to bear more sons, if that is your wish.' Malia licked her lips and stroked her stomach. 'I certainly plan on creating more daughters to ensure I have a suitable body to replace this one when it is no longer young and attractive.'

I gasped, stunned both by her callousness and her complete faith she would be keeping Emily's body.

'No need to look so shocked, Tyler. I'm merely being practical. Without wings, I am not immortal. But now that I know how to get a new body there is no reason I cannot live forever.'

Malia's smile sent shudders through my body. I stormed over to the door and wrenched it open. 'Get out.'

She sashayed past me. The temptation to rip her soul out of Emily's body was so strong I gripped the edge of the door to keep from doing so. Malia was a monster, but I couldn't kill her and she knew it. As long as Grimm had Emily's soul, my hands were tied.

'Twenty-four hours, Malia. If anything has happened to Emily's soul, I'll do everything in my power to make sure your precious clan dies with you.'

Her back stiffened, but she didn't look back. A white sedan pulled up at the kerb and a tall, well-built man with black hair hopped out of the driver's seat and rushed around to open the passenger door for her. I watched him, a wave of familiarity sweeping over me as he bowed his head while Malia spoke to him. She climbed inside the car and he gently closed her door before returning to the driver's side. Seconds later, Malia gave me a wave as they drove off.

I went back into the lounge room. Rhonda sat on the couch, staring at the blank television screen, despair etched on her face. She looked up at me and the despair was replaced by anger.

'This is your fault. Connor is going to die because of you.'

I shook my head. 'You do not get to blame me for all of this. I screwed up, I know, but maybe if you hadn't lied to me my entire life things would be different now. You're the one who put Connor in danger when you didn't tell me about Grimm and Malia and their plans for me.'

Rhonda's shoulders slumped. 'You were doomed the moment your mother died. Nothing I could have said would have changed that.'

'That may be so, but if I'd known, I wouldn't have let Grimm put this around my neck.' I slapped my hand against the necklace. 'And I wouldn't have agreed to be a reaper and I wouldn't have discovered how a soul could bring a dead body back to life. Malia wouldn't have been able to take Emily's body. She would never even know she existed, and Connor would be safe.'

My entire life had been built on lies and Rhonda sat there looking at me as if I was the monster. I forced myself to take a deep breath, and another, as I relaxed my hands and unclenched my jaw. I couldn't change the past, no matter how much I wanted to. I had to work with the facts as they stood.

After another calming breath, I took a seat opposite Rhonda. 'Tell me everything you know about Grimm and Malia. There has to be a way to stop them, and we're going to find it.'

Rhonda looked at me as though I was crazy. 'You want to go up against the Grim Reaper?'

'I already have.' I shrugged.

'And look how well that turned out. I saw the news this morning. Wraiths are killing people all over Easton. Some crackpots are calling it the zombie apocalypse. And you heard what Malia said; Grimm can have his wraiths killing people all over the world just like that.' She snapped her fingers. 'Because of you he's focusing on Easton, but if you threaten his supply of souls he'll be sure to branch out.'

'We need to stop the wraiths from killing more people. Is there a way we can block them from the astral plane, and trap them in the Underworld?'

Rhonda shook her head. 'Grimm has complete control of the Underworld, and all the souls in it. As for the astral plane, there's no way to block access to it that I know of.'

'So we have to get to Grimm, if he's the key.' My stomach churned at the thought of facing him again, but I pushed my fear down. 'What are his weaknesses? I know he gets his strength from souls, but cutting him off from them only weakens him, it doesn't kill him. There must be something; some way to stop him.'

'Grimm can have all the souls he wants as far as I'm concerned. I'm only interested in saving Connor.'

I wanted to shake her. 'Don't you get it? Connor will never be safe. None of us will, unless we can stop Grimm and Malia. You heard her. If Almorthanos gets out of Demania and into a new body, they're going to restart the war with Cade. Even if they don't take his body, do you really think Malia and Almorthanos will let you and Connor live in peace?'

She frowned at me. 'Fine, we need to stop Grimm's wraiths. But that's easier said than done.'

'That guy who picked Malia up, Talaom, is he a Tr'lirian as well?'

'Yes. After your mother died he was ordered to give up his wings to help me keep an eye on you.'

I frowned. 'He looked familiar.'

'He should do. He's spent much of the last twenty-five years following you around.'

A shiver swept over me at the thought of a stranger's eyes watching me without my knowledge. Like Killian, he'd be able to slip into the astral plane at any time to avoid detection. So could Rhonda.

My eyes widened. 'That's how you always knew when I'd done something wrong. You or this Talaom were watching me from the astral plane.'

She stiffened. 'What are you talking about?'

'You're a full blooded Tr'lirian. I know you can still slip into the astral plane even though you don't have wings anymore.'

'Who told you?' Rhonda's nostrils flared.

'It doesn't matter how I know.' I didn't want to explain about Killian, or that Chris could see into the astral plane, not sure how far I could trust her. 'Are there more of you, living among us, who won't want to follow along with Malia's and Almorthanos's plans? And what about the ones who are still immortal, where are they?'

Rhonda shrugged. 'As far as I know, six more of our clan were persuaded to give up their wings to enable them to live in Easton. The rest of our clan still resides in Angellin, but you'll find no help there. They are forced to endure humiliation and deprivation under Cade's leadership. If Almorthanos rises from Demania they will flock to the physical world to join him.'

I shook my head, picturing hundreds of winged Tr'lirians descending on Easton and the havoc that would cause. Unlike those without wings, who were only able to access the astral plane, they would be able to travel to them all and would still be immortal. 'We can't let that happen.'

'I don't see how we can stop it.' Rhonda stood up. 'But I can't just sit around waiting for them to steal my son away from me. I have to find Connor.'

I nodded and got up as well. Connor needed to know the danger he was in. I was just glad I wouldn't be the one to tell him. That was his mother's job.

Rhonda got her handbag from the kitchen, but before we could leave, the front door opened and Dad walked in. He wore his usual frown as he stomped over to his armchair and sank into it.

'Rhonda, I'm hungry; go get me something to eat.' He didn't even look at her, too busy glaring at me. 'What are you doing here, girl?'

I didn't get a chance to reply. Rhonda planted herself in front of Dad's chair, bag slung over her shoulder, arms crossed in front of her chest. 'You want something to eat, go get it yourself. I'm done being your slave.'

The shock on Dad's face was almost comical. He opened his mouth and spluttered as he attempted to spit out words. He cleared his throat and had another go. 'Here now, what's all this rubbish you're talking, woman? Is this some kind of joke?'

He scrambled out of his chair and shook a fist at me. 'Is this your doing, girl? Some silly prank you've got my wife involved in, is it? Well, it's not funny and you can stop it right now.'

Rhonda, a satisfied smirk on her lips, said, 'as of this moment I'm no longer your wife. You're nothing but a chauvinistic bully and I've had enough of you. I'm leaving.'

Understanding followed by anger crossed Dad's face. He lunged forward and grabbed Rhonda's arm. 'Don't be stupid. You're nothing without me. You have nothing. The house, the car, everything; it's all in my name. You've got nowhere else to go.'

'That's where you're wrong. I'm moving in with Tyler.' She wrenched her arm free and smiled at me. 'You can entertain your father while I pack.' She strode from the room, moving with a spring in her step.

I watched her disappear down the hall and into the bedroom she had shared with my dad for the last twenty-four years. I wasn't sure what shocked me more; finding out Rhonda was a Tr'lirian or watching her walk out on Dad. A hard shove sent my head spinning and I scrambled backwards, out of Dad's reach.

'What have you done to my wife?'

'I didn't do anything to her.'

'Of course you bloody well did. She was normal when I left this morning. Now look at her. You've gone and filled her head with nonsense, and I won't have it. You hear? Go find your mother and make her see sense.'

I took a deep breath, squared my shoulders. 'She's not my mother, and you're the one who needs to talk to her. Not me.'

Maybe he could talk her out of her insane plan to move in with me. No way did I want to be sharing the flat with my step-mother, even if I understood why she didn't want to live with Dad any longer.

Face red, Dad roared at me. 'Don't you take that tone with me, girl. She's your mother if I say she is.'

I stood my ground, refusing to be cowed even though I had

never seen him this angry. The veins in his temples stood out like purple snakes, emphasising how red his face had got.

'My name is Tyler, not girl, and I already have a mother.' I let out my breath, fighting the urge to grin, euphoric to be standing up to him.

Dad sneered as he loomed over me, trying to intimidate me into backing down. 'You killed your mother and your brother too, after turning him into a psycho.'

Heat blazed inside me. 'That's it. I've had it with being the scapegoat for everything that has gone wrong in this family. I did not kill Mum. She died in a car accident, and it was not my fault Andrew got himself killed.'

'Now you listen here–'

'No.' I poked him in the chest, forcing him to take a step back. 'It's your turn to listen. You want someone to blame for Andrew, look in a mirror. You treated him even worse than you did me, just because he didn't fit your image of the perfect son. I'm not saying you turned him into a monster; he was obviously sick for a long time before he started killing people, but you didn't help. Maybe if he'd felt loved when he was a child, and if his mum hadn't abandoned him, he wouldn't have turned out so bad.'

'How dare you talk to me like that?' His breath was coming in gasps.

'Why not? It's how you talk to everybody else.'

'Get out. Get out of my house.' He shoved me and I stumbled backwards. I dodged a second shove as I scooped up my handbag. 'You're not welcome here. You're not my daughter. I disown you.'

I retreated to the door. 'Andrew's dead, Rhonda's leaving you, and you disowned me years ago. One of these days Connor will realise what kind of man you are and turn his back on you too. Or worse, he'll turn out just like you and ruin even more lives.'

'Get out.'

His roar pushed me through the doorway and I ran to my car, hands shaking as I unlocked it. I wanted to drive off, to just start the engine and keep driving until I ran out of petrol. But as much as I disliked her, I couldn't leave Rhonda stranded. I sat in the car and waited for her to come out of the house I had grown up in, the house I would be happy to never set foot in again.

I was done trying to make Dad like me, to make him proud and to have him accept me as an equal. He was never going to change, but I had to. Connor, Emily, and even Rhonda; they depended on me to save them from Malia and Grimm.

It was time for Daddy's neglected little girl to grow up.

CHAPTER 15

Rhonda emerged from the house lugging two suitcases. Dad watched on from the doorway as I got out and helped her put one in the boot and one in the back seat. Rhonda didn't spare him a glance as she got in the car, but I did and squashed the momentary flash of pity at the forlorn figure he cut. Shoulders sagging, all his bluster gone, he didn't move as we backed out of the driveway and out of his life.

'Finally, I'm free.' Rhonda reached up and pulled her hair out of its tight ponytail. She tossed her head from side to side and let her hair tumble around her face. I blinked, surprised by how much younger she looked with her hair down. She glanced over at me.

'What?'

I shook my head. 'Where do you want me to take you?'

'To your flat, of course.'

'Wouldn't you feel more comfortable somewhere else, like with Connor?' I asked, trying not to show how much I wanted her to say yes.

Rhonda wrinkled her nose and gave a carefree laugh. 'Connor wouldn't want me cramping his style, and neither would his housemates. And I certainly don't want to stay with a bunch of young men, who'd no doubt expect me to cook and clean for them. It would be worse than living with your father.'

I snorted. 'Seriously, if that's your excuse I don't buy it.'

She rolled her eyes at me. 'Fine, if you want the truth, here it is. I don't like you and I also don't think you have what it takes to keep Connor safe, but you're the only hope I have. So I'm going to go where you go, and make sure that when Grimm and Malia tear you down you don't take my son with you.'

'Thanks for the vote of confidence.'

She raised her eyebrows. 'What have I got to be confident about? You let Malia trick you into telling her how to get a new body, practically handed your cousin to her on a plate, and endangered Connor in the process.'

'And maybe none of that would have happened if you hadn't kept what you knew to yourself.' I wasn't going to be Dad's scapegoat, and no way in hell was I going to be hers.

She tossed her head. 'It doesn't matter now. What's done is done and unless you find a way out of the mess you landed us all in, you're going to die. Grimm will make you release Almorthanos from Demania and then he'll come for Connor.'

'So, help me. Tell me everything you know about this necklace and how I can use it to stop them.'

'Fine, but I doubt it will do you any good.'

I pulled into the driveway of the flat and helped Rhonda carry her suitcases into the spare room. Emily's stuff was strewn all over the place and I carefully packed it in her suitcase, hoping one day soon I would get to return it.

I carried Emily's suitcase into my room and stashed it in the back of the wardrobe. I tossed the shoes Malia had left on the floor back in the bottom of the wardrobe and shut the door. Not so easy to shut out the memories. Emily had been in my life for only a short time, but she'd made a big impression, lightening my heart with her constant chatter and good nature.

What if I couldn't get her back? How could I face her parents and tell them I had let a bitch like Malia take over her body?

I couldn't tell them, not the truth, and I hoped it wouldn't come to me having to come up with yet another lie to explain to Emily's parents why their daughter was never coming home.

I trudged into the kitchen and found Rhonda making herself at home. She was rummaging through the cupboards, looking for a glass to go with the bottle of white wine she'd found in the fridge.

'Isn't it a little early in the day to start drinking?'

'It's never too early. How else do you think I managed to stay with your father for so long?' She found my wine glasses, filled one to the brim and downed half of it in one gulp before topping it up again. Then she turned to me. 'Want one?'

'No, thanks. I prefer to keep a clear head while facing the end of the world as we know it.' I sat at the table as she brought the bottle over and joined me.

'I'd have thought that was the best excuse to start drinking, and never stop.'

'Do you want to find a way to protect Connor or not?'

'Of course I do. But I'm realistic enough to know I'm on the losing team.' She saluted me with her glass before taking another gulp.

'Rhonda.' I slapped my hand on the table.

She emptied her glass, refilled it, and put it on the table in front of her. 'Fine, here's what I know. After Malia was made mortal, it became her life's mission to get her wings back. She hated the thought of dying. She had all of us scouring the world for any tales of magic, shamans, witchdoctors; anyone she thought might be of use to her. When we found a possible candidate she would travel through the astral plane to visit them, and persuade them to spill their secrets.'

Rhonda took a long swallow of wine, grimacing as if it tasted bad. 'Not everyone was keen to share and Malia quickly discovered seducing them got better results. That's how your family line was conceived, so you can thank her search for power for your existence.'

It was my turn to grimace and Rhonda gave me another salute with her now empty glass before she poured the last of the bottle into it.

'Anyway, one of the shamans taught Malia how to imbue her body with aether, which was supposed to make her live forever. It didn't work out that way. She died at a very bitter old age and all the power she had hoarded was fused into your necklace when her body was cremated. It didn't look anything like the way it does now.'

'It changed after I used it against Grimm.'

'Malia was furious it no longer responded to her, wasn't she?' Rhonda wore a satisfied smirk. 'In fact, I'd say she was even more furious than when she found out she couldn't use it to bring herself back to life. One of her pet Tr'lirians finally found it and delivered it to her in the Underworld several weeks ago, and she was not happy to find out it wouldn't work for her. Then she had to wait until Grimm had one of his wraiths prepped to kill you.'

I shook myself, dispelling the horror of the night I'd been murdered and focused on Rhonda, frowning as I considered her words.

'Malia didn't have a body to go back to. Why did she think the necklace would bring her back to life? And I thought it was only supposed to work for her eldest female descendant.' Me.

Even then, from what Chris had told me, it would only resurrect me if no one took it from my body before the power had time to kick in.

'Grimm controls everything in the Underworld. He made her a body out of nether that looked and felt as real as you or I. They thought that as the necklace had come from her original body it would bypass the whole descendant thing. But the necklace wouldn't fasten around her neck. So they decided to kill you, to see if it would work. Bet they're regretting that now, along with their decision to get you to find Grimm's missing reaper before they got you to release Almorthanos.'

Rhonda double checked the empty bottle of wine. 'Got anything else to drink?'

Someone pounding on the front door saved me from answering.

'What the bloody hell is going on?' Connor pushed past me when I opened the door. 'Dad said you stole Mum.'

'Hello to you, too,' I said as he marched over to the table.

'Connor, my darling son. How lovely of you to join us.'

'Have you been drinking?' Connor scowled down at her and then turned his displeasure on me. 'Did you get her drunk?'

'She did that on her own, and I'll let her tell you all about it.' I scooted into the lounge, grabbed my phone, keys, and handbag and raced outside before either of them could stop me.

'Damn.' Connor's car was parked behind my Corolla. I wasn't going anywhere, not by car at least. But no way was I going to stay here and get dragged into Rhonda's mess. She could fill Connor in on all the gory details without any help from me.

I pulled my phone out of my bag and started to dial Chris's number.

'Oh no.' I stared at the gold BMW that pulled up at the kerb, with Sam behind the wheel. I stuffed my phone back into my bag and took several deep breaths as he got out of the car and strode towards me. He had sunglasses on so I couldn't gauge his thoughts, but his purposeful movements and tense shoulders suggested this wasn't a social call.

'We need to talk.'

'Now is really not a good time.' I fiddled with my handbag, deliberately letting my fringe slide over half my face. 'I'm in the middle of a family crisis.'

'That can wait.'

'I wouldn't be too sure about that. My stepmother just left my father and has decided to move in with me, and Connor just showed up so it is all going to get messy.'

'Tyler, enough. I don't want to have to arrest you. It will make both our lives that little bit easier if you just come with me.'

'Arrest me? What for?'

He shrugged. 'Obstruction of justice, aiding and abetting. Whatever I can make stick.'

'But that's crazy. I didn't do anything wrong.'

'You want to know what's really crazy,' he said, shaking his head, 'I've got dead bodies escaping from the morgue and going on killing sprees. Dozens of people have been murdered in the last twenty-four hours and not all of them have stayed dead. It's like a goddamn zombie movie, and they're talking about putting the whole town under quarantine in case it's some freak virus doing people in. I know you're connected to it and you are going to tell me everything you know.'

'I don't know anything.'

'Then how do you explain this?' He pulled an evidence bag out of his pocket and I froze when I saw the contents; my teardrop, from the birthday party massacre.

I swallowed down my nerves. 'I don't see what a trinket has to do with me.'

Sam's smile didn't reach his hazel eyes. 'I had it analysed by a friend of mine at the university. Clever man, he can do things with his equipment the guys in our forensic labs can only dream about. This "trinket" is a crystallised tear, and when I gave him a DNA profile to compare it to he got a one hundred percent match. Want to guess whose DNA it is?'

CHAPTER 16

Shaking my head, I backed away but Sam caught hold of my arm and held me in place. 'This ends now, Tyler.'

Numb, I let him lead me to his car. He opened the car door and I slid inside. I closed my eyes and leaned into the seat, unresisting as he stretched across and buckled me in. The gentle touch on my chin as he angled my face upwards surprised me into opening my eyes.

He'd taken his sunglasses off and I could see the war going on inside him as the man fought with the homicide detective.

The man won.

He pressed his mouth against mine and I parted my lips, welcoming his kiss, the firmness of his touch. I drank him in, his tongue stroking inside my mouth, and heat flared low in my belly.

I reached up to wrap my arms around his neck, wanting him closer, needing to feel his body pressed against mine. But he broke off the kiss with a groan, peeling my hands away and placing them in my lap, leaving me breathless and wanting more.

He pulled his head back and put his sunglasses on, the emotion leaving his face as he closed the door. Breathing ragged, pulse pounding in my ears, I didn't look at him as he hopped into the driver's seat and started the engine. We travelled several blocks before my brain started to function and I realised just how much trouble I was in.

I rummaged in my bag for my phone, opening up a search engine.

'What are you doing?'

'Ah… I'm just letting Rhonda and Connor know where I am.'

He reached over and took the phone away from me, a wry smile curving his lips as he read out what I had typed in. 'Can you get DNA from tears?'

He tossed the phone into my lap and I scrambled to stop it sliding off, not sure if I should risk reading the answers the search engine had come up with. His tone had been suspiciously mild and I wondered if I had made another major blunder.

'For your information, yes, you can get DNA out of tears, though I doubt any laboratory would come up with a result this fast. And they'd need some of your DNA to compare it to.'

'You were bluffing.' I shook my head.

'Not really. You were there last night. I might not have been able to see you, but I heard you, and I could sense your presence. I don't know how you did it, but with zombies on the loose I'm learning that anything is possible in this town.'

I put my phone back in my bag and looked out the window for the first time. 'This isn't the way to the station.'

'I'm taking you somewhere quiet where we can talk without interruptions.'

Somewhere quiet turned out to be the lookout on top of Mount Pilbeam, named for one of Easton's founding fathers. Years ago an outdoor café had operated at the lookout, but now it sat empty, its popularity dwindled since more upscale venues opened in the town centre.

Sam escorted me to one of the picnic tables out the back of the café. Large trees cast shade over the picnic area and birds called to each other as they announced our arrival to every living creature in the vicinity. I took a seat and gazed out over Easton, conscious of Sam's presence beside me but not ready to acknowledge him.

Beside me, Sam gave a quiet sigh and twisted in his seat to face me properly. 'Why don't you start at the beginning?'

I shook my head, refusing to look at him. 'Please, Sam, you don't know what you're asking.'

'Some crazy shit is happening in this town and you're right in the middle of it. People are dying, Tyler, and I don't buy the Health Department's line that it's some kind of mutated virus. This is murder, and it's my job to catch whoever is responsible. But I can't do that if you won't help me.' He gently turned my head.

I avoided his eyes, looking over his shoulder and focusing on the white car pulling into the car park beside Sam's unmarked. The doors opened and four men climbed out and went around to the back of the car. The driver's tall frame looked familiar, but he was too far away for me to pick out his features. He opened the boot and the others crowded around him.

'Tyler.'

I glanced back at Sam and the depths of care and compassion in his eyes caught at my heart. He took both of my hands in his and squeezed. 'I can't help you if you won't let me in.'

I shook my head, hair falling forward and covering my face. He let go of one hand and gently pushed my hair back behind my ears. 'No hiding, remember?'

I wanted to close my eyes, to concentrate on the scent of him, so clean and crisp, the strength residing in the hand holding mine, savouring the moment before I ruined it by lying to him yet again. With a shaky breath, I gave him a nod. 'Okay, I'll tell you everything.'

Sam's shoulders relaxed and he gave me such a beautiful smile it was all I could do to stop myself from bursting into tears. My mouth was dry and I swallowed a couple of times, delaying the moment I would destroy the last thing that was good in my life.

'I was…' I scrambled backwards, dragging Sam with me, eyes wide as a golf club swung at his head. It missed him by an inch and he reacted quickly, jumping to his feet and pushing me behind him.

Mottling covered the faces of the three men standing on the other side of the table. In the background, I saw the driver leaning against the bonnet of his car and his swarthy features came into focus.

Talaom.

The three wraiths came around the table, all of them brandishing golf clubs.

Sam backed up, still keeping me behind him. We were nearing the edge of the lookout, a log fence standing between us and a steep incline covered in trees and shrubs and dotted with large rocks. We could break our necks trying to navigate it on a good day, let alone with wraiths after us.

Sam tried to move us sideways, but one of the wraiths blocked our path. The other two spread out until we had one on either side and one directly in front. They hefted their clubs and attacked. Sam pushed me to the ground, standing over me as he ducked and weaved. He managed to avoid two of the clubs but the third clipped him on the side of the head. He grunted and staggered, but didn't fall. Two of the wraiths swung their club at his legs, while the other one aimed for the torso.

Sam grabbed the club aimed at his middle and wrenched it out of the wraith's hands, but the other two clubs connected with his legs and he fell to his knees. I struggled to get up but Sam pushed me down with one hand, swinging the club he'd managed to snatch in the air in an attempt to ward the wraiths off.

But they didn't feel pain. The two still armed with clubs swung them at him while the third dived forward and rammed his head into Sam's stomach. Sam landed on his back and the other two wraiths raised their clubs, ready to bring them crashing down onto his unprotected head.

'No.' I flung myself across Sam, one hand gripping my necklace and the other outstretched as I summoned up every ounce of aether I could, and channelled it into my necklace. My ears buzzed and my skin tingled as I sliced my hand through the air, lightning streaking out of my fingertips in a horizontal line. Their bodies jolted when the lightning cut into them and black shards blew out of their throats, flying through the air towards us.

The wraiths' stolen bodies reeled, then hit the ground with sickening thuds.

I collapsed on top of Sam, shielding his face with my arm. When the rain of soul shards ended I struggled to lift my head, looking for Talaom. He stood by the open door of his car, watching, smiling, and gave me a wave.

'Malia sends her love. She'll be in touch.' He threw something on the ground in front of his car before climbing in and speeding away, a plume of dust kicked up in his wake.

Sam groaned. I dropped my head back onto his chest and was reassured by the steady beat of the heart beneath my cheek. I closed my eyes, content to lie there and listen to his heartbeat.

I felt his arms come around me and smiled as he held me tight, unable to resist the urge to nestle in even closer. Regardless of how I got here, I knew this was where I belonged. The world faded away and I was happy to let it. Just for now, this moment, exhausted and unable to move, I wanted to drink in the feel of Sam beneath me, the warmth of his hands on my back.

Too soon, reality intruded. Sam groaned again and rolled me over on my side before he struggled into a sitting position. 'Tyler, are you okay?'

I fought to open my eyes to look at him. My eyelids were so heavy, they kept closing of their own volition. I stopped trying to open them and sighed as I felt Sam manoeuvre me around so my head rested in his lap.

'Open your eyes, Tyler. You need to stay with me.' Sam changed position, the muscles in his legs flexing, and I frowned as my head rolled from side to side.

'Sorry,' he said, 'but I need to get my phone out of my back pocket so I can call an ambulance.'

'No,' I forced my eyes open and met his worried eyes. 'No ambulance.'

'Tyler.' He frowned down at me. 'Something is seriously wrong with you.' He held his phone in one hand and stroked my face with the other.

'You look worse than me,' I said. Blood trickled down the left side of his face from a nasty gash on his temple.

Sam didn't answer, his eyes never leaving mine. 'I'll be fine. You're the one I'm worried about.'

'You don't need to be. I'm just really, really tired. I'll be fine once I get some energy back.'

'Energy, like the lightning you shot out of your fingers,' he said, shutters coming down on his expression.

I winced. 'You saw that.'

'Saw it. Don't understand it, but can't deny it worked.' He pointed at the three dead bodies the wraiths had used. 'Mind telling me how you managed to blow the stuffing out of these guys with a wave of your hand?'

I sighed, and took the first step towards losing him. 'My necklace allows me to harness aether, the psychic energy created by all living things, and use it as a weapon against wraiths.'

'Wraiths?'

'Dark reapers who can temporarily reanimate dead bodies.'

'Fair enough.'

I stared up at him, surprised by his bland tone. 'You're taking this extremely well.'

'What did you want me to do; rant and rave and tell you what you're saying is impossible and there's no such thing as wraiths or dark reapers?'

'That's kind of what I was expecting, yeah,' I said with a frown.

'I just saw you annihilate three zombies with a lightning bolt. At this point I'm open to anything.'

'Oh.' This was not the way I thought this conversation would go.

'Could your old necklace kill zombies too?'

'They're wraiths, not zombies, and this is my old necklace.'

'Doesn't look like it.' Sam traced a finger along my collarbone, and then picked up the necklace. 'As I recall, the other one looked as if it belonged on a heavy metal rocker. This one suits you better; it's beautiful and yet mysterious, almost otherworldly. It looks delicate but it's deceptively strong, like you.'

I dropped my gaze, disconcerted by both his words and the way his hand kept stroking my collarbone. 'It... ah... changed after I managed to link with it.'

'Hmm.' Sam withdrew his hand and gazed into my eyes. 'Feeling better?'

'Uh huh.'

He helped me sit up, and immediately my head started spinning. He wrapped both arms around me and I leaned into him, eyes closed, as I waited for my equilibrium to return to normal. Snuggled as I was in Sam's arms, I hoped it wouldn't happen anytime soon. I did not want to move out of his embrace and face the rest of the questions that must be filling his head. He was being kind and considerate now, but that would change when he knew I was up to a more rigorous interrogation.

With what Sam had witnessed, and what I'd already told him, there was no point trying to hide what I was anymore.

CHAPTER 17

'I'm a reaper,' I said, 'I reap the souls of people who are dying.'

Sam stiffened. He eased me back from his chest and peered down at me, eyes narrowed to slits. 'You're the Grim Reaper?'

'He's my boss. At least, he was my boss up until I refused to reap a soul for him and sent him back to the Underworld.'

'I see.'

'No, you don't.' I gave a bitter laugh. 'Everything is so messed up, and it all started the night I went to buy a packet of *Oddfellows*.' I gave him a sad smile when his eyes narrowed.

'You were at the service station that night, when the dead drug addict killed the truck driver and the owner.'

'She was a wraith, and she killed me too.'

Sam went still for a moment, and then he let me go and stood up. I bit my bottom lip as I watched him pace in front of me while running his hands through his close-cropped brown hair.

After a moment he stopped pacing and pulled me to my feet. He steered me around the dead bodies and led me back to the picnic table. He got me to sit down and stood in front of me.

'Tell me everything.'

I looked into his hazel eyes, the eyes of a homicide detective, and told him about being murdered before I was recruited and then resurrected by Grimm, and the task I'd been given. Throughout it all his eyes never left mine, his expression remote, giving nothing away about how what I was saying made him feel. The only time he reacted was to clench his fists when I told him Chris Bradbury was the lost reaper Grimm had ordered me to find.

My voice faltered as I described the night Grimm had come for Chris's soul, and how I'd had to sacrifice my mother's soul to save him. 'Only, she wasn't my mother after all. She was Malia.'

'The sister of the guy you said is stuck in Demania, Hell?'

'Oh my God.' I scrambled off the seat. 'She sent these wraiths.' I pointed at the black shards littering the ground around the three dead bodies. 'Talaom said she'd be in touch and threw something on the ground.' Legs shaking, still not recovered from taking out three wraiths in one go, I wobbled as I moved towards the car park.

Sam took my elbow, steadying me as I searched for the object Talaom had thrown towards me. He spotted it first, scooping up a basic mobile phone. He inspected it before handing it over to me. 'No numbers in the contact list. No way of tracing anything back to her.'

I nodded, grateful when he wrapped his arm around me and helped me over to his car. I leaned against the bonnet as I told him the rest of the sorry tale, voice catching when I explained Chris's role in my mother's death.

'So that's why you broke up with him.'

I shook my head. 'We were never together, not really. We were more like partners, thrown together by the need to fight Grimm.'

Sam didn't say anything and I looked up at him. He was gazing out over Easton, seemingly lost in his own thoughts. Then he cast his eyes over the three dead bodies. 'I need to call this in. The longer I leave it, the harder it will be to explain.'

'Okay.' I gulped, not looking forward to being involved in another police investigation. 'What do you want me to say?'

'Say?'

'About what happened here? It's not as though I can tell them the truth.'

'You told me.'

'That's different. You were here, and you deserved to know the truth.'

'What changed your mind?'

'Excuse me?' I frowned, not liking the flat tone or the hard stare he was giving me.

'I'm wondering if your decision to tell me the truth has anything to do with needing a new partner, one who wasn't involved in your mother's death.'

I stiffened. 'How can you say that?'

'What else am I supposed to think?' He shrugged. 'You can't trust Bradbury anymore, so who else can you turn to except for the dumb cop who has stupidly let his feelings for you get in the way of doing his job.'

'That's not true,' I said, eyes stinging. I resisted the urge to wipe them, not wanting him to see how much his accusation hurt.

'Isn't it?'

'You're right, I don't trust Chris anymore. But I have always trusted you.'

'Then why is this the first time you've been honest with me? Why did it take me nearly being taken out by a bunch of zombies and watching you zap them with lightning for you to finally confide in me? Explain to me how you suddenly confessing comes on the heels of you breaking away from Bradbury, but isn't connected to him in any way.'

'I didn't want to get you involved. The Grim Reaper, Malia and her followers, are dangerous. I was trying to protect you.'

He banged his fist on the bonnet, making me jump. 'Damn it, Tyler. I'm a homicide detective. It's my job to do the protecting.'

'Exactly. You're a homicide detective and I'm a reaper. You deal in facts; evidence. Would you have believed me, if you hadn't seen it for yourself?' I shook my head. 'Either way, I didn't want to draw you into my world and put you in this position.' I waved a hand at the dead bodies. 'They came after you because you were with me.'

He took hold of my shoulders. 'No more trying to protect me. I can take care of myself.'

'As you did today?'

'I might not be able to shoot lightning bolts out of my fingers, but I'm not helpless. Now that I know what I'm dealing with I can take precautions.'

I threw my hands up in the air, scrambling for a way to get through to him. 'It won't be enough. The bodies the wraiths take over are already dead. The only way to hurt them is to go for the soul, and no amount of guns or precautions can stop them. Only I can.'

'We'll figure it out, but first I need to get you out of here before someone else decides to visit the lookout.' He tapped away on his phone and held it up to his ear.

'Bradbury. Get your arse to the Mount Pilbeam lookout. Tyler needs you.' He listened for a moment and then barked into his phone. 'No time to explain. Just get here, and come alone.' He hung up and met my eyes, no doubt reading surprise in them.

'I don't like him, don't trust him, but he's the only one who knows enough about all this reaper stuff to have a chance of protecting you while I sort this mess out. When I'm done I'll come to get you and together we can work out a plan of attack, because I am sure as hell not sitting back and letting a bunch of zombies have free rein in my town.'

I nodded and the tension left his shoulders. 'Do you really think you can put Emily's soul back in her body?'

'I hope so.'

He went silent for a moment, rubbing his chin. 'What's it like, reaping a soul?'

'At first I was terrified; didn't want to do it at all, but I realised these people needed me. Their souls would be left to wander the astral plane if they weren't reaped, or worse, taken by one of Grimm's dark reapers. And for the most part, they seem at peace. I get a sense of well-being and it kind of soothes me, almost makes up for watching them die.'

'So it's not so bad, being a reaper?'

'Not so bad.' I didn't tell him about the penalty for reaping a soul I had not been called for. The idea of discussing the pleasure that engulfs me immediately afterwards made me shift uncomfortably, even if it was immediately followed by pain. There were some things about being a reaper Sam did not need to know.

Before Sam could question me further, Chris arrived at the lookout.

He gave a low whistle as he took in the scene. 'Do I want to know what happened here?'

'No.' I wrapped my arms around my torso and bit down on my bottom lip before immediately letting it go. It throbbed from earlier teeth marks.

'Tyler can fill you in on the way down the mountain,' said Sam. 'I need you to get her out of here before the police arrive.'

Chris raised one eyebrow. 'You are the police.'

'Yeah, so do as I say before I change my mind and arrest you both for withholding evidence.' He held up a hand to forestall any more of Chris's questions, and turned to me. 'Be careful and stay with Bradbury. I don't want you on your own if any more of the Grim Reaper's zombie pals turn up.'

I grimaced and he took my hand. 'Promise me you'll stay with Bradbury until I can come and get you.'

'Fine, but don't take too long.'

'I'll be there as soon as I can.' He leaned forward and brushed his lips against mine, a soft promise that lifted my heart despite the problems we were facing. He squeezed my hand and stepped back as I reluctantly climbed into Chris's car. I placed my handbag at my feet, dreading the coming drive, not ready to discuss my relationship with Sam.

To distract him, I pointed at his sling. 'Should you be driving?'

'It's an automatic.'

He backed the car out of the park and steered us onto the start of the winding road that led down the mountain before he spoke again. 'I can't believe you told Lockwood about Grimm.'

'How else was I supposed to explain killing three wraiths right in front of him?'

'I'm sure you could have come up with something, if you'd really wanted to.'

I sighed. 'I didn't want to lie anymore. Everything has got out of hand, and it was time he knew the truth.'

'How much did you tell him?'

'All of it.' I twisted in my seat to face Chris before I told him what had happened with Malia. Tears ran down my cheeks. 'I got Emily killed, and I need Sam's help to get her back.'

Mouth drawn in a firm line, Chris glanced at me. 'What happens now?'

I held up the phone Talaom had tossed on the ground. 'I wait for Malia to contact me and force her to give up Emily's soul. Then I rip her out of Emily's body and hope like hell for a miracle.' I don't know what I would do if the transfer didn't work a second time.

'Have you been able to track down Killian?' He was my last hope for finding a way to force Malia to give up Emily's body and soul.

Chris frowned. 'I found him, but I'd hold off on going to him for help. He's moved to a property out past Greenlakes. It's huge, with plenty of room and privacy for any number of Tr'lirians to hide out.'

Greenlakes was a sprawling housing estate ten minutes north of Easton, with five acres the minimum block size, giving its residents a rural setting that was still close to the amenities offered by Easton. Some of the blocks were closer to twenty acres, offering plenty of room to hide.

'You really think there are more of them?'

'I know it.' He reached into the centre console, pulled out a yellow envelope and handed it to me. 'Had a hell of a job convincing my private investigator this was a set for a movie.'

The envelope was crammed with photos of winged Tr'lirians, all of them holding weapons. There were also plenty of armed people without wings, and one of them was Killian.

'There are dozens of them.'

'I know, and it looks as though they're preparing to go to war,' said Chris, his deep voice grim.

With Killian wanting us dead, it would be suicide for either of us to go near the compound. Now how was I going to save Emily?

$\mathcal{A}$ loud beeping made me jump, and I fumbled for the call button on the phone Talaom had left for me. 'Hello?'

'Do you think it was a good idea to leave your friend up on that mountain all alone? You know what happens to people you care about when you're not there to protect them,' said Malia.

I gasped. 'What have you done to Sam? If you've hurt him I'll–'

'He's fine, but unless you and I come to a new arrangement that could change. It would be terrible if something bad were to happen to such a handsome young man. He's rather tasty, isn't he? I'm not surprised you chose him over Chris. Although I understand your former lover is quite the catch in his new body.'

'Where is Sam?'

'He's busy on his phone explaining to his colleagues how he managed to subdue three wraiths without help, although I am led to believe he calls them "zombies". Talaom had to explain to me what your young man was referring to. Nasty creatures. Wraiths are much more civilised.'

'Civilised? They're murdering innocent people.'

'There are no such things as innocent people. Everyone ends up with blood on their hands at some stage of their life.'

My fingers hurt from gripping the phone. I wanted to throw it out the window, to deny Malia any control over my life, but with Sam in jeopardy I couldn't afford to. 'What do you want?'

'I'm keeping this body. I've grown to like it and I will not give it up. Try and take it from me and my people will swoop on your precious Sam within seconds. They are watching him from the astral plane and he will never see them coming.'

I shook my head, unable to believe I was back in almost exactly the same position I'd been in on Thursday night. I would have to sacrifice Emily's soul to keep Sam safe.

I gulped down my horror at what I was about to say, hoping I wouldn't live to regret it. 'No deal. I want Emily back. If you don't give me proof her soul is safe before ten o'clock tomorrow morning, I will come after you.'

'Do that and Sam is a dead man. He will be dead, and so will you, and nothing will stop Almorthanos from taking your brother's body.'

'Almorthanos is never getting out of Demania, not while I hold the key.'

'That necklace is part of me and I will get it back, and when I do your pathetic attempts to stand in our way will come to an end.' After that parting shot, she hung up.

I faced Chris. 'Turn the car around. We have to go back.'

Chris shook his head. 'Not happening. Lockwood wants you as far away from the crime scene as possible.'

'He's in danger. Malia said she'll kill him if I try to get her out of Emily's body.'

'The worst thing you can do right now is run up there and get yourself into trouble with the police.' He pulled over and I realised we'd come down the mountain and were now at a small parking area that marked the end of a walking track snaking along the road leading to the turnoff.

No sooner had he stopped than two police cars and an ambulance roared past, taking the turnoff and heading up the mountain.

'Lockwood will have company soon enough and I doubt Malia is going to make a move on him today. She was just trying to shake you up, let you know you have more to lose on this than she does,' he said, his reasonable words doing nothing to stem my fears.

I rubbed at my temples, trying to rub away the dull ache building behind them.

'Migraine?'

I shook my head slowly. 'Not yet.'

'You left some of your medication at my place.' He wore a grim smile. 'Guess you were in such a hurry to escape my company you forgot to pack it.'

I dropped my hands and stared out the window. 'I can't stand the thought of Malia roaming around in Emily's body. Who knows what she'll do to it?'

'Ah, so we're avoiding the topic. I know you think you hate me but if we're going to work together on getting your cousin back and keeping Lockwood alive, we're going to need to talk about what happened.'

I sighed. 'I don't hate you, Chris. But I don't trust you anymore.'

'If that's the case, why is this the second time in as many days I've received a call to bail you out of trouble?'

'Sam called you, not me.'

'Lockwood didn't call me last night, you did,' he said with a knowing smile.

I shot him a haughty glare. 'Only because I had no one else to call.'

'Are you sure about that? I know I hurt you, and you have no idea how sorry I am for that, and for my part in the accident that killed your mother. But my feelings for you have not changed. I love you, Tyler, and no matter how much you try to fight it, how angry you are about what I did, I know you have feelings for me too.'

'You're damn right I'm angry. I have every right to be. All my life my father has treated me like rubbish, telling me over and over again how I was responsible for my mother's death. That I was not worthy. To find out twenty-five years later that it was your fault, after I'd just sacrificed what I thought was my mother's soul for you, it burns.' I growled. 'There are no words for how angry I am.'

'But it wasn't your mother's soul.'

'I didn't know that at the time.' I threw my hands up in the air.

'Would you have really handed me over to Grimm, if you'd known what I'd done and that your mother's soul was never in danger?'

'That's not the point.'

'Sure it is. You couldn't bring yourself to sacrifice my life because you have feelings for me. I know it, you know it, and so does Lockwood. That's why he called me to come and get you.'

I rolled my eyes at him. 'He called you for the same reason I did. There was no one else to call.'

'No way.' Chris shook his head with apparent relish. 'He knows I'm the only one who can share in every part of your life. He certainly can't. No matter how reasonable he's being now, the minute the reality of you being a reaper sets in he'll back off, back to his safe and predictable little world.'

'You're wrong. Sam wouldn't do that,' I said, worried he would turn out to be right. It didn't help that he'd nailed the main reason I'd been so determined to avoid telling Sam the truth. Despite all my talk about protecting Sam, I'd really been protecting myself from the possibility of rejection.

I gave another low growl, furious at him for making me doubt

Sam's ability to understand and accept who I was, needing to lash out and hurt him back. 'I wouldn't have handed you over to Grimm because I didn't want him finding out how to get Almorthanos a new body. But that doesn't matter now because I screwed up and Emily paid the price. They don't need you anymore or I'd trade you for her in a heartbeat.'

'No you wouldn't. Though, I'd be happy to let you trade Lockwood for Emily.' He gave me an apologetic smile. 'Malia will make you choose between them. When it comes down to it, who will it be? Lockwood or Emily?'

I glared at him, hating to hear it stated in such bald terms. But he was right. Malia would not hesitate to kill Sam if I attempted to get her out of Emily's body. As horrified as I was by Emily's death, I wouldn't risk Sam's life to bring her back.

'Well?'

I leaned my head against the headrest. 'There has to be another way.'

Chris reached over and took hold of my hand and brought it up to his lips. 'And we'll find it, together.'

I pulled my hand free and crossed my arms in front of my chest. 'Can you please not do that? We're working together, that's all.'

He gave me an intense look. 'For now. But I'm not giving up on us and I promise I won't let you down again.' He finally pulled out onto the road and neither of us spoke during the drive back to his penthouse.

Once we were inside, he handed me my migraine tablets and I swallowed one with water, hoping it would be enough to stop my headache from becoming a full blown migraine and not make me drowsy. I couldn't afford to have my wits dulled.

I started to pace, but Chris interrupted me after my first lap of the lounge. 'Come and sit down and we'll go over what we know, and figure out what resources we have.'

I huffed out a sigh. 'Fine.' I flopped onto one of the chairs at the dining table and he took a seat opposite me.

'Don't sound so enthusiastic.'

'I want to be doing something, like tracking down Malia so I know where she is for when I get Emily's soul back. Not stuck here wondering if Sam is okay or if Grimm is about to launch another wraith attack.'

Chris snorted. 'Lockwood can take care of himself.'

I scowled at him. 'Three wraiths just tried to kill him.'

'But you stopped them, and I want to know how.'

'I told you, I blasted them with a burst of aether. But taking out three of them left me exhausted. If there'd been four, Sam and I wouldn't have been so lucky. I need to find out what else my necklace can do if we are to have any hope of taking on Malia.'

'I bet she was pissed off to discover it could bring you back to life, but not her because she had no body to go back to,' he said with a smirk. 'Of course, if they hadn't burned her body, the necklace would never have been created.'

'I don't imagine she'd have been happy even if she could have been resurrected. She was old when she died, and she'd still have been old if she'd been resurrected. But now, thanks to me, she has a plan that will keep her looking young and beautiful forever.'

'Reproduce and create a never-ending supply of bodies to hop into whenever her old one starts to wear out. It could work.'

'I know,' I said with a groan, 'and that's why I can't stand the thought of her in Emily's body. What if she's out there now, trying to get pregnant to create her next victim? What if I manage to get Emily's soul back into her body and then I have to explain to her why she is suddenly having a stranger's baby?'

Chris shook his head, a smile on his face. 'I doubt Malia would do anything of the sort, at least until she has got Almorthanos out of Demania.'

'You don't know that. You didn't see her prancing around in my white dress, minus her underwear. She didn't strike me as the kind of woman who would hold off if she found a man who caught her eye.' I shuddered at the thought of the things Emily's body might be subjected to.

Chris threw his head back and laughed, a deep belly laugh that had his broad shoulders shaking.

I scowled at him. 'It's not funny. How would you like it if somebody like Cade took over your body and did who knows what with it?'

At the mention of his body's biological father, his laughter petered off. 'Okay, I see your point,' he said with a frown. 'Although, I'm in the same situation as Malia. This body isn't the one I was born with.'

'No, but you got tangled up in it by accident. You didn't murder the original Chris Bradbury just so you could come back to life.'

'I can't honestly say I wouldn't have if I'd known it was possible. The chance to live again and do all the things I cheated myself out of in my first life would have been an incredible lure.' He gave me an apologetic shrug. 'I'm sure lots of people wouldn't hesitate if given the same opportunity.'

'No, no way. I would rather die than take over someone else's life.' The very idea made my stomach churn.

'Yeah, well, not all of us are as noble as you,' he said with a strange look in his eyes. Before I could decipher whether he'd meant his comment to be complimentary or sarcastic, someone knocked on the door.

'Sam.' I got up from my chair and ran across the lounge, throwing myself into his arms once Chris let him in. 'You're okay.'

He smiled down at me. 'Was there a doubt?'

Chris cleared his throat. 'Malia called Tyler and threatened to have you killed if she tried to get Emily's soul back.'

'Hey,' said Sam, his arms tightening around me. 'I'm not that easy to kill. You do whatever you have to do to get your cousin back. I can handle a couple of zombies.'

'You don't understand.' I wanted to shake him, make him take this seriously. 'She had Tr'lirians watching you from the astral plane.'

He frowned. 'Are they watching us now?'

I glanced over at Chris and he shook his head.

Sam's eyebrows rose as he stared at Chris. 'Don't tell me, you've got Tr'lirian detectors set up in this place?'

Chris smirked, leaving it to me to explain. 'He can see into the astral plane.'

Sam looked back down at me. 'Can you and Connor do that?'

'Connor has never mentioned seeing things, and as Killian didn't know it was possible I'm guessing Chris having been a reaper gives him the edge. As for me, I might be a reaper but my Tr'lirian blood is more diluted. It's only because of the necklace I can enter the astral plane when I'm called to reap.'

Sam pursed his lips. 'It also lets you zap zombies. What else can it do?'

'That's what we were just discussing,' said Chris as he retook his seat at the table.

Sam kept a hand at my back as we walked to the table, only removing it when we sat down across from Chris.

'We know Malia's power is stored in the necklace, but so far I have only managed to use it to draw on aether,' I said. 'But the power must still be in there or she wouldn't want it back so badly. I just need to figure out how to access it.'

'Didn't it zap her, when she tried to take it from you?' Chris leaned forward.

'Yes, but I can't count on that stopping her. It may have changed shape and colour after I used it to fight Grimm, but it is still a piece of her and she seemed confident it would respond to her once she had a chance to reconnect with it.'

'Let's make sure that never happens.' Sam nudged my shoulder with his.

'You got it.' Despite my bravado, fear nibbled its way into my head. There was so much we didn't know about what we were dealing with and time was running out for all of us.

CHAPTER 19

e discussed possible scenarios for what seemed like hours, but when I looked at the clock it was early in the afternoon. So much had happened, that it felt as though I'd lived a lifetime of ups and downs in one day. As time passed, sure Malia was solidifying her position, a ball of dread formed in my stomach. It was almost a relief to have my necklace go cold.

'I have to go,' I said. 'Someone is dying.'

Sam shot to his feet. 'Where? Who are they?'

'I won't know until I get there.' Reluctant to take to the astral plane with Sam watching on, I turned to Chris. 'Can I use the guest room?'

'Of course.'

Sam followed me down the hall. 'Is it okay with you if I stay? I'd like to know what it's like, to reap.'

'It's not that exciting,' I said as I entered the bedroom and lay down on the bed. 'You won't actually get to see anything.'

'I still want to be here for you, for when you come back.'

'Oh, okay.' I took a deep breath and closed my eyes, trying to pretend he wasn't watching me as I took hold of my necklace.

113

Immediately, I was pulled out of my body and floated up and through the ceiling. I streaked across the sky, looking down at Easton and its citizens as they continued to live their lives oblivious to what was going on around them.

Shapes flitted around me once again, lost souls, their form not as distinct as mine, though occasionally I caught a glimpse of a face. Their mouths were moving, arms waving at me, as if they were trying to tell me something. I could tell they were scared, but had no clue as to what it was they were so afraid of.

The lost souls vanished in an instant, and I had a new escort. Five black winged Tr'lirians appeared around me, all male, chests bare. They flew in v-formation, the astral plane casting a light haze over their bodies. They flew in close and the flap of their wings buffeted me about. If I'd been one of the lost souls the wind they created would have sent me reeling through the sky, but the draw of my client kept my course steady.

My silent escort followed me all the way to my client and hovered over the man sprawled on the grass in the middle of a hockey field. They set down, wings furled, and watched me.

I glanced over at the creek where I had found the body of one of Andrew's victims almost a week ago. That was the night I'd discovered Chris was the reaper Grimm had me searching for. I pushed those memories aside and made my way between the still silent Tr'lirians and moved over to the dead man.

'Oh no.'

Logan Miller, my ex-boyfriend, lay flat on his back, arms spread. A large knife stuck out of the middle of his chest, a knife that looked exactly like the largest one from the set in my kitchen, the one I'd used that morning to slice bananas for breakfast.

I heard movement behind me and spun around, hovering protectively over Logan's body.

Talaom stalked towards me, dark and brooding, features hazy. He was in the astral plane with me.

'For every day you delay us a person close to you will die, and each death will be laid at your door.' He smirked.

'You won't get away with this.'

'We have been getting away with this for centuries. You and your pet detective are no match for us. In fact, he might be the next to die.'

A chill wind swept through my diaphanous body. 'Leave Sam alone.'

'Give Malia what she wants and your boyfriend will be safe. Cross us and you'll lose everyone you care about. Your friends, your family, even your work colleagues. They'll all die and you'll get the blame for their murders. Malia will take everything from you, and with nothing left to live for you'll beg us to kill you too.'

'I will never give Malia what she wants.'

'I wouldn't be so hasty to throw down the gauntlet. Sleep on it, watch as Grimm's wraiths continue to feed on the people of Easton, and then decide if your miserable life is worth the cost to preserve it.' He clapped his hands and a swarm of dark reapers swooped over me; the wind raised from their passing whipping through me like a blast of arctic cold.

I spun around. An empty hole gaped where Logan's soul should have been. The knife that had been used to kill him was also gone. The draw of my physical body kicked in and I was dragged back to Chris's apartment, my Tr'lirian escort shadowing me the entire way.

I floated through the roof and my spirits lifted at the sight of Sam. He sat on the bed beside my body, stroking my hair. I choked out his name and he frowned, eyes scanning the room. I reconnected with my body and waited impatiently for my senses to return and my muscles to react.

Sam helped me sit up and I clutched his arms. 'Malia had Logan killed, and I'm going to get the blame for it.'

'Miller is dead?'

I nodded. 'He was lying in the middle of the hockey fields, the ones at Archer Park. He had a knife sticking out of his chest and I think it's the one I used to slice up a couple of bananas this morning.'

'How could you tell? Lots of people would have the same knives, and why are you so sure Malia had Miller murdered?'

'Talaom was there and five winged Tr'lirians.' I looked into Sam's worried eyes. 'He said you could be next.'

'I already told you, I'm not that easy to get rid of.'

I frowned. 'This is serious, Sam. You could die, and so could everyone else I care about. Talaom said they would kill someone every twenty-four hours, unless I hand myself over to them. How many more innocent people are going to die because of me?'

Sam stood up, pulling me up with him, his hands gripping my elbows. 'None of this is your fault. You haven't hurt anyone. All these deaths, they're on Malia and Grimm. Not you.'

Intellectually, I knew he was right, but that didn't lessen the guilt I felt over every death since Grimm had first turned me into a reaper. 'If I give myself up, I can save people. I don't want you to die, Sam.'

'I won't, I promise.' He wrapped his arms around me. 'I'm not going anywhere.'

Though I let him comfort me, and drew strength from his touch, I knew a simple promise wouldn't keep him safe. Only I could do that.

After a moment, Sam let go and started to pace. 'If it was your knife that killed Logan, how did Talaom get access to it?'

'He's a full blooded Tr'lirian. He can enter the astral plane whenever he wants and slip through walls. No number of locks could keep him out.' I gasped. 'Connor and Rhonda; I left them at the flat.' I launched myself off the bed, racing to the door and wrenching it open.

'Don't panic,' said Sam as he followed me. 'You don't know that anything has happened to them. Your stepmother is Tr'lirian. She'd be able to use the astral plane, just like Talaom.'

I raced into the lounge, snatched my handbag off the coffee table and pulled out my phone. Hands shaking, I dialled Connor's number. 'Connor can't, and Malia wants his body for Almorthanos.' I clutched the phone, listening to it ring, holding my breath. After ten rings it stopped, and I feverishly dialled Rhonda's phone, only to get the same result.

'They're not answering. She's got them.'

'Maybe they just turned their phones off, to have some mother and son bonding time.' Even as he said it, the look on his face told me he didn't believe it. 'We'll go to your flat. See if we can find them.'

'What is it? What's happening?'

I'd forgotten all about Chris. He stood in front of the large window in the dining area, frowning as he looked from Sam to me.

Sam started to reply but his mobile rang and he moved away to answer it.

I filled Chris in on what I'd found when I'd been called to reap and said, 'Talaom has to have been in my flat. When Sam picked me up this morning, Connor and Rhonda were there, and now I can't contact them.'

Chris strode forward. 'Lockwood's right. No need to panic until we know what we're dealing with.'

'Tyler.' Sam's voice was tight and I spun around, hand to my mouth as I prepared myself for bad news.

'They've found Miller. I have to go, and make sure there's nothing at the scene that links you to him.' His jaw clenched. 'I'll do my best to keep your name out of the investigation, but if anyone else, a witness, friend or family member, mentions your name, I'll have to bring you in for questioning.'

I nodded. 'Of course, thank you.' I gave him a grateful smile, aware a simple thank you would never make up for what he was about to do. His decision to shield me from the investigation not only risked his reputation and career, it went against everything he stood for. I would reward that loyalty in the only way I could, by making sure he never became a casualty of Malia's machinations.

I took a deep breath and crossed over to him, not caring that Chris was watching as I placed my hands behind Sam's neck and kissed him goodbye. Both of us were breathing heavily when the kiss ended. Then Sam looked over my head at Chris.

'Take her to the flat, but do not leave her side. If anything happens to her–'

'It won't, I promise.'

'I'm holding you to that.'

'I don't need Chris to babysit me.'

Sam cupped my face. 'He can see into the astral plane. You can't. I need to know you're safe or I can't go and do my job. Promise me you'll stay with Bradbury?'

I took a deep breath, aware of what he had already given up for me, and gave a slow nod. He kissed me again, a quick, hard, hungry kiss, and then he was gone and I was left to face Chris.

'Shall we go?' Chris's face was suspiciously bland as he scooped up his keys and strode to the front door.

An awkward silence filled the elevator as it took us to the hotel's underground car park. Finally, as he drove out into the traffic, Chris adjusted his sunglasses and flashed me a sad smile. 'Don't you think you've punished me enough?'

'I don't know what you mean?'

'You're doing exactly what I did. Kissing that woman at *Remy's Black Cat Club* to make you jealous, asking Sarah out on a date instead of you after the last time I caught you kissing Lockwood. You're punishing me for lying to you.'

I shook my head. 'My kissing Sam has got nothing to do with punishing you.'

'Really? Because, I have to say, seeing you in his arms is killing me.' Chris stopped the car for a red light. He removed his sunglasses and rubbed his eyes before looking at me. 'I wish to God I'd been honest with you from the start. Maybe everything would have turned out differently and looking at you wouldn't make me feel as if my heart is being ripped out of my chest.'

I dropped my eyes, not liking the effect his pain was having on me. I did not owe him anything. I took a deep breath and stared straight into his reddened eyes. 'I'm sorry if you're hurting but we can't go back in time, and you and I were never together. A couple of kisses, that's all it was, and only because of the situation throwing us together all the time.'

'The way it is now?'

I huffed out a sigh. 'The only reason I'm in this car with you is because I promised Sam and, like it or not, we need your help. That doesn't mean I've forgiven you for the part you played in my mother's death, or for lying about it.'

'Don't I get credit for telling you everything when you asked me for the truth?'

'You only came clean because Killian forced your hand. You would never have told me otherwise.'

'And we'd still be together,' he said with a wry smile before putting his sunglasses back on. 'You see why I might have been hesitant to reveal all.' The light changed to green and he drove through the intersection.

While I couldn't deny I'd been attracted to Chris from the start and I'd enjoyed his kisses, there had always been a part of me that doubted his intentions. When he'd declared his love for me the first time, I hadn't been able to block the thought he was more in love with my necklace than me. He'd even admitted his initial interest in me had been sparked by his recognition of it and all it represented.

But none of that mattered. 'You and I were never together, and my future is with Sam,' I said.

The car halted at a stop sign and he looked over at me, eyes hidden behind his sunglasses. 'Lockwood's a cop. Discovering the truth and serving justice are what he lives for. He's never going to be able to reconcile that part of him with your life as a reaper.'

I didn't reply as Chris started driving again, not liking the picture he was presenting or the questions it posed in my head. But the fear Sam would one day reject me paled in comparison to the fear I would fail to save him if I didn't find a way to access my necklace's full capabilities.

I needed to be able to get to the core, and find a way to use the power Malia had hoarded. If I couldn't do that, I couldn't keep everyone I cared about safe. I rubbed my eyes with the heels of my palms, wanting to block out the image that appeared in my head, of Sam lying dead in a field. I would not let that happen. No matter what I had to do, I would keep him safe.

Time ran out for me to come up with a solution to all my problems. We had arrived at the flat.

Connor's car was still parked behind mine and as Chris pulled in at the kerb I saw that the front door of the flat was open.

I steeled myself for what I would find inside.

CHAPTER 20

I reeled, the sight of my lounge room hitting me like a physical blow. Barely conscious of Chris's presence, I stepped into the ruin that had been my home.

The couch and armchairs were upside down, the lining slashed to ribbons, cushions ripped apart and stuffing strewn everywhere. The coffee table had also been demolished, one leg resting on top of the shattered remains of my television. Every DVD and CD I owned had been broken in half and dumped in the middle of the floor, the cases cracked.

My eyes stung, and I wrinkled my nose at the stench as I moved further inside, gagging on the fumes of what smelled like paint mixed with spoiled milk and rotten eggs. Glass crunched under my feet as I stepped around the remnants of an armchair and saw the fridge on its side, door open, contents left to leak out all over the linoleum. My empty knife block sat in the middle of the dining table, the only piece of furniture left intact, all the chairs around it smashed beyond repair.

Eggs had been cracked and smeared all over the kitchen bench tops, left to rot in the heat of the day, and I retched, stumbling towards the hall.

Chris caught my arm. 'Let me go first,' he said.

I was too distressed to protest, following blindly, my feet catching on the contents of the linen cupboard. Every towel I owned had been shredded and dumped in the middle of the hall, useless even as rags.

Chris scanned the bathroom and then the laundry before disappearing into my room.

Each step I took felt as if it covered thousands of miles, time slowing as I approached the door to my room. I averted my eyes from the bathroom, but caught a glimpse of the cracked mirror and the bathroom tiles smeared in makeup. I turned away, not wanting to see any more, helpless to keep myself from continuing.

The laundry had received the same treatment, the tap in the tub beside the washing machine left on. Water flowed over the sides to pool on the floor and spill out in all directions. The carpet under my feet squelched as I trudged to where Chris stood, blocking the doorway of my bedroom, the expression in his eyes telling me my personal belongings had not been spared. I tried to brush past him, but he caught my arm.

'You don't want to see it.'

'Is it Rhonda?' Dread pooled in my stomach, mixing with nausea from the worsening paint smell. I'd never grown to love my stepmother, but I didn't want her to die, and I'm sure she would never have let anyone take Connor while she was alive.

'There's no one here.'

I shook off his arm and this time he didn't stop me entering. A split-second later I wished he'd held me back and forced me to walk out of the flat. My room was red, the bed, walls and even the ceiling covered in a thick red substance. At first I thought it was blood, but my bemused brain finally recognised it as the source of the cloying paint smell.

Only patches of carpet near the door and parts of the curtains had been spared.

The wardrobe doors were open and a film of red coated every piece of clothing I owned. Even the shoes were ruined. I had nothing left and still no clue as to what had happened to Connor and Rhonda. I dreaded what answers I would find when I forced myself to look inside Sarah's old room. I stumbled along beside Chris as we made our way to the end of the hall.

The bedroom door was closed and Chris reached for the handle.

'No. I'll do it,' I said, swallowing down my fear and the urge to vomit as I twisted the handle and pushed the door open.

I blinked, unable to take it in.

The room was immaculate; all of Rhonda's belongings untouched. I glanced down the hall, casting bleak eyes over the destruction of everything that made the flat my home, and then back into the pristine environment in front of me.

It made no sense, a bizarre oasis in the middle of chaos. Was this a message, a way of showing me Rhonda was still alive but I was doomed?

The front door slammed shut, setting my heart racing. I bolted down the hallway as fast as I could without getting tangled up in the ruined linen, Chris at my heels.

'Connor. Rhonda. Is that you?' I burst into the lounge, eyes frantically scanning the room, only to be yanked backwards by Chris.

A knife banged into the wall just in front of me and then fell to the floor.

'What the hell?'

Four men appeared in the middle of the lounge, all with dark hair and swarthy features. Talaom's men. They had to be.

I had no time to think, only to react as four more knives were flung at us.

Fingers clutching my necklace, its heartbeat throbbing throughout my body, I thrust out my free hand and pushed at the air in front of me. I had no idea what I was doing, only that it felt right.

The effect was instantaneous. Three of the knives bounced off an invisible barrier, falling harmlessly to the ground. The fourth had been thrown high, sailing over top of the barrier and hitting the ceiling above me. Its point clipped my right forearm as it fell to the floor. I winced at the sting but did not take my eyes off the Tr'lirians.

Eyes wide, they stared at me, shock on their faces.

One of them stepped forward. 'Get her,' he roared as he charged towards me, slipping into the astral plane as he went. The others followed suit, rendering them invisible to me.

I focused on my barrier, willing it to expand, strengthen, so that it covered the opening. I saw a slight shimmer in the air as it obeyed my command and I hoped it would be enough to stop them breaking through.

I heard a grunt, followed by a whoosh of air being forced out of lungs as one of them collided with the barrier. More grunts, pained groans and curses followed. I could feel them pushing, searching for weakness. Muscles tense, sweat beading on my brow, I fought to hold my creation in place.

Several long minutes later the pressure lifted and silence filled the flat, but I did not drop the barrier until Chris put his hand on my shoulder and said, 'They've gone.'

I sagged against the wall, exhaling loudly.

'How the hell did you do that?'

I shrugged. 'I don't even know what it was I did, let alone how. I just wanted to stop the knives from hitting us.'

'It was aether, at least that's what it looked like. A solid wall of it.' He ran a hand through his hair. 'But I've never heard of anyone being able to manipulate it like that.'

'What about Grimm?'

'He can build whatever he wants out of nether; it's what the

Underworld is made of after all. But he can't utilise the positive energies.'

'Which is why he only wants the souls of those who have died violent deaths.'

Chris gave a bleak smile. 'Exactly.' Then he frowned. 'You're hurt.'

I inspected the cut on my arm. Two centimetres long, it wasn't deep but it was bleeding. I pushed off the wall and went into the bathroom, feet squelching as I reached over and turned off the tap in the basin. Then I searched the floor for my first aid kit. I always kept it in the cupboard under the basin but who knew where it was now.

'Looking for this?' Chris handed me the small white container with the red cross on the lid and I hunted inside it for an antiseptic wipe and a bandage. After I'd treated the cut I glanced at the cracked mirror.

My heartbeat stuttered and I gripped the bench as my knees threatened to buckle.

A death's head, bisected by cracks, stared back at me.

I wanted to believe it was Grimm, playing tricks on my eyes, but the way the skull moved, mirroring my every movement, I knew what this meant. Just like the young woman in the bathroom and the other patrons at the steakhouse, this was a portent.

I was going to die.

'What is it? What's wrong?' Chris grabbed my arm and swung me around to face him.

I shook my head, struggling to find my voice as I tore my eyes away from my doomed reflection. 'Everything. It's all so screwed up. People are dying. Connor and Rhonda are missing, and we just got attacked by four Tr'lirians.'

I sucked in a deep breath, fighting to stamp down on my panic. I would not just sit back and wait for death to claim me.

'I want to see Killian.'

Chris glared at me. 'You are not going anywhere near him.'

'What if he knows something? He could be my only chance of saving my family.' And maybe myself.

'No. No way.'

I put all the conviction I could muster into my voice. 'Killian has the manpower and resources to find them. We don't. Besides, you were willing to take me to see him last night.'

'Risking a confrontation with Killian while he was alone in his hotel room would have been bad enough. Walking into his compound, where he's surrounded by dozens of Tr'lirians, all of them armed… That's a suicide mission.'

I shook my head. 'Not necessarily, not if we play it right.'

'There is no right way to play this, not when it comes to Killian. It's not happening.'

I put my hands on my hips and glared at him. 'I am not asking your permission. I will do this, whether you come with me or not.'

He stared at me for a long moment, eyes never leaving mine. Then he rubbed the back of his neck. 'All right, what's your plan?'

Mouth dry, pulse racing, I wiped sweaty hands on my jeans as Chris pulled up in front of a large wrought iron gate. An electronic box rested on top of a short pole on the driver's side. Chris wound down his window, stretched out his arm and depressed a button at the bottom of the speaker.

Moments later a distorted voice could be heard. 'State your name and business.'

'I'm Chris Bradbury and I'm here with Tyler Morgan. We want to see Killian.' No trace of nerves showed in Chris's deep voice, and his expression was equally cool as he waited for a response.

'Drive straight up to the house; any detours will result in your death.' A loud click was followed by a buzz as the gate slowly drew open.

'Friendly fellow,' said Chris, as he navigated his way through the gap.

I glanced over my shoulder, watching with a fair amount of trepidation as the gate swung closed behind us. Then I sat up straight, conscious of the armed guards who stood beside the driveway and watched us drive by. Men and women, dressed in black combat gear, faces hard, were just waiting for us to give them an excuse to pull the trigger.

'I hope you know what you're doing.'

'So do I,' I said, earning a faint smile from Chris. But there was no time for further talk. We pulled up in front of the house and four armed men, two with white wings, waited for us to get out of the car.

None of the men surrounding us spoke as they led us inside the house. I walked with my head held high, eyes fixed on our destination.

We were marched down a long hall, until a wooden door barred our progress. One of the men without wings slipped through the closed door, and moments later it opened from the inside.

I stepped forward without being prompted, Chris at my side, and walked over to where Killian stood with his back to an unlit fireplace. He had a sword in his hands and a predatory smile.

'You're early. I was not expecting you to lose all hope for a few days yet,' he said with a sharklike grin. 'Not that I am averse to putting an end to your misery now.' He hefted the sword and swung it in an arc in front of him.

'We didn't come here so you could kill us. We need your help.' I struggled to keep my eyes on him, and not watch the sword as it swung back and forth.

'Then you came on a fool's mission, one I will not hesitate to take advantage of.' He nodded at the men standing behind us and hands grabbed my arms, holding me in place as Killian stalked towards me.

I glanced to my left to where Chris cursed as he struggled to break free of the two men holding him. I faced Killian once more and gambled our lives on a hunch.

'Malia is alive.'

Killian froze, fist clenching on the hilt of his sword, fury burning in his eyes. 'What did you say?'

'Malia's soul has been trapped in the Underworld ever since she died. Last night she had my cousin killed and then stole her body.'

'How is this possible?'

'How it happened doesn't matter. What matters is the woman who caused a war between your people is roaming free, and she's planning on using my half-brother's body to get Almorthanos out of Demania.'

Killian walked over to a large desk set in the middle of the room, picked up a plain scabbard and sheathed the sword, body tense as he stood with his back to us. He whirled around and barked orders at one of the winged Tr'lirians in their own language. The Tr'lirian winked out of view and I watched Chris's eyes narrow as he tracked his progress through the astral plane.

Killian stalked towards me and grabbed my chin in a punishing grip. 'Tell me everything you know about the treacherous bitch.'

I shook free of his grip. 'First we make a deal.'

'Do you really believe me stupid enough to make a deal with one of Malia's blood? And why would I?' He grabbed my neck, squeezing just enough to make the threat clear.

'Kill me and the first thing I'll do will be to tell Grimm that you and Cade are here, waiting to kill Almorthanos the second he's free. Help me get my cousin back, protect the people I care about, and I will give you everything you want.'

He squeezed harder and I struggled to breathe, sure he was going to kill me. I'd hoped I'd have more time, not knowing how long before death the portent appeared in the mirror. To die now, with nothing resolved, made regret burn in my stomach.

He abruptly released me. 'Let her go,' he said to his men, 'but not him. Kill him if she tries anything.'

As soon as my arms were released I massaged my neck.

Killian stiffened. 'Touch your necklace and Bradbury dies.'

I slowly lowered my hand, swallowing several times to lubricate my throat, grimacing at the pain of each movement.

Killian did not give me time to recover. 'Why should I keep you alive and not rip your throat out?'

Voice croaky, I gave him what he wanted. 'I will free Almorthanos for you, as long as you give me what I want.'

'Tyler, what are you doing?'

I refused to look at Chris, blocking out the horror in his deep voice, never taking my eyes off Killian. His eyes narrowed; scepticism in his bearing.

'A moment ago you said you would warn Almorthanos of our presence if I were to kill you. Not that his being aware of us would change the outcome, but losing the element of surprise would prolong the conflict.'

'A quick war or a long one, the choice is yours.'

'What is it you want?'

'Malia out of my cousin's body, and your assurance my family and those I care about will be safe. Promise you'll protect them and I will let Almorthanos out of Demania and not reveal your presence to him.'

'Tyler, no, you can't do this. I won't let you.' Chris struggled to break free from his captors, anguish in his voice. 'There has to be another way.'

I shook my head. 'This is the only way to make sure you and the others are safe, of getting Emily back and stopping Almorthanos from taking Connor's body. I don't have a choice.' I was going to die anyway. At least this way it would count for something.

'I won't let you kill yourself.' Anguish filled his words.

I turned away from him and faced Killian. 'Do we have a deal?'

'I will need to discuss your proposal with Cade. In the meantime, the two of you will enjoy our hospitality.' His shark grin made another appearance. 'In case you get cold feet and wish to renege on your promises.'

I lifted my chin. 'If you keep us here, Malia will know something is wrong and you will lose your element of surprise.'

He pursed his lips. 'Very well, you may leave, but first you will tell me everything.'

Two hours later, Killian's men led Chris and me back to the car, wrung out by his interrogation. Chris stalked beside me, the heat of his fury pouring out of him. But he didn't speak until we were outside Killian's compound, heading for home.

'You little fool. Do you really think that I, or Lockwood, would let you sacrifice yourself for us?'

'I don't want to die, but I have no choice.' I was reminded of this each time I glanced in the side mirror to see a skull looking back at me.

'We keep fighting. We find a way to unlock that goddamned necklace of yours and we fight.'

'And in the meantime more people will die. They already have Connor and Rhonda. Emily is dead. I wouldn't be able to bear it if something happened to you or Sam. I know you think I'm giving up, but I'm being realistic. We can't win, not on our own.'

'Your dying won't save anyone.'

'Yes it will. It has to.'

'If Malia already has Connor, Cade and Killian won't be able to protect him, and there's no way she'll give up Emily's body without a fight.'

'The next time she contacts me, I'll tell her I will free Almorthanos as long as she gives Emily her body back and finds someone else to be her brother's host.'

'You're placing a lot of faith in matters you can't control.'

'I am not going to sit back and watch Grimm's wraiths turn Easton into a graveyard.' I shuddered, remembering the wraith attacks I had already been witness to.

'Not all reapers are capable of reanimating a dead body, and with the rate it rots the brains of those that can, Grimm is bound to be running low on troops. You've probably taken out over half of his wraiths as it is.'

'You don't know that, and Malia said Grimm has wraiths all over the world. Whether he's killing people in Easton or somewhere else, people are still going to die.'

The ring of my mobile phone cut off Chris's reply and I fished it out of my bag, half-convinced it would be Malia and time to put another nail in my coffin.

But the caller ID showed Connor's name.

CHAPTER 22

'Connor, where are you? Are you okay?'

A long silence set my heart pounding. Then Connor's voice sounded impossibly loud in my ear.

'I'm fine, but Mum's ready for the loony bin. She keeps telling me I'm only half-human and that she used to have wings. What the hell did you do to her?'

Relief made me lightheaded. 'I didn't do anything to her, and she's not crazy.'

He snorted. 'Then she's been smoking something. Why else would she come up with such a ridiculous story?'

'Where are you?'

'At the League's Club. I thought a meal might sober her up.'

'But your car is still at the flat,' I said, an echo of the panic I'd felt at not finding them bubbling in my stomach.

'We caught the courtesy bus. It's impossible to get a park on a Saturday.'

'So you're okay?'

'Why wouldn't we be?'

'I tried calling you earlier, and neither of you answered the phone.'

'Give me a break. They've got a live band playing. We didn't even hear our phones ring.'

'You're still there?'

'We're on the bus again, heading back to the flat.'

I clutched the phone tight. 'Don't go to the flat. It's not safe. Get the bus driver to take you to Chris's hotel.' I gave him the address.

'But my car's there.'

'You can get it later. Please, Connor, I'll explain everything when you get here.'

After I finally got Connor's agreement, I ended the call and smiled at Chris. 'Malia didn't have them after all.'

'Meaning you didn't need to offer yourself to Killian on a platter.'

I stiffened. 'Just because Malia didn't have them this time doesn't make them safe. They're still in danger; all of you are.'

Chris tossed me a knowing smile. 'Not as much danger as you'll be in once Lockwood finds out what you're planning.'

My heart skipped a beat. 'Promise me you won't tell him.'

'He might have better luck than me in talking some sense into you.'

'Give me twenty-four hours and after that I'll tell Sam myself. Then the two of you can gang up on me as much as you like.' Not that it would do any good.

'One day, that's all I ask.' One day to spend with Sam without the knowledge of my impending doom hanging over our heads, tainting our last moments together.

Chris frowned, jaw clenching. 'All right. But make no mistake, I will never let you sacrifice yourself no matter how many lives you think it will save.'

'It will be okay. You'll see. Everything will work out.'

Chris steered the car into the hotel car park and switched off the engine. He ruefully shook his head as he cupped my cheek in his hand.

'I'm not an idiot, Tyler. I know you're just saying whatever you think will get me to back off. But you need to know that I will do whatever it takes to keep you alive. I would throw the entire population of Easton to the wolves if I thought it would save you, and I have a feeling Lockwood would do the same. So whatever plan you're hatching isn't going to happen, and I'm giving you twenty-four hours to come to terms with that.'

His thumb slid across my bottom lip, soft and sensuous. His eyes, filled with love and determination, never left mine as he leaned in close. His hand moved to the back of my neck, pulling me forward as his mouth covered mine. His kiss was sweet, light, and a smile played around his eyes when he let me go.

'Now then, let's go ruin your half-brother's day.'

I followed Chris into the reception area, biting at my bottom lip as I scanned the large space for any sign of Rhonda or Connor while Chris asked the doorman if he had any visitors.

Expression neutral, Chris returned to my side. 'They must still be on their way.'

'It would only take five minutes to get here from the League's Club.' The hair on the back of my neck stood up. 'Something's wrong.'

'You don't know that. They could be stuck in traffic, and who knows how many stops the driver had to make before this one.'

I stepped through the sliding doors and out into the under-cover area that housed the hotel's circular driveway. No cars were on it, though a faint trace of petrol fumes and grease lingered. I stared down the road, willing the courtesy bus to appear.

My phone rang and I whipped it up to my ear. 'Hello?'

'You need to come to the flat, right away. It is seriously messed up. Mum is freaking out; she's practically hyperventilating.'

'Connor, I told you not to go there. You need to leave, now.'

'I needed my car. Whoever trashed your flat is damn lucky

they didn't touch it. I'd have found the sons of bitches and smashed them up something shocking.'

'Get Rhonda in the car and get to the hotel. Before they come back.'

'Okay, okay. Don't get your knickers in a knot. Mum's just packing her stuff. We'll head over as soon as she's done.'

'She doesn't have time to pack. Drag her to your car and strap her in if you have to.'

Connor snorted. 'You know what Mum's like when she gets an idea in her head. She's not leaving until she's good and ready.'

'Connor…' My voice broke, but I forced myself to keep going. 'The people who did this, they killed Logan and they've threatened to kill you and Rhonda.'

I heard Connor grunt, and when he spoke his voice was subdued. 'We'll be right there.'

He hung up and I turned to Chris. 'How's that for ruining his day,' I said, eyes stinging.

'Tyler.' Chris moved to embrace me, but I held up a hand to ward him off. I didn't want comfort. I had to be strong, for all our sakes.

We stood side by side until Connor's car pulled up in front of us. His face was pale as he got out of the car.

'I'm so sorry, Connor.' He was still as I hugged him, arms hanging limp at his sides.

Rhonda got out of the car, glared at me, and pulled Connor out of my arms. 'Come on, honey, let's get you inside.' She took the keys out of his hand and tossed them at Chris. 'Take care of his car.'

Without a word, Chris handed me the keys to the penthouse before he climbed into Connor's car and drove it away. I was left to follow what was left of my family inside. The air-conditioning felt like a slap on my face, cooling the hot tears I hadn't realised I was shedding.

I wiped my eyes and strode over to the elevator. None of us

spoke on the ride to the top. I looked over at Connor and quickly averted my gaze when I saw the bleak expression on his face. I felt bad for not feeling as wretched as he did over Logan's death.

Logan had been my boyfriend for three months before I found him in bed with Sarah. Three months, and until that day I'd never seen him for who he really was. Being a jerk didn't mean he'd deserved to die but, surrounded by death as I was, I found it hard to summon up an appropriate sense of grief. I had to focus all my care and concern on the living, and make sure no one else died because of me.

I unlocked the door to the penthouse and stood aside so Rhonda and Connor could enter. They went straight to the couch and sank onto it. Connor put his head in his hands, while Rhonda rubbed his back. I remained by the open door, waiting for Chris, not ready to face my family on my own.

The welcome ding as the elevator arrived lifted my spirits and I greeted Chris with a smile. It might have wobbled, but it was a smile. He assessed the situation in his lounge room.

'I think we all could do with a drink.'

Connor looked up as Chris headed into the kitchen, eyes unfocused as he gazed around the penthouse, almost as if he didn't know how he came to be there.

Chris returned with four glasses in one hand and a bottle of scotch in the other. He placed them on the coffee table before pouring a generous measure of scotch into each glass. He held one out to Connor, who stared at it blankly.

Connor leaned forward, ignoring the glass Chris was offering him, and took the bottle instead. He took several deep gulps before placing it back on the table.

His eyes, clearer now, found mine and his expression hardened. 'How did he die?'

'He was stabbed in the chest,' I said, giving him a moment to process my bald statement before I hit him with the rest. 'He was murdered by Tr'lirians who want me to free their clan leader from Demania, Hell, and they plan on using your body to house his soul.'

Connor screwed up his face. 'Not this shit again. Have you been smoking the same stuff as Mum?'

'It's all true. I wish it wasn't, but it is. Rhonda is a full Tr'lirian and you are half, the same as Chris.'

Connor's gaze flicked over to Chris, who stood beside me sipping his scotch. He raised his glass in a salute.

Connor grabbed the bottle and took another gulp. 'This is bullshit,' he said, wiping his mouth. 'Logan's dead and you lot are raving on about flying aliens.'

'We aren't aliens. We're the original inhabitants of Earth,' said Rhonda, sounding affronted. 'We lived here long before humans showed up and spread their filth all over the world, ruining our paradise. We fled to Angellin to avoid their stink.'

'Really, Mum? You sound like one of those crazies who reckon they've been abducted by a UFO.'

Rhonda sniffed. 'I'm not crazy. I'm telling the truth. Why won't you believe me?'

'Show me your wings, and then I'll believe you.'

'I don't have them anymore. I told you, I had to give them up so I could watch over Tyler's mother.'

'That's convenient.' He lifted the bottle of scotch to his lips once more.

Rhonda's face had gone red and her hands arched into claws.

'Have you shown him how you can slip into the astral plane?'

'What?' Rhonda stared at me, eyes wide. 'No, I... ah... didn't think of that.' She gave me a defiant glare. 'I've spent so many years making sure no one knew what I could do, it never even occurred to me.'

'Chris and I already know what you can do. Now you just have to show Connor.'

Rhonda stood and straightened her skirt, looking self-conscious as she faced her son. 'Connor, honey, I don't want you to be scared but I am going to disappear. Don't worry, I'll be in the astral plane. I'll be able to see you; you just won't be able to see me.'

'Come off it, Mum. I'm not five.' Connor waved the bottle of scotch in her direction. 'Just do your magic trick so we can get this farce over with.'

Rhonda glowered at him. 'Do not take that tone with me, young man. I may have put up with it when I was with your father, but no more. You will show me the respect I deserve. Do you hear me?'

Connor gave a start. 'Ah, sure.' He put the scotch on the coffee table and scratched at his head. 'Do your thing.'

Rhonda took a deep breath, squared her shoulders, and vanished from sight.

Connor shot up from the couch, waving a hand in the air in front of him. 'Holy shit. Where did she go?'

I couldn't see her, but watched as Chris tracked her progress through the astral plane. At one point it looked as though he was going to reach out and touch her. I shook my head, not ready to trust her with what might be our one advantage over Malia's Tr'lirians. I had no doubt that if it came down to it, Rhonda's determination to protect Connor would see her hand Chris and me over to Malia in a heartbeat.

Rhonda reappeared on the other side of Connor and he jumped sideways. She wore a self-satisfied smirk. 'Now do you believe me?'

Connor sank back down on the couch, hands on his knees, eyes roaming over all of us. 'Will someone please tell me what the hell is going on here?'

'Rhonda can fill you in,' I said. I'd had enough of delivering bad news. Before she could protest, I moved over to Chris and led him into the kitchen.

'I want to find Malia. I need to know where she is staying for when I get Emily's soul back.'

He shook his head. 'It's too dangerous.'

'You could get your private investigator to find her.'

'Why don't we wait for Lockwood to return, and then we'll decide on a course of action?'

'We don't have time.'

'There's always time.'

I glared at him before stomping back into the lounge room. Connor was shaking his head as Rhonda filled him in on the freak show his life was about to become. I could sympathise with him. It had been mere days since darkness and death had entered my life, revealing hidden worlds both above and below. I was still struggling to come to terms with what that meant for me. But at least Connor's awakening wasn't as violent as mine, nor had he been chained to the Underworld.

I, on the other hand, faced an eternity of reaping souls, my quota increased by one thousand every time I reaped the soul of a wraith, destroying its hope of rebirth. I hadn't stopped to calculate what my quota now stood at, not wanting to face my future head on. I paced in front of the dining table.

'You're a reaper? What does that mean?'

I stopped pacing and looked over at Connor, who was peering over the back of the couch at me.

I heaved a deep sigh and took a seat in one of the plush armchairs. 'When a person is dying, this necklace goes cold to let me know. Then, when I touch it, my astral form leaves my body and I am pulled through the astral plane to my client. I reap their soul, place it inside the necklace, and return to my physical body.'

'You're carrying dead people around your neck. Gross.'

'They're souls, and mostly it's not too bad. They're content, peaceful, waiting for rebirth.'

'Was Logan content?' His eyes hardened. 'Monique? Sarah?'

I forced myself not to look away. 'Monique is at peace. Her soul is safe, in my necklace, until I release it. Then she'll be reborn. Sarah's soul is there too.' I left it at that, not wanting to explain how Sarah had become a wraith and attacked me or how she would never be reborn.

Connor's face paled. 'What about Logan?'

'One of Grimm's dark reapers took his soul before I could reap it, so I don't know where it is.'

Connor washed this information down with the last of the scotch. He stood, staggering as he navigated his way around the coffee table. 'I need to lie down.'

Rhonda took his arm and I showed them to the third bedroom. Connor stretched out face down on the mattress and was snoring in seconds. Rhonda removed his shoes and sat on the bed beside him, stroking his hair, stern expression dissolving as she watched him sleep.

I sneaked out of the room and found Chris clearing away the glasses and empty bottle of scotch.

'Connor is sleeping off your scotch and Rhonda is keeping him company,' I said.

'I'd be driven to drink too if I suddenly found out I'd been lied to my entire life.'

I nodded but didn't reply, his comment hitting a little too close to home. 'I'm going to lie down as well. I have a feeling tonight is going to be busy.' I tapped a finger on my necklace. 'Can you wake me when Sam gets back?'

His mouth firmed into a line before he gave a slow nod. 'Enjoy your nap.'

He brushed by me and I didn't turn around until he left the kitchen. I headed to my room and lay down, wishing my words hadn't hurt him.

CHAPTER 23

I'd barely got myself settled on the bed when the call to reap came and I was drawn to a housing area opposite Easton University. One of the newer estates, brick homes were squeezed into tiny blocks and juvenile trees provided limited shade for the kids playing in their yards. Cars slowly wound their way through narrow streets, dodging people out for a stroll. A typical Saturday afternoon in suburbia.

The pull of my client drew me towards the backyard of a gleaming two storey monstrosity. I rounded the corner of the house and at first I could see nothing to warrant my presence. Washing fluttered on the clothesline, an empty basket resting on the ground beneath it. Then the clothesline turned in the wind, revealing white sheets splattered in blood.

On the other side of the clothesline, sprawled on the grass in front of a large outdoor entertainment area, lay the body of a middle-aged man. Blood seeped from dozens of deep slashes on his arms and legs. Rents in his shirt and shorts showed similar wounds to the rest of his body. But it wasn't the sight of my client's injuries that made me gasp.

Two people stood over him. The male, young and muscular,

tossed a blood-drenched knife on the grass beside the dead man. He peeled off thick gloves and placed them in a plastic bag the pretty young woman beside him was holding open. They shared a passionate kiss before he took the bag from her and moved to the back of the entertainment area. He used a brick barbecue as a step ladder to scale the six foot fence.

The second he was out of sight the woman dropped to her knees beside the man on the ground and let out a long wailing scream. A shudder swept through my astral body as I moved closer, revolted by the look of satisfaction on her face as she surveyed her lover's handiwork. I shifted my focus to my client, resisting the urge to let loose with my own scream as I placed my hand below the bloody rent in his neck.

His soul answered my call, its light subdued as I placed it in my necklace.

I was equally subdued as I travelled back to Chris's penthouse. Though the man's death was not related to Malia or Grimm's wraiths, it was still disheartening to witness the levels of violence mankind was capable of perpetrating on one another.

I swept into my body, tears leaking from closed eyes as I waited for my senses to come back on line.

Sound returned first, and my pulse kicked up a notch when I heard movement in the room. I forced my eyes open, blinking rapidly to clear my vision.

Sam's smiling face greeted me, and my own lips curved up despite what I had just witnessed.

'Hey,' he said. 'Sorry I woke you. You looked peaceful.'

'I was reaping.' I sat up and reached for the bottle of water I'd put on the bedside table.

'Bad?'

'I've had better times.'

He sat beside me and put a hand over mine. 'Bradbury told me what happened at the flat, and with Connor. How are you doing?'

I forced myself to maintain eye contact, hoping Chris hadn't mentioned our visit to Killian's compound. 'I'm doing lots better than the man whose soul I just reaped. He was murdered, and I know who did it.' I gave him the details, fascinated by the cop face he wore as he questioned me further.

Finally satisfied with my descriptions of the murderous lovers, he stood up. 'I'll need to take care of this, and make sure the detective handling this case knows what to look out for. The first couple of hours of any investigation are the most crucial. I don't want to give the perpetrators a chance to get rid of the evidence.'

I followed him down the hall, wishing he didn't have to leave but understanding why he had to go. 'What about Logan? Was there any evidence at the scene to identify who killed him?'

He sighed, rubbing his chin. 'So far all we have is one set of footprints leading to the body, which preliminary tests suggest are Miller's. There's no sign anyone else was there, and his car is missing. My guess, one or more of your winged friends forced Miller to walk into the middle of the field, while they flew along beside him, never leaving any trace of their presence.'

'When I was drawn to reap his soul they gathered around his body, but they were all in the astral plane. No footprints when you're not in solid form.' He must have been so scared, marched to his death by beings beyond his comprehension. No one deserved to die like that.

Sam gave a nod. 'We searched Miller's place. One of my colleagues recognised you in a photo on the mirror in his bedroom. I need to take a statement from you, from Bradbury as well, to make it clear you were here at the time of the murder.'

I gave him a sad smile. 'You were here too, but I guess that doesn't count.'

'I can't tell them that, Tyler. They'll take me off the case, and I need to be on top of every discovery they make, otherwise I wouldn't have found this before anyone else could bag it for evidence.' He reached into his shirt pocket and pulled out a silver charm bracelet that had my name spelled out in sparkling letters. Sarah had given the bracelet to me for my twenty-first birthday.

I stared at it; at the evidence he had removed from a crime scene to protect me. All my doubts about getting involved with a homicide detective, soothed by his easy acceptance of my life as a reaper, came back with a vengeance. I forced myself to meet his eyes as I took the bracelet from him.

'Thank you.'

'We'll get them. I promise,' said Sam.

Chris cleared his throat as we entered the lounge. 'I wouldn't be making promises you can't keep. Even if you did manage to find out which one of them did it and bring them in, it would be impossible to keep them locked up.' He gave a grimace. 'They'd slip straight into the astral plane, never to be seen again.'

'I'll deal with that when I find them.'

'Why, Lockwood, are you proposing to deliver your own brand of justice to our Tr'lirian murderer?'

'I will do my job, Bradbury, and I'm counting on you to do yours. Tyler's just filled me in on an unrelated murder. I'll be back after I get her information to the lead detective. With who knows how many Tr'lirians running around, this is probably the safest place for Tyler. Keep her here. Keep her safe. Do not leave her side.'

'Understood.' Chris tipped his head.

'Hey, I'm right here.' I glared at both of them in turn. 'I am not a child. I don't need a babysitter and I get to decide where I go and what I can do, not the two of you.'

'Tyler, this is for your own protection,' said Sam.

'We just want what's best for you,' said Chris.

I straightened my back. 'Right now that means finding a way to stop Malia. I need the two of you on my side, backing me up. Not standing in my way.'

I settled my gaze on Chris. 'I'm going to check on Connor and

Rhonda. While we wait for Sam to get back, I want to go over what we know and make a plan for where we go from here.'

Neither of them spoke as I stormed away. I kept my momentum up as I made my way to the last bedroom down the hall. Outside the closed door, I took a couple of deep breaths before slowly twisting the knob and peeking inside. Connor lay on his back, a deep snore echoing around the room. Rhonda had dragged an armchair beside the bed and was curled up in it, facing her son, also sound asleep. She might not be the easiest person to like, but she definitely loved her son.

I quietly closed the door and tiptoed back to the lounge room, my anger at the way Sam and Chris had talked over me fading. I should never have got angry with them, but they had to understand that this was my fight. They couldn't lock me away and hope the situation would sort itself out. I had to take the fight to Malia before I died, again. To have any hope of doing that I needed Killian and Cade on my side.

I returned to the lounge and found Chris sitting at the dining table.

'Is there any word from your investigator about where Malia and Talaom are hiding out? I need to be able to tell Killian when he calls.'

His expression darkened. 'I hope he doesn't call, that way you won't live to regret offering yourself to him like a sacrificial lamb.'

'I did what I thought was right. I'm still not convinced there's another way to stop Malia and Grimm.' I sat down opposite Chris, avoiding my reflection and the ever-present death head in the mirror on the wall behind the table.

'Don't give up hope yet. We faced down the Grim Reaper and lived to tell the tale. We can do this, together.'

His eyes were intent on mine, deep emotion in the vivid blue. I glanced away, relieved when my phone rang.

I checked the caller ID, hoping it was Killian with Cade's answer.

I frowned when I realised it was my boss's number. I hit the talk icon. 'Hello?'

'Please help me, Tyler.' Anne's voice was frantic, breathless, barely recognisable. 'He said he'll kill me if you don't come to the office immediately.'

'Anne, are you okay? Who's there with you?' I stood, knocking my chair to the floor behind me, conscious of Chris's worried gaze.

'I don't know. He's wearing a mask. He has a gun. Please, Tyler. Hurry.' The line went dead.

'We have to go. My boss is in trouble.' I bolted to the front door and wrenched it open.

Chris grabbed my arm before I could push the button for the elevator. 'Wait up a second. What's going on?'

My voice was as frantic as Anne's had been as I told him what she'd said.

Chris's expression hardened. 'You can't go. It's a trap.'

'I don't care. He's going to kill her.'

'Better her than you.'

'How can you say that? Her life wouldn't even be in danger if it wasn't for me.'

He swung me around to face him, still keeping a firm grip on my arm. 'I'm not saying we don't help her. I just want you to stop and think about this. Call Lockwood. Get him to check it out first instead of rushing in blind.'

My stomach clenched at the thought of Sam falling into the hands of whoever was terrorising Anne. I shook my head. 'No. I don't want Sam involved.'

'Way too late for that,' he scoffed. But he did let go of my arm.

I pushed the elevator button, relieved when the doors imme-diately slid open. I bounded inside and hit the button for the carpark. My relief faded when I turned around and saw Chris had his phone out.

'This is Chris Bradbury. I want to speak to Detective Lockwood.' His brow creased as he listened to whoever had answered the phone.

'I see.' His eyes shot to my face; his voice suspiciously bland. 'Well, when you find him can you please let him know I called and the matter is urgent?' He hung up the phone and stared at me, expression cautious.

I wrapped my arms around my middle, a chill sweeping over my body. 'Who were you talking to? Why didn't Sam answer his phone?'

'Constable Ward found Lockwood's phone fifteen minutes ago, on the front lawn outside a crime scene. But she has so far been unable to locate him to return it.'

I braced myself against the side of the elevator, head shaking from side to side. 'No. He can't be missing.' I still held my phone, from when I'd answered Anne's call. I dialled Sam's number, hanging up without saying a word when I heard the constable's voice.

'We don't know he's missing. He probably just dropped his phone. Ward will find him any minute and he'll ring us back. There's nothing to worry about.'

I rubbed my eyes, desperate to believe him. But deep down I knew he was wrong. Constable Ward would have found him by now if he was at the crime scene. And Sam wasn't the type to lose his phone.

They'd taken him.

CHAPTER 24

The elevator doors opened onto the carpark and I rushed over to Chris's car, waiting impatiently for him to unlock it so I could slide inside.

He started the engine and looked over at me. 'Where to?'

I wanted to say the crime scene, to find Sam, but knew it would do me no good. '*The Chronicle.* Maybe whoever has Anne will know where Sam is.'

The short drive to the office seemed to take forever and I peered at the front windows as Chris drove past. The lights were off, making it impossible to see inside.

Chris parked half a block away and scanned our surroundings. 'There's no one here, Tr'lirian or otherwise.'

I bounded out of the car and ran to the front door, tugging on the handle.

Locked.

I banged on it, willing it to open.

Chris reached my side and put his face against the glass while I continued to bang.

'Tyler. Tyler. Stop. There's no one here.'

149

Chris's words took a while to sink in. I turned to him, shaking my head. 'That's not possible. Anne rang me. Said to come here.'

'Call her. Maybe they're out the back.'

I feverishly dialled her number, counting the rings before she picked up.

'Anne Porteous speaking.' The clipped words struck me silent. She sounded like her usual self, no trace of panic or fear in her voice.

'Hello, is anyone there?'

'It's Tyler. You rang me, begged me to come to the office. Said you needed my help.'

'I just got out of the shower. I couldn't possibly have called you.' Confusion filled her voice.

'So you're okay? Nothing's wrong?'

'I'm perfectly fine. I don't know why you think I called you, but I do appreciate your willingness to help if needed. I'm looking forward to having you back at work in a week's time, and putting all this unpleasantness behind us.'

I said goodbye in a daze, head spinning, unable to comprehend what had just happened.

'It was a hoax,' said Chris. 'They were messing with your mind.'

He drove us back to his apartment block to check on Connor and Rhonda. From here on, I wanted us all to stick together so they couldn't pick us off one by one. Worry for Sam ate at me as I tried to call him again, this time getting his message bank. Not knowing where he was or what was happening to him, it made me what to hit something, someone, yell and scream. He had better be okay or I would do whatever it took to make whoever had him pay.

Thoughts of revenge fled when we arrived back at the penthouse and I spotted Talaom looming in the open doorway.

Shock leaching my voice, I brushed past him, running into the lounge and skidding to a halt when I found two black winged

Tr'lirians standing over an unconscious Rhonda. I rushed over and kneeled beside her, Chris at my side.

'I apologise for our rough handling of Rallani, but as she is full Tr'lirian it was necessary to take her out to maintain our element of surprise,' said Talaom, his grin showing all of his teeth. 'Surprise.'

I scanned the room. 'Where's Connor?' Heart thudding, I gripped my necklace, ready to throw a shield of aether around Rhonda, Chris and me. I couldn't risk blasting Talaom or his men until I knew where my brother was.

'Your brother will be enjoying our hospitality while we prepare for the arrival of Almorthanos. He will not be harmed, and neither will your detective.'

Terror sucked strength from my limbs, and I fought not to show how hard it was to stay calm. 'Give Sam back to me. Now,' I said, standing and facing Talaom.

'That will not be possible. Consider Detective Lockwood a down payment on your debt to Malia.'

'I don't owe her anything.'

'You stole her necklace, turned it against her, and she intends to collect payment for it one way or another. But he will not be harmed, I give you my word,' said Talaom.

'You really think I would trust your word?'

'You don't have a choice.' With that parting shot, Talaom and his Tr'lirians vanished.

I collapsed to my knees, clutching my stomach, unable to move as Chris crouched beside me. 'Lockwood is smart, resourceful. He'll be fine.'

Desolate, I met his eyes, and saw the worry he was desperately trying to mask. I shook my head. 'They have Sam, and my brother. This is the beginning of the end.' My time had run out.

Rhonda groaned, and I dragged my eyes away from Chris as she heaved herself into a sitting position.

'Where's Connor? Where's my son?' She scrambled to her feet

and swayed, one hand going to the purple bruise on her temple as she scanned the room with desperate eyes.

'I'm sorry, Rhonda, they took him,' I said as Chris helped me to my feet.

'You promised you'd protect him, that you wouldn't let them have him.' Rhonda flew at me, enraged, and only Chris's quick reflexes stopped her attack.

He caught her fist as she aimed it at my head and then spun her arm behind her back. 'This is not helping. You need to calm down.'

'They have my son. They're going to kill him.' Rhonda struggled against Chris for a moment, but was unable to break free and her body sagged in his grip, tears streaming down her face.

'There's still time. They have to keep him alive until Almorthanos is free. If you want to get your son back before that happens, you need to control your emotions. Blaming Tyler won't get you anywhere, and you have no idea what she is willing to do to save your precious son.' He let go of her arm and gave her a slight push.

She straightened up and peered at me, hope blooming in her eyes. 'What is he talking about? Is there a way to save Connor?'

'We don't have the resources to go up against Malia and her followers on our own, but I know someone who does.' I took a deep breath, wondering if I could trust Rhonda with the truth. She had been on Malia and Almorthanos's side up until they threatened her son, and she could easily baulk at allying herself with her ancient enemies. Then again, like me, she had nothing left to lose.

'Cade can do what we can't.'

'Cade.' Rhonda's features contorted into one of distaste. 'He would never lift a finger to help me or my son. He'd be glad to get rid of us.'

'Having met his right hand man, Killian, I don't doubt he would happily destroy anyone related to Malia and Almorthanos.

But we have something he wants. I'm hoping that will be enough to get him to help us.'

Her eyes narrowed. 'What could you possibly have that Cade would think is valuable enough to warrant aiding an enemy?'

'If he promises to protect Connor and the rest of you, I will let Almorthanos out of Demania so he can kill him once and for all.'

Rhonda sank down onto the arm of the couch. 'To do that you would have to die. That's the only way the key will work.'

'I know.'

'And you'd be willing to do that, die, to keep Connor safe?'

'Yes.'

She pushed herself to her feet. 'All right then, what are we waiting for?'

Chris shook his head and grabbed my arm. 'You do not have to do this, and you don't even know if Cade has accepted your offer.'

'We'd better go and find out then, because I am not going to leave Sam and Connor in Malia's hands for a second longer than necessary.'

His grip on my arm tightened. 'I am not going to stand by while you offer to die to save everybody else. That is never going to happen, even if I have to tie you down.'

'You can't stop me.'

Chris opened his mouth to argue the point, and then his gaze focused on something behind me, eyes wide. 'You.'

I spun around, and hurriedly backed up as six men appeared in the middle of the apartment. One of them was Killian. The other five had white wings and swords sheathed at their hips. I recognised four of them from when we'd visited the compound. I had never seen the last man before. Like all the winged male Tr'lirians I had seen so far, he went bare chested, and his tall, muscular build, dark blond hair and deep blue eyes were so like Chris's that I knew who he was.

'Cade, I presume.'

He gave me a sharp nod, shimmering white wings sparkling in the light of the crystal chandelier hanging over the dining table. He took a step forward, bypassing me to confront Chris.

'Hello, son.'

Rhonda gasped, while Chris glowered at Cade. 'You are not my father.'

'You are my son, in every way that counts, and as such I have the right to question why you have become entangled with the likes of these.' With an arrogant flick of his wrist, he pointed at Rhonda and me. 'They are beneath you, and yet here you are, conspiring with them to stop me from vanquishing our family's enemy.'

Cade turned his attention on me, reaching out to grasp my chin. 'Remarkable, the likeness, and when I first got here and saw Talaom and his rabble entering the hotel I believed you to be just as treacherous as the one whose face you bear.'

I pulled free of his grip. 'I'm nothing like her.'

'So Killian has assured me. He advised me to wait, to watch and see what they wanted with you. He was most insistent, and made me curious as to what manner of woman you were that my second in command would place such faith in you, despite your unfortunate lineage.'

I slid a sideways glance at Killian, whose handsome face remained deadpan. I thought back on all our encounters so far, the demeaning way he'd treated me. He was the last person I would expect to support me.

Cade smiled; a humourless smirk that carried a hint of menace. 'Your adamant announcement of your intention to honour the deal you offered me indicates his assessment of your integrity was correct.'

'Do you accept?'

'Tyler, no.' Chris tugged on my arm. 'I won't let you do it.'

Before I could say anything Cade waved his hand and said, 'Silence him.'

Two of the Tr'lirians jumped on Chris, pulling him away from me. He fought back, cursing, hitting out at them with his good arm. One of them dug his fingers into Chris's injured shoulder. He cried out, colour leaching from his face, sagging to his knees. His opponents kept him there as another Tr'lirian moved forward with a gag.

I dragged my eyes away from Chris and met Cade's cold gaze. 'Do we have a deal?'

'Though it pains me to let any of Malia's tainted clan live, it will be as you wish. I will forgo my desire to scourge this world clean of their ilk. As Rallani is already exiled here in the physical plane, to let her and her half-breed son live out their lives will be of no consequence.'

Rhonda stepped forward. 'What about the rest of my clan? Will you still let them live in Angellin?'

'Those who do not wish to join you in exile will be executed. That is the price I demand for saving your son. Will you pay it?'

Rhonda blanched, but squared her shoulders. 'Gladly.'

'Then let us begin.' He pulled his sword out of his sheath and faced me. 'Time to die.'

CHAPTER 25

'Wait.' I backed up as Cade stalked towards me.

'I thought you were ready to die?'

'I am, but not like this. It has to be done in front of Malia if we are to save Sam and my brother, and get my cousin back.'

Cade lowered his sword. 'What do you propose?'

I took a deep breath and told him my plan.

He listened in silence, frown deepening. Then he sheathed his sword. 'Call her so we can finish this.'

Rhonda gave me Talaom's number and I punched it into my phone. With a deep breath, I hit the call button.

'What took you so long?' Talaom's gravelly voice sounded in my ear.

'I want to talk to Malia.'

'She's busy entertaining your detective. She gave instructions that they are not to be disturbed. Once he satisfies her... curiosity, she'll call you back.'

Ice settled in the pit of my stomach at the image his words sparked, of Malia and Sam with limbs entwined, bringing back memories of the night I'd found Sarah and Logan in bed together.

I made my voice harsh. 'If she wants her brother out of Demania, she'll talk to me now.' I hung up the phone, hands shaking.

I looked over at Chris and had to avert my eyes at the naked despair in his. I focused on my breathing, steadying my hands as I waited for my phone to ring, struggling not to think about what Malia was doing to Sam in the time it took her to call back.

Cade and Killian conversed in low tones in the corner of the room. Rhonda paced, biting her nails and checking her watch. The other Tr'lirians crowded around Chris, keeping him immobile, though I noticed they kept wary eyes on Rhonda and me.

Fifteen excruciating minutes later the phone rang, making me jump, and I fumbled to answer it. 'Hello?'

'I do like your detective,' said Malia, her voice a sexy purr. 'He will be the perfect father for my daughters.'

'You are not going to touch him.'

'Oh, Tyler, I already have.'

She was lying. She had to be. Sam would never do that. I swallowed down my jealousy. 'I am ready to let your brother out of Demania, after you release Sam, Connor and Emily.'

'You know that isn't possible. I need this body, and my brother needs Connor's if he is to be truly free.'

I fought down my revulsion at what I was about to suggest. 'Connor is only half Tr'lirian and Emily has barely any Tr'lirian blood at all. If you switch over to full Tr'lirian bodies you'd be able to enter the astral plane again, no longer chained to the physical world.'

'You expect me to sacrifice two of my people just to save your brother and your cousin?'

I forced a note of incredulity into my voice. 'I'd have thought their loyalty to you would have them volunteering. I'm willing to die for the good of my family. Are you telling me no one in your family is ready to die for you?' I held my breath, willing her ego to bite.

After a long silence she said, 'Very well. Your life in return for theirs. I'll be in touch with the details of the trade.' The line went dead and I grasped the nearest chair to stop myself from toppling over.

I forced my head up and met Cade's eyes. 'You better hold up on your end of this deal or I swear I will haunt you for an eternity.'

He sneered at me. 'Watch your mouth, little girl. I could snap you in two any time I want.'

'And Almorthanos would remain beyond your reach. I don't trust Malia, and I have no choice when it comes to trusting you. You hold yourself as better than her, better than all of her clan. Prove it. Keep my family safe and show me your high opinion of yourself is warranted.' I turned away before he could reply and went over to the Tr'lirians holding Chris.

'Let him go.'

They looked to Cade and when he nodded they released their hold on Chris. He ripped off his gag and launched himself to his feet. He clutched me to him, fingers digging into the flesh of my upper arm.

'Don't do this. Please, Tyler. I can't bear to lose you.'

'Control yourself. You are acting the fool, and over a woman from Clan Davila. No son of Clan Godden has ever fallen so low.'

Chris ignored Cade's outburst. Eyes locked onto mine, he kneeled at my feet. 'I'm begging you, do not throw your life away like this.'

A watery smile on my lips, I sank to my knees. 'I'm sorry,' I said, my words little more than a whisper. 'It's the only way.'

His chest rumbled with the force of the denial that burst from his lips. 'No. I will not let you die.' He crushed me to him and then stood up, pulling me along as he strode for the front door.

Cade's men appeared in front of us, blocking the door.

'Get out of my way,' said Chris. Fury radiated out of him, but it had no effect on the four stone-faced Tr'lirians barring his path.

Cade appeared on our left, while Killian positioned himself on our right. 'Do not make me regret releasing you, son.'

'I am not your son.' Chris shot Cade a black glare, chest heaving, a snarl on his lips.

Cade's form blurred and he reappeared with his sword in his hand, the tip pointed at Chris. Killian latched on to my arm, pulling me away from Chris. He swung me around so my back was against his chest, one arm clamped around my waist, the other holding his sword against my throat.

'He'll kill her now, and any hope her family has will die with her,' said Cade.

'No.' The denial came from Rhonda. She hurried to Chris's side, taking hold of his arm and tugging him around to face her. 'You have to let her go. My son will die if you don't.'

'I don't care about your son.'

'I do,' I said, drawing Chris's eyes back to me.

Emotional pain poured out of him, to be overtaken by a steely determination. 'If I can't be with you in this life, then I'll join you in the Underworld. I'll become a reaper again.'

'If you do that, I'll never forgive you. I'll reap your soul; destroy any hope you have of rebirth.'

'I'd rather that than to live without you.'

'Enough of this.' Cade swung his sword.

The hilt slammed into Chris's head. He dropped to the floor, eyes closed, blood streaming from a gash on his temple.

Killian released me and I fell to my knees beside Chris, feverishly checking his pulse. A strong and steady beat calmed my fears. Cade crouched beside me, his wings casting shadows over Chris's unconscious body.

'The sooner you are dead and gone from my son's life the better,' he said.

'You won't let him kill himself after I die?' I asked, refusing to be cowered by his hatred.

'We take care of our own. You no longer need concern yourself with him.' He stood and two of his men scooped Chris up.

I remained on the floor as I watched them carry Chris to his bedroom, shutting the door behind them, closing a chapter of my life at the same time. I dragged myself to my feet, striving to keep all emotion out of my voice and off my face. 'Let's do this.'

I strode over to the table and scooped up my phone, dialling Talaom's number. 'You've had enough time to come up with a place,' I said the second the call went through, not giving whoever was on the other end time to speak.

'The hall at the hockey grounds,' said Talaom. 'You have ten minutes.'

I hung up the phone and turned to Cade. 'Time to go.'

I scooped up Connor's car keys and then travelled down to the underground car park with Rhonda and Killian. Cade's insurance, Killian slipped into the astral plane as soon as he took a seat in the back of Connor's car. He would ride with us to the hockey grounds and rendezvous with Cade. The rest of his Tr'lirians were to station themselves around the hall, ready to annihilate Malia and Almorthanos once they were in their new bodies.

Rhonda and I did not speak as I drove to the hockey grounds, and it wasn't just Killian's invisible presence in the backseat that stilled our tongues.

What do you say to someone at a time like this?

But this would be the last time I would ever see the woman who had been my stepmother for almost my entire life. As I waited at the lights at the end of the bridge, waiting to take the right hand turn that would lead me closer to my final death, I glanced over at her.

'What will you do now?' I asked.

She shrugged, the glow from the dash doing little to illuminate her silhouette. 'Move, I guess. Take Connor and find a place where no one knows us, build a new life.' She turned to face me, her expression bleak. 'I'm betraying my clan. Any one of them would kill me on sight if they were to find out what I've done.'

'What about Dad?'

She snorted. 'He can rot in that stinking armchair of his for all I care, or find himself a new wife to be at his beck and call. I am done with him.'

'Connor might not feel the same way.'

'Connor will adapt to life without his father. He will have no choice.'

The traffic light changed to green and I drove around the corner. Three sets of lights later I turned left, heading for the small side street that wound around the hockey grounds. After Killian slipped out, I pulled into the car park beside Talaom's car. The large doors on the side of the hall were open, and I could see several figures grouped together in the middle.

I switched off the ignition. 'Maybe you should stay in the car,' I said to Rhonda.

'Like hell I will. I'm not sitting back while my son's life is in danger.' She climbed out of the car and slammed the door shut.

I got out and joined her, glad she was with me, a bitter sweet smile on my face. This would be the first time we'd stood side by side for anything.

Without giving myself time to think, I strode towards the hall, eager to finish this once and for all, comforted to know my enemies would go down with me.

CHAPTER 26

My eyes went to Sam first. He sat in a chair, thick ropes pinning his arms to his sides. Malia stood beside him, one hand on his shoulder. When she saw me watching she grabbed a handful of his hair with both hands and wrenched his head up before covering his mouth with her own. Sam tossed his head, but she tightened her grip, forcing him to endure her foul kiss.

When she finally released him she ran a hand over her lips, and gave me a sultry smile. 'He really is quite delicious. It will be a shame to let him go before I have fully enjoyed the delights his body has to offer. Perhaps once you are dead I can persuade him to return to my bed.'

'Never going to happen,' said Sam before I could respond. He spat at her feet. 'You taste like shit.'

Malia's face darkened and she slapped him across the face. His head rocked back from the force of her blow, but he made no sound. She lifted her hand, ready to hit him again and I took a step forward, both hands on my necklace.

'Leave him alone.'

Malia glared at me, but did lower her hand. Her eyes flicked to Rhonda, who had moved to where Connor was also tied to a chair.

'Rallani, you disappoint me. I never thought you would betray me like this, siding with your stepdaughter over your own clan.'

'I'm not siding with her. I'm here for my son.'

I flinched at Rhonda's words, though I'd known all along Connor was her priority.

Malia laughed; a dark and twisted laugh that sent a chill down my spine. 'Poor little Tyler. Nobody loves her. Everybody is just waiting for her to die.'

'I love her.' Sam's steady gaze met mine. He turned his gaze on Malia. 'You're nothing, a pale imitation, a knock-off. Only Tyler is the real deal.'

'Silence,' Malia roared at Sam, hitting him across the face over and over again.

I jumped forward, only to have Talaom spring out of nowhere and block my path. He pushed me back. I stumbled and fell to the ground, while he spun around and pulled Malia away from Sam.

'That's enough. We have a trade to make, or have you forgotten why we're here?'

Malia wrenched herself out of his grasp and straightened her dress. She still wore the white dress from the Underworld and it swirled around her feet with each movement as she fought to control her emotions.

Features contorted with rage, she pointed at me. 'I want that bitch dead, now.'

I grabbed my necklace and climbed to my feet as I was surrounded by black winged Tr'lirians. 'Anyone touches me before the trade is made and I will destroy every one of your souls. You know I can do it,' I said to Talaom. 'You saw what I did to your wraiths on top of Mount Pilbeam.'

He gave a sharp nod, and the Tr'lirians moved back three metres. 'They will not harm you, as long as you live up to your end of our bargain,' he said.

'I will, as long as you do the same.'

He gave another nod and two of the Tr'lirians left the circle around me, knives appearing in their hands. They moved over to Sam and Connor, cutting the ropes that bound them. Rhonda helped Connor to his feet and pulled him towards the nearest door.

'I'm not leaving,' he said, wrenching his arm free. 'Tyler needs me.'

'You have to leave,' I said, before Rhonda could speak, 'and you're taking Sam with you.'

Sam had got to his feet and was trying to get to my side, but the Tr'lirians surrounding me kept shoving him back. Blood trickled from the corner of his mouth, yet he refused to back down.

'You have to go, Sam. Please, I have to know you're okay.'

'Not happening.' He ducked under a wing, quick strides bringing him to my side. He took me in his arms, shaking his head slightly as he gazed down at me. 'You're crazy if you think I'd leave you alone with this lot.' He dipped his head, lips finding mine.

I savoured the taste of him, the strength of the arms holding me. I pressed my body against his, losing myself in his kiss. When our lips parted we remained in each other's arms, content in that moment to just be.

I pulled back, not wanting to let go but needing to see his face, look into his eyes one last time. 'Please, Sam. I need you to leave.'

He gave me a grim smile, cradling my face in his hands. 'I am not walking away from you, ever. I know you made a deal with these people but I didn't, and there is no way I'm going to let them hurt you. I will do whatever it takes to keep you safe. You got that?'

I stifled a sob, wishing there was some way I could make it through this alive and have a future with Sam. I knew it was an impossible wish. I was going to die, and the best I could hope for was that Sam not be hurt in the process.

I managed a nod, even forced out a tremulous smile, and he moved until we stood side by side, holding hands.

His body was tense as he surveyed the room. 'Where's Bradbury?'

'He tried to stop me, so I had to knock him out.' I couldn't tell him what really happened, not with Malia and Talaom watching on.

Sam snorted. 'You realise I'm going to have to kill him next time I see him. I told him to keep you safe.'

I smiled through my tears and Sam squeezed my hand. I marshalled my courage and looked over at Malia. 'I want Emily back, now.'

Malia glared at me, but gave Talaom a nod. He made a signal with his hand and a winged Tr'lirian appeared beside him, a young woman hanging limp in his arms. She had short, spiky brown hair and as the Tr'lirian laid her on the ground in front of Malia, I saw blood on the back of her shirt.

I swallowed down my revulsion. The bloodstains were positioned where her wings had once been and from the bruising around her neck, and on what I could see of her arms, she had not given them up willingly.

My resolve to see Malia destroyed strengthened as she laid herself down on the floor beside the unconscious woman.

I couldn't see the reaper that took her soul, but I saw the effect it had. Malia's body arched up, a gasp escaping her lips, followed by an agonised scream. It was less painful for the other woman, already unconscious and spared the agony of having her soul ripped out. My actions had led to this atrocity. My suggestion had seen her stripped of her wings and her body.

I tore my eyes away from her face, focusing on Emily's body, waiting for some sign it had reunited with her soul, waiting for her to come back to life. Malia's new body stirred first, a process as painful to watch as the extraction of her soul had been, and my heart ached for the pain Emily would soon feel.

Talaom helped Malia to her feet and she winced as she ran her hands over her new body. 'Somebody get me something to dull the pain. I'd forgotten how much having your wings ripped off hurts.' She stripped off the bloodstained shirt and dropped it on the floor, a look of distaste on her face as she inspected the pink vest that covered her breasts. 'And find me some new clothes while you're at it.'

Talaom immediately pulled off his shirt, revealing a muscular bronzed chest. He offered his shirt to Malia but she shook her head, eyes gleaming, as she stretched out a hand and traced the trail of dark hairs that led down to the waistband of his jeans.

He stood there, towering over her, smirking at me until Malia dropped her hand. He flung his shirt over one shoulder.

Malia stepped over Emily's body and confronted me. 'Satisfied?'

'Not until I know Emily is alive and well.'

Emily groaned, and then wailed as the pain of reconnecting with her body hit. I let go of Sam's hand and rushed to her side, helping her to sit up.

She blinked; eyes confused as she gazed around the hall. 'Where am I?'

'It's okay, Emily. You're going to be okay.'

Her expression cleared when her eyes met mine. 'I had the weirdest dream. I was fast asleep, dreaming about your brother, and all a sudden I was screaming and everything went black and when I came to I was floating in space, surrounded by billions of stars, and it was so cold. It felt I was hanging there for hours, in the darkness, and then the pain came back and I woke up here.' She cast another look around the hall. 'Or am I still dreaming?'

I smiled, her stream of words convincing me this truly was Emily. I hugged her, tears filling my eyes, happy at least one thing had gone right. Now for the rest.

I helped Emily to her feet and led her over to Connor. 'Take care of her for me,' I said.

He gave me a solemn nod, wrapping an arm around her waist.

I kissed him on the cheek. 'Your mother is right. You have to leave. You have to get as far away from here as possible, and take Emily with you.'

'I'm not going to desert you, Tyler.'

'You're not deserting me. You're fulfilling my last wish. Now go, before this lot try to stop you.'

He wrapped his free arm around me and hugged me so hard I was sure I'd be bruised. He let go, firming his grip on Emily and leading her from the hall. Rhonda followed them, stopping at the door and looking at me.

'Thank you,' she said, and then she too was gone. Moments later I heard the familiar roar of Connor's engine as he sped away into the night.

I took Sam's hand once more. 'Who will be Almorthanos's host?' I dreaded the thought another unwilling Tr'lirian would be stripped of his wings and his life because of the deal I had made to save Connor.

'I will,' said Talaom, stepping up to stand beside Malia, 'in return for the privilege of killing you.' His hand whipped up.

Sam shouted my name, tugging on my hand as he moved to shove me behind him, even as something slammed into my chest, pushing me backwards. He leaned over me, horror in his hazel eyes. Only then did I realise I was on the floor. People crowded in around Sam; Talaom holding a gun, Malia with a gleeful smile and two winged Tr'lirians who latched on to Sam's arms and dragged him away.

Then I saw him. The Grim Reaper, come to collect my soul.

The Tr'lirians parted, averting their eyes from where he stalked towards me. His voluminous cloak billowed around him, hood obscuring his face. A skeletal hand gripped his scythe and the mist followed in his wake, a roiling sea of nether that blocked the hall and everyone in it from view. All I could see was the Grim Reaper as his bony fingers pulled back his hood to expose his skull.

Fire burned in his empty eye sockets and his jaw creaked as a maniacal laugh boomed out of him. 'This is going to hurt,' he said as he gripped my neck and squeezed.

I screamed, back arching, heels drumming on the ground as he ripped my soul out of my dying body.

Everything went black.

CHAPTER 27

Onsciousness dribbled in piece by piece. I couldn't move, couldn't open my eyes, unable to do anything to alleviate the pain racking my body. Deafened by the screaming in my head, I begged for the sweet mercy of oblivion.

Hands gripped me, digging into the flesh on my lower legs and dragging me across the ground. Icy fingers poked and nipped at my body; a cold burn left in their wake. Whoever had been dragging me shifted their grip to my ankles and wrenched them up in the air, suspending me upside down. Frozen hands covered my eyes, and when they were removed I could once again see.

I hung over a black chasm, dim light flashing off jagged needles of ice that jutted out of the walls. Nether roiled and swirled among the ice, constantly moving, obscuring what lay at the bottom of the chasm. The black mist expanded, bursting out of the chasm, over and around me.

My paralysis ended and I twisted my head, looking up and meeting the Grim Reaper's malevolent stare.

'Told you it would hurt,' he said, a cruel smirk thinning his lips even further. 'You're here in the flesh. Ripping you out of the physical world was the only way we could guarantee your necklace wouldn't resurrect you. What happens to you here is real, no illusion, and I have an eternity to make you regret crossing me.' He let go of my ankles.

The scream trapped in my head burst out of my mouth, its echo following me as I fell, arms flailing, down, down, down, to the bottom of the Underworld.

I slammed into the ground, splinters of ice piercing my skin. I lay on my back, body twisted, waves of agony sweeping over me, forced to watch as the Grim Reaper, nether wrapped around his skeletal form, landed lightly beside me.

He flicked his wrist and nether swarmed over me, grabbing hold of my broken limbs. I arched my back and screamed as they pulled and twisted my body back into shape. Then they let go and I flopped, gulping in air as the pain in my mended body ebbed away with excruciating slowness.

'On your feet, reaper.' The Grim Reaper kicked me in the ribs, forcing the air out of my lungs, and I rolled to the left when he kicked out at me again.

Clutching my side, I dragged myself to my feet, staggering and almost falling as pain shot through my chest with each movement. His kick must have cracked some of my ribs. Bad as the pain was, I refused to cower before him. I straightened, unable to stop myself from groaning at the fresh wave of agony that swept over me.

The Grim Reaper glared back at me; his terrifying visage partially hidden by his hood. Then he morphed, his form taking a shape that was familiar but no less frightening; Jonathon Grimm.

'Hello, Tyler,' said Grimm, his glacial voice unable to compete with the soulless expression in his eyes. 'Welcome to Hell.' He waved a hand and the nether that surrounded us parted, forming a long hallway.

At the end of it was a door, forged of a dull black metal that repelled the eyes and induced nausea so strong it doubled me over.

Grimm grabbed hold of my hair, twisting it around his fist and pulling me with him as he marched towards the door. The closer I got, the worse I retched, eyes streaming, stomach muscles aching. I collapsed and he dragged me the remaining distance, the fire in my scalp pale in comparison to the agony besetting my body as my ribs grated against each other.

Grimm let go of my hair and grabbed me under the arms, lifting me up and holding me in front of him so that I faced the door. Bile dribbled down my chin, strands of hair sticking to my face. I kept retching, but there was nothing left in my stomach to come out, and I drew up a shaking hand to wipe my mouth.

Grimm shook me and I cried out, blackness hovering on the edge of my vision at the pain in my torso.

I forced down my nausea and twisted away from him, staggering and then steadying myself on the chasm wall, fighting back a scream when one of the spikes of ice pierced my palm. I focused on the pain, welcoming it, using it to block out the debilitating stench emanating from the door. Breathing heavily through my mouth, I dragged my hair out of my eyes and glared at Grimm.

He ignored me, moving forward to run his hands over the door. 'It is time, Master.'

A boom sounded from the other side of the door and it made the walls of the chasm shake. Grimm's eyes rolled back in his head, thin lips parting in a smile, as his body quivered. I turned away, sickened by his gasps of pleasure.

He turned his head and licked his lips. 'Soon you will long for our master's touch, beg to receive it, and then you will be His for eternity.'

'No.' I forced the denial out, throat dry, lips cracked. 'Never.'

He let go of the door and clapped his hands.

The mist of nether burst into movement, surrounding me, pushing me forward. It forced me to stand in front of the blighted door and I cringed, convinced one touch would taint me forever.

'Fulfil your destiny. Open the door.'

I shook my head, unable to bring myself to touch it; sure whatever lay on the other side should never be released. But the nether twined itself around my wrists, forming thick ropes that pulled and twisted until my left hand touched my necklace, while my right hand stretched out towards the door.

I struggled against the ropes, whimpering at the pain in my ribs as my hand was inexorably drawn closer to the door. I curled my fingers into my palm, forming a fist. Grimm moved to my side and wrenched my fist open, and nether swarmed around my fingers, splaying them out so that the palm of my hand lay flat against the centre of the door.

The nether seeped away, removing the barrier between flesh and cursed metal.

Cold fire blasted into my hand. I convulsed and slumped to my knees; palm still fused to the door. My other hand clutched my necklace, which started to heat up and, no matter how hard I tried to let go, I couldn't make my fingers move. The necklace began to pulse, its beat synchronising with the rapid beat of my heart. The cold from the door swept through my right arm, across my chest, and flowed down my left arm. I screamed when it reached my hand and smashed its way into the necklace. The necklace retaliated, blasting the cold fire with a surge of power that flowed like molten lava.

Blinded by the steam that erupted from my skin as the lava fought to dominate the cold fire, I whimpered as the war continued to rage inside my body. The lava sizzled out of my palm and spread over the door. The metal beneath my hand bubbled, boiling my skin along with it. But the cold fought back, fighting to regain dominance, and the melting door froze over.

The steam dissipated and I moaned when I saw my hand, the bones fused together by the lava, still connected to the door. My skin was blackened, peeling away in places to reveal charred flesh.

I no longer felt pain; the lava had burned away my nerve endings, and all for nothing.

The door still stood, locked.

Relief swamped me. It hadn't worked. Almorthanos was still trapped in Demania; the world spared his evil presence.

I sensed movement beside me and turned to see the Grim Reaper with his scythe raised above his head. He swung it at the centre of the door. A loud clang sounded and it shattered inwards at the same time as my necklace exploded and ripped through my throat.

Flung backwards by the simultaneous explosions, I landed on my back, helpless to do anything but watch as Almorthanos stepped through the ruined doorway. Tall, with black hair and even blacker eyes, clad only in dark pants, he strode over to where Grimm, once more in his human guise, kneeled.

Almorthanos patted Grimm on his head. 'Rise, my faithful servant. You have earned your place at my side.' He grimaced and twisted around to inspect his back.

Blood seeped out of two large gashes, one on each of his shoulder blades, wounds inflicted thousands of years earlier when Cade had ripped his wings off. Time stood still in Demania so the wounds had never healed.

'Thank you, Master.' Grimm stood, devotion on his gaunt face, and looked over at me. 'Shall I heal her?'

Almorthanos pursed fleshy lips as he considered my burned and disfigured body.

'Not yet. First she must prove her worth.' He crouched beside me and took my head in his hands. 'Will you obey me, child of Davila, and accept me as your master?'

His eyes bored into mine and I felt a pressure in my skull, as if a hand rummaged through my brain, seeking to rearrange it. I sought to wrench my head out of his grasp, but could not move. I attempted to close my eyes and block out his penetrating stare, but my muscles would not respond.

Helpless, frozen, unable to fight him off, I used the only thing I had left to me.

I pitched my will against his. I could not speak my denial of his dominion over me, but I could think it. In my head, I screamed defiance. His eyes narrowed and the pressure in my head grew. It hammered at me, seeking to bash its way through, so strong it obliterated every thought, except for one.

I must not yield.

Almorthanos abruptly released me, and my head slammed into the ground. He staggered as he got to his feet, and Grimm rushed to his side.

'Master?'

Almorthanos waved him away. 'Do not fear, Grimm, it is merely the vagaries of time, catching up with this body. Has a new host been selected?'

'Yes, Master.'

'Then take me to him so I may once again walk at Malia's side.'

'What about her?'

'Leave her here. She is stubborn, stronger than I had planned for, and it will take time to break her spirit. But break it I will.' He leaned over me, black hair now liberally streaked with grey, lines on his once smooth face, as old age caught up with him.

'Make no mistake, girl. You will be mine.' He smiled. 'Use this time wisely or when next we meet I will not be so pleasant.'

Nether wrapped around him and Grimm and I watched as they rose out of the chasm, leaving me lying broken and discarded on the ground with only the doorway to Demania to keep me company. I glanced at the door, horrified to think of what else lay beyond it. What other horrors might use it to escape?

Confusion and then relief washed over me. The door was

whole, with no sign it had ever been blasted to pieces. The stench remained, not as strong as before, but building up as I lay there, trapped in my broken body.

How long would it be before they came back for me so Almorthanos could fulfil his promise to break my spirit? As nausea gripped my stomach I realised any amount of time was too long. Each second I lay there the door's emanations grew stronger, flowing over me, penetrating my pores.

If I didn't get out of there soon, Almorthanos wouldn't need to break me. The doorway to Demania would do it for him.

CHAPTER 28

'Wake up, Tyler. You must wake up. We need you.'

I came to with a start and instantly retched as the emanations from the door hit me anew. I wanted to sink back into unconsciousness, escape the torment of being this close to Demania.

Pale mist swirled above me, and I welcomed the thought that Grimm had come back to collect me so Almorthanos could batter his way into my head. At least then I might get out of this chasm and away from the soul-destroying door.

Faces appeared in the mist, insubstantial and transparent, but nonetheless familiar. They were the souls of the people that had been stored in my necklace. They floated above me, constantly moving, whirling as one face was replaced by another, until I had seen all of their faces, except one.

That one was Sarah, my former best friend, whose soul I had reaped after she'd become a wraith and tried to kill me. Chris had told me that to reap the soul of a wraith meant they died a final death, no longer able to be reborn into a new body.

The mist parted, and there she was. Unlike the souls in the

mist, she appeared solid, though she hovered a foot off the ground. She kneeled in the air beside me.

'You have to get up, Tyler.'

'I can't move,' I said, surprised at the sound of my own voice. Why could I speak now when I could not during Almorthanos's attempt to impose his will on me?

'You have to let go. Your body is holding you back. Release it and you will be free,' said Sarah, with a gentle smile.

'I don't understand.'

'Your body is dead, but your soul is not. You can rise out of this place, but first you have to let go.'

'Will I be like you?'

'No. My soul is dead. I am part of the Underworld now.'

'I'm so sorry. I never meant to hurt you.'

'Shush.' She stroked my face. 'It's all right. You did nothing wrong. I brought this on myself. I let Grimm use my jealousy to turn me against you. Can you forgive me for what I tried to do?'

'Of course I forgive you. I love you, Sarah.'

'I love you, too. But you must get out of here. Grimm is sending reapers to kill your family as soon as his master has a new body. They never intended to honour the bargain they made with you.'

'I knew they'd betray me, but I took precautions,' I said, reluctant to name Cade. Grimm had fooled me once with a fake soul. This could be a trick to get me to divulge what I knew, or to break me.

She shook her head. 'Grimm will do whatever it takes to destroy those you love. You humiliated and weakened him, and stopped him from accessing the physical world. He will never forgive or forget. And now his master is free, together they plan to enslave mankind and wage a war that will destroy the world. You must stop them.'

'How?'

'You must break free of your body, and rise to the world above.'

'But I'm dead, and my necklace was destroyed. I won't be able to do anything.'

'You are a reaper, and in the world above people are dying. Go to them.'

She made it sound so easy, but I'd never reaped a soul without my necklace before, and it had exploded, ripping my throat out in the blast. How was I supposed to reap a soul without it to guide me?

But the belief shining in Sarah's eyes meant I had to try.

I closed my eyes, focusing on where my necklace had rested against my collarbones, the place where the soul resided in every human being. I still couldn't move any part of my body but I could feel warmth as my soul responded to my intent. I was a reaper, and it was time to reap.

I lifted free of my body, choking back a cry as I saw myself for the first time. Blackened and broken, patches of bone and singed flesh visible, I was a vision from a nightmare. A light touch on my arm drew me away and I looked over at Sarah.

Her smile was radiant. 'I knew you could do it,' she said. She pointed behind me and I glanced over my shoulder and gasped.

Silvery wings, as insubstantial as the rest of my astral form, grew out of my back, each feather shining brightly, pushing the darkness away. I marvelled at them until Sarah tugged on my arm. The wings flexed and then lifted me into the air with gentle sweeps as Sarah drew me with her, out of the chasm. The souls of those I'd reaped eddied in the air around us. We rose higher and higher, into a dense blackness, the only light coming from my wings. Soon the souls fell away and only Sarah and I continued on.

Pinpricks of light appeared above us, filling the black sky, thousands of them, twinkling and shining, the sight of them filling me with joy.

'What are they?'

'They are the souls of every living being in Easton,' said Sarah, hovering beside me, 'and now you must go to them.'

I looked back at the souls, frowning when one dimmed before it disappeared.

'Hurry, Tyler,' said Sarah, as she began to descend into the depths of the Underworld. 'Time is running out.'

I looked back at the souls, finding the place where the light of one had been extinguished, and saw another soul had begun to dim. I focused on it, on the draw to reap, and felt myself propelled forward. I passed through the black veil separating the Underworld from the physical world, and slipped into the astral plane.

I streaked over Easton, fear gripping me as the soul drew me towards the hockey fields. How much time had passed since I died? Surely Sam and the others were well clear by now? A sickening feeling made a mockery of my attempts to convince myself nothing was wrong. Cade had promised to protect my family. They had to be safe.

I skimmed over the trees bordering the creek that meandered its way around the hockey fields, and skirted the hall.

I entered a warzone.

The car park was filled with the dead and dying. As I watched, two black winged Tr'lirians ripped the wings off one of Cade's men, tossing them on the ground before stabbing the now mortal man in the chest. They left him to die in the dirt and lifted into the air in search of other prey.

I could see Cade, fighting back to back with Killian, warding their foes off with swords. White winged Tr'lirians battled their black winged counterparts in the air above their leader, while men with guns shot at any who came too close. I couldn't see Malia or Almorthanos, who was presumably in Talaom's body by now. Grimm was also absent, but it was what I did see that terrified me.

Connor's car, all four doors open, stood in the middle of the road leading out of the car park. I zoomed over to it and peered inside. Empty.

I scanned the car park, hovering over the bodies of the fallen, searching for anyone I knew. The hollow below my throat warmed and I allowed it to direct me, praying it was not taking me to reap the soul of someone I loved.

It led me back to the hall and I steeled myself before I floated inside.

I gasped and Sam spun around, a bloodstained knife in his hands. 'Tyler,' he said, 'is that you?'

'Yes, Sam, I'm here,' I said, tears falling at the sight of Connor, Rhonda and Emily crouched behind him.

Sam's eyes tracked the tears as they crashed to the ground at my feet. He looked up at where they had come from. 'Wish I could see you.'

'Me too,' I said, smiling through my tears. My smile faded. I'd felt the call of a dying soul, and it had led me here. But Sam and the others were the only ones inside the hall. Whose blood was on the knife?

I brushed against Sam as I floated past him. He shivered and rubbed his arm.

'No.' I sank to the ground and stared at where Connor cradled Emily in his arms, while Rhonda held a blood-soaked cloth over her chest. Emily's face was pale, eyes closed, dark lashes fluttering as her life leeched out of her.

'It was Malia,' said Sam, as he kneeled beside Rhonda. 'She sent her men after them as soon as you were... gone. They brought them back here and she stabbed Emily. She was going to kill all of us, but Cade showed up and I guess getting away from him mattered more to her than killing us.'

He heaved out a sigh. 'I'm sorry. I tried to stop her.'

I tore my eyes away from Emily and saw he was also hurt. The front of his shirt was slashed, blood and skin showing through the gap. I moved over to him, concentrating on making my hands solid as I slid the fabric aside so I could inspect his wounds.

Sam sucked in a breath. 'Cold,' he said, gritting his teeth as my ghostly fingers roamed over his chest. I let the remnant of his shirt fall back into place, relieved to find his wounds were not serious. Emily had not been so lucky. I turned away from Sam and touched her chin.

She opened her eyes and gazed up at me.

'Tyler,' she said in a voice less than a whisper. 'You're beautiful, like an angel.' She stretched out a hand and ran her fingers over one of my wings, setting a shiver over my astral form. Her hand dropped away as the light in her eyes went out.

I cried, and Sam's hand stretched out to catch my tears as they fell.

Connor hugged Emily's body tighter, tears wetting his face while Rhonda, eyes red, rubbed his back.

I placed my hand on Emily's chest, above the wound that had taken her life, and drew forth her soul. It hovered in the air in front of me, the purity of its light simply stunning. I gazed at it in wonder, getting a sense of Emily's infectious laughter as the light expanded to touch every one of us.

Sam, Connor and Rhonda all lifted their heads, and from their expressions I knew they could see it too and were just as amazed as me.

I didn't want to touch Emily's soul, to dim her radiant light, and I froze, wondering what I was supposed to do now. I had always placed souls in my necklace, but that had been destroyed.

A wave of reassurance came from Emily's soul, drawing me in, and I reached out to tap it with one finger, intending to carry it back to the Underworld with me. Maybe Sarah would be able to tell me what to do next, how to send Emily's soul on for rebirth. No matter what happened, I would make sure Grimm never got his hands on it.

The second I touched Emily's soul it grew brighter, its light expanding to fill the entire hall. Then it vanished, leaving me with a sense the next journey for Emily had already begun. I hoped her next life treated her better than this one had.

I readied myself for the journey back to the Underworld, where I would be reunited with Sarah once more.

A whirlwind reached out and took hold of me, spinning me every which way. I cried out and Sam shot to his feet.

'Tyler, what's wrong?'

I had no breath to answer him, sucked into a maelstrom of darkness that blotted out everything. Pain filled me, as intense as anything I had ever experienced before, shooting into me from every direction, pushing and pulling at me.

The wind released me, and I twitched as the pain subsided. I groaned, fighting to open my eyes, sure this must be an attack from Grimm. I had to get up, draw him away from Sam and the others. I forced my eyes open and confusion sent me into a spin.

I was in Connor's arms, his blue eyes wide as he stared down at me, while Sam and Rhonda peered over his shoulders.

'Emily, you're alive,' said Connor, a smile blooming on his face.

I gasped, horror sweeping over me.

I'd stolen Emily's body.

CHAPTER 29

My eyes sought Sam. 'This wasn't supposed to happen. I didn't want this.'

His eyes widened. 'Tyler?'

Connor let me go, confusion on his face as Sam helped me stand. Hands shaking, I poked at my chest where blood soaked through the white silk dress and could find no trace of the injury that had killed Emily.

'You took her body.' Rhonda sounded as horrified as I felt.

'I didn't mean to. It just happened.' I hung my head, biting at my bottom lip.

Sam gently coaxed my head up. 'It doesn't matter how it happened, what matters is that you're alive.'

'It matters to me. I'm no better than Malia, taking over someone else's body. Emily is dead because of me, and now I do this to her.' I waved a hand over my new body. 'It's disgusting.'

'You are nothing like Malia,' said Sam, eyes intent on mine, 'and what happened to Emily isn't your fault.'

'I'm the one who put her in danger. I'm the one who told Malia how to get a new body, and now I've done exactly the same thing.'

'No, this was an accident. I'm sorry Emily died, but I'm not sorry her death brought you back to life. You're alive, Tyler. After everything you've been through, you've got a second chance.'

'I can't live like this. I don't want to live like this.'

'You have to. We need you. I need you.' He ran a hand through his hair, mouth set in a grimace. 'Talk to Bradbury. Maybe he can help you adjust.'

I took a deep breath, shuddering as I contemplated a future stuck in someone else's body. Nausea engulfed me and I doubled over, retching as the contents of my stomach were expelled. Sam stoked my back as my shudders subsided. When I straightened up, he handed me a neatly folded handkerchief and I wiped my mouth.

I was just about to thank him when a loud explosion went off outside the hall. I raced to the large double doors at the end, with Sam, Connor and Rhonda close behind me. A huge cloud of dust hung over the car park, chunks of metal and other debris raining down on the people below.

'My car,' said Connor, running ahead of me. 'The bastards blew up my car.'

As the dust settled the wreckage of his Commodore became visible, torn to shreds by whatever explosive had been used. Bodies were strewn on the ground around the wreckage, thrown several metres by the force of the blast. Those with wings were groggily getting to their feet, while many of the bodies without wings remained ominously still.

I scanned the car park, noting the lack of black wings. I hunted for Cade and found him in the middle of the chaos, helping a bloodied Killian to his feet. I raced over to them.

'Cade, what happened?' Did you get Malia and Almorthanos?'

He glared at me. 'Go away, little girl, or there will be one fewer child of Clan Davila in the world, no matter what I promised Tyler.'

'I am Tyler.'

Cade stiffened. 'What madness is this?'

'Malia killed my cousin and when I reaped her soul I got sucked into her body, bringing it back to life.'

Cade's eyes narrowed as he scanned my new form. 'But you no longer wear the necklace. How is this possible?'

'I don't know, and right now that's the least of my concerns. Did you win? Are they dead?'

Cade's nostrils flared. 'We had them cornered and I was sure they were about to surrender and justice for my sister would finally be delivered. Then that vehicle exploded, and they used it as cover to flee the battlefield. Cowards.' He spat on the ground.

I hugged my arms around my chest, looking at all the bodies still sprawled on the ground. So many dead, and all for nothing. Worse than nothing. Almorthanos was free and reunited with his sister, and together they planned on taking over the world.

'We have to find them.'

'We will, but not today. My men need time to rest. But mark my words, Tyler Morgan, your part in this war is not done.' Cade tightened his grip on Killian as the two of them stepped into the astral plane. I watched as the rest of his men did the same, those with wings carrying the bodies of the fallen or supporting the wingless Tr'lirians that still lived.

As one, they lifted into the air and flew off in the direction of the compound. I watched until I could no longer see them, not sure how I felt about suddenly being able to see into the astral plane from the physical world. I scanned the rest of the bodies scattered over the car park, leaving Rhonda to comfort Connor over the loss of his beloved car as I walked among the dead.

Sam came with me and together we searched futilely for any signs of life. It was surreal, stepping over broken wings, the black and white feathers liberally coated in blood, discarded after they had been ripped from the backs of those fighting for either Clan Davila or Clan Godden.

Sirens sounded in the distance and Sam's expression hardened. 'We need to leave,' he said. 'If they find us here, with this lot,' he waved a hand over the car park, 'we'll be locked up and questioned for hours.'

I sighed, sad he had to hide from his colleagues because of his involvement with me. I turned around and walked back to Connor and Rhonda. 'We have to go. The police are coming.'

Rhonda gave a weary nod, eyes bleak as she surveyed the dead.

Connor frowned. 'Where are we going to go? Those sirens sound close and we don't have a car.'

On cue, headlights appeared at the main entrance to the car park and rolled towards us. My heart leaped at the sight of Chris in the driver's seat. Sam ushered me over to the car and opened the passenger door as soon as it came to a stop beside us.

'We need to get Tyler out of here, now.' Sam pushed me into the seat and closed the door, and then climbed into the back with Connor and Rhonda.

'Tyler?' Hope filled Chris's eyes as he gazed at me. Blood trickled down the side of his face from where Cade had hit him. His brow creased. Then his eyes went wide. 'You're in your cousin's body?'

I nodded, miserable, too choked up to talk.

'We don't have time for this, Bradbury,' said Sam. 'Get us out of here.'

Chris put the car into drive and gunned the accelerator. The car shot forward, leaving a trail of dust behind as he drove out the other side of the car park, away from the sirens. Within minutes we had rounded the hockey fields and were back on bitumen, navigating the back streets. Chris turned onto the main road heading to the bridge and shortly after crossing the river he pulled into his parking space in the underground carpark at the hotel.

My hands were shaking so much it took three attempts before

I could undo my seat belt. Sam opened my door and helped me out. I couldn't stop shivering even though it was a mild evening.

'Here, put this on.' Sam took his shirt off and guided my arms into the sleeves before doing up the buttons. Warmth radiated from him and I leaned closer. I wrapped my arms around him, feeling the smooth movements of his muscles beneath my palms. I nestled in even closer, pressing my face into his bare chest, needing his heat to chase away the chill that had settled into my body.

No. Not my body.

Emily's body.

I pulled away from Sam, hands clenched into fists. He took hold of my right arm and led me over to the elevator, with Chris, Connor and Rhonda at our heels. No one spoke on the ride to the penthouse. I hugged Sam's shirt to me, his scent rising from it, soothing me. Chris brushed past me to unlock his front door. He stepped aside so we could all shuffle in.

The second I stepped over the threshold Chris crushed me to his chest. 'Thank God you're alive. I thought I'd lost you.'

I pushed him away, shaking my head. 'This is not a good thing. This was not supposed to happen.' Tears spilled down my cheeks. 'Emily was supposed to live. Not me.'

'To hell with Emily. You're the only one I care about.' He tried to take me in his arms again and I sidestepped.

'I can't do this,' I said, the words bursting out of me, teeth chattering and my shivering intensifying.

Chris moved towards me again but Rhonda stepped in front of him. 'Just leave her be. Let me take care of her.'

Chris grimaced, but he stepped back as Rhonda took my arm and tugged me along with her. I kept my head down, not wanting to meet anyone's eyes as she led me from the room. She took me to the bathroom nestled between the two guest rooms and got the shower running. She pushed me towards the shower.

'You get clean while I find you something else to wear.' She slipped out of the room, leaving the door slightly ajar.

I undressed and stepped into the shower cubicle. Blood ran down the front of my chest and turned the water pink. I retched at the smell and hurriedly poured a glob of shower gel into my hands and rubbed it all over me. I tried not to think about what my hands were touching, unable to reconcile the juxtaposition between Emily's body and my soul.

I did not belong in this body.

I stood under the shower, letting the hot water wash away the soap suds. I started in on my hair, making sure I washed away any trace of blood. But I still didn't feel clean. No matter how much soap or shampoo I used, no matter how hot the water was, I couldn't wash away the stench that clung to every pore.

I was no better than a wraith, the rot invisible and yet insidious. My actions had put Emily in danger, stolen her future from her, and now I had taken her body as well.

I crumpled, falling to my knees, hot water streaming over me as I cried. Great big shuddering sobs ripped out of me as I rocked backwards and forward, wanting to die, to end this horrible twisted nightmare.

The water stopped flowing and I looked up through wet tangles of hair as Sam placed a towel around my shoulders. He lifted me out of the shower and cradled me in his arms. He carried me into my bedroom and sat on the bed with me still in his arms, all without saying a word.

He held me, his chin resting on top of my head.

I closed my eyes, letting out a deep shuddering breath as I relaxed into him, listening to his heartbeat.

I didn't want to move, ever, to open my eyes and face what my life had become. But I didn't have that luxury. Malia and Almorthanos were out there, plotting who knows what, and I was responsible for unleashing them on an unsuspecting world. It was up to me to make this right.

Somehow.

CHAPTER 30

I forced my eyes open and wriggled out of Sam's embrace to stand beside him.

'Thank you,' I said, pulling the towel more firmly around me, suddenly conscious of my state of undress. And I wasn't the only one in need of new clothes.

Droplets of water clung to Sam's bare chest, glistening in the light. I shivered, and not from the cold. I dragged my eyes away and focused on a spot over his shoulder, not ready to meet his eyes.

'I'll, uh, get dressed and be out in a minute.'

'Tyler.' Sam, hand outstretched, stepped towards me and I shuffled back.

'I'll be okay. I'm fine.' I shrugged.

'You're not fine,' he said. 'But we'll deal with that later. Right now I need you to look in the mirror.' He pointed over my shoulder at the mirrored doors on the wardrobe.

I shook my head, not ready to look into Emily's eyes.

'Tyler, you have wings on your back.'

I whirled around, letting the towel drop down to expose my back.

The tattoo started just above my shoulder blades and swept down past my waist. The wings were silver, just like the ones I had when in astral form, and shimmered with each movement I made.

'That's new, right?'

I nodded, swallowing down a lump. 'The same thing happened to Chris, when he came back to life, only his wings are black.' I had run my fingers over his wings, fascinated by how lifelike they were, but I had no desire to touch my own set.

I dropped the towel, no longer caring about Sam still being in the room as I scooped up the clothes Rhonda had laid on the bed for me. I pulled the underwear on with jerky movements, breathing heavily. I tugged on the nightshirt, finding little comfort in knowing the wings were covered.

'Malia didn't have wings tattooed on her back.'

I froze, peering at Sam. 'When did you see her back?'

He cleared his throat.

I shook my head, forcing away the image of Malia prancing around naked in front of him. 'Never mind. I don't want to know.'

I grabbed the towel and dried my hair. I combed out the tangles, expecting it to take longer than it did. Emily had kept her hair shorter than me. I put the comb back in my toilet bag and faced Sam.

'Malia was never a reaper, so she wouldn't have wings like me and Chris.'

'That explains it then,' he said, giving me a wry smile. His expression sobered as he stared at me. 'You can do this. You're stronger than you think. If Bradbury can adapt to living in a different body, so can you.'

'It's not the same, and you know it.' I rolled my shoulders.

'Give it time. Take it slow.' He moved until he stood right in front of me, tilting my head back and gazing intently into my eyes.

'I know you feel like an intruder but when I look into your eyes I see you, not Emily. It is the soul that breathes life into the body, not the other way around. You are Tyler Maree Morgan, and I love you.'

He dipped his head, lips covering mine in a kiss so sweet it brought tears to my eyes.

I pulled away. 'I can't,' I said, shaking my head. 'It's not right. This isn't my body.'

I brushed past him and opened the door.

Chris stood in the doorway; hand raised to knock again. He looked over my shoulder at Sam and then fixed his blue eyes on me. 'How are you doing?'

I stepped out of the room. 'I've had better days.'

Chris caught my arm before I could walk away. 'I know it's a shock to find yourself in somebody else's body, but it does get easier.'

I didn't want it to get easier. I wanted it to end. But I knew I couldn't say that to either Chris or Sam.

I tossed my head as I strode down the hall. 'What will make it easier is making sure the person responsible has been punished. Malia and Almorthanos are both going to pay for what they have done.'

Connor leaped to his feet when I entered the lounge. 'Glad to have you back, sis,' he said, bounding forward and hugging me. 'Though I was getting used to the idea of being an only child and getting more presents at Christmas.'

I forced out a laugh. 'You already get more presents than anyone else.'

'True, but a few more wouldn't hurt.' He gave me a cheeky grin.

I eased out of his arms. 'Sorry about your car.'

'Nah, it's fine,' he said, shrugging. 'I was getting bored with it anyway. I'll buy a better one with the insurance money.'

'I doubt your policy covers explosions,' said Rhonda. She

stood up and smoothed down her linen skirt. 'But I'm sure we can work something out.'

She stepped over to my side and cleared her throat. 'I'm truly sorry about what happened to your cousin, Tyler. But, as your detective said, I'm not sorry you are alive again. After everything you did for Connor, sacrificing yourself to keep him safe, to keep all of us safe, you really do deserve a second chance. Thank you.'

Before I could say anything she grabbed me, hugging me so tight it hurt. When she finally let go, my shoulder was wet from her tears. All my life she had treated me with disdain, barely tolerating me as her stepdaughter. To see acceptance and even approval in her eyes now was both bitter and sweet.

Chris handed me a glass. 'You look as if you could do with this,' he said, his voice suspiciously bland.

I gulped half the glass, the scotch slipping smoothly down my throat and warming me from the inside out.

'Steady on,' he said. 'You're supposed to sip it, not guzzle it.'

'After what she's been through, Tyler has every right to get plastered,' said Connor.

'What about what we've been through? What I went through, regaining consciousness to find you gone, forcing Cade's lackey to tell me where you were, racing to the hockey grounds praying I wasn't too late to save you, to stop you throwing your life away?' No longer bland, his voice vibrated with fury.

I lifted my chin. 'I did not throw my life away. I did what had to be done.'

'Bullshit.'

'That's enough, Bradbury.'

Chris whirled around and pointed at Sam. 'You let her die. You threatened to kill me if I let anything happen to her, and then you just stood by and watched as that bastard Talaom shot her.'

'That's not what happened.' I stepped between them. 'Sam tried to protect me, but he couldn't. No one could.'

Chris glared at me. 'You should never have been there in the first place. If you'd listened to me, never made that bloody deal with Cade, I could have got you away, taken you somewhere where no one could hurt you ever again.'

'I had no choice.'

'There's always a choice.'

'Then this was mine, and I'd do it again if it was the only way to save the people I love.' I stepped over to Chris and placed my hand on his chest. 'I know you're angry with me but this was always my choice to make, not yours.'

'I need another drink,' he said, stalking off to the kitchen.

I let out a sigh, shaking my head. Sam appeared at my side and I gave him a light smile, resisting the urge to take shelter in his arms.

'What happens now?' Connor asked.

'We get some rest,' said Rhonda. 'Andrew's funeral is on Monday. After that we'll start packing, and decide where to go from here.'

'Packing?'

'Easton is no longer safe, Connor. Malia and Almorthanos know I betrayed them. And Cade's promise to protect us will hold little weight in the middle of a warzone. We need to leave, and start new lives somewhere far away from here.'

'You're kidding me? I can't just walk away. I have a life, a job, friends.'

'You can find a new job. Make new friends.'

'I'm not letting those arseholes run me out of my own town.'

'Rhonda is right. Easton isn't safe for you anymore. You should go,' I said.

'What about you, and Dad?'

'I helped create this mess. I can't just walk away.'

'You could, you know. You could leave. Become a different person, like Bradbury did.'

I spun around to face Sam. 'I am not going to pretend to be

Emily.' My stomach burned at the thought, making me regret downing so much scotch in one go.

'It's just an option. Or you could go with your family, all of you starting over together. Let those winged bastards fight it out among themselves.'

'What about you? Are you going to walk away and let Almorthanos and Malia turn Easton into their own personal playground?'

He slowly shook his head. 'I have to make sure they are brought to account for their crimes.'

'So do I.'

'No, you don't. You've done enough.'

'I'm not leaving, Sam. Cade said my part in this wasn't done, and he's right. I have to make sure no one else gets hurt because of me.'

'I'm not leaving either.' Connor put his hand on my shoulder. 'You can run away if you want, Mum, but I'm staying here.'

'Connor, no, you don't understand how bad it will get. I've lived through the horror of war once before, when I lived in Angellin. Almorthanos and Cade will turn Easton into a waste-land, thousands will die.' Tears streaked Rhonda's face; her eyes filled with dread.

Connor moved to her side and placed his arm around her shoulders. 'Mum, it will be okay. No more running away.'

Her shoulders slumped and Connor led her over to the couch. She sank onto it, hands kneading her skirt.

'Are you going to be okay for a while?' Sam touched my elbow. 'I need to go to the station. They've called half a dozen times, but I didn't want to leave until I knew you were okay.'

I forced a smile. 'I'll be fine. I'll probably just go to bed. Tomorrow is going to be a big day, with Andrew's funeral and finding a way to put an end to a war that's been going on for centuries.'

His mouth curved into a crooked smile as he leaned forward and kissed me on the forehead. 'Sleep well.'

He said goodbye to Rhonda and Connor and left. Chris hadn't come back from the kitchen and, cowardly, I retreated to my bedroom. I huddled under the covers, trying not to think about being in Emily's body. Every muscle pulled taut; it was impossible to sleep and I lay awake in the dark staring at nothing.

How was I going to fix this?

I closed my eyes and the last image I had of Emily filled my head. She'd been at peace, the light of her soul as bright as her personality, but it didn't give me any comfort to know she had accepted her death and moved on. She didn't know I'd taken over her body. I didn't want to die, again, but the thought of remaining as I was made me shudder. I couldn't live like this.

I drew a shaky breath. No matter how much I hated being trapped in Emily's body I couldn't do anything about it until after I had taken care of Malia and Almorthanos. Almorthanos had been free for mere hours and already people had died, with worse to come, according to Rhonda.

I had no idea how to deal with a centuries old war and stop it spilling over onto Easton's streets, and with the necklace destroyed I wouldn't be able to use aether. If Grimm sent more wraiths, the only way to stop them would mean reaping their souls and earning more penalties. I'd do it if I had to, but I hoped it wouldn't be necessary. Somewhere, someone had to know of a way to stop them that didn't require me staying a reaper for all of eternity.

I closed my eyes, willing my muscles to relax so I could at least grab a few hours of sleep.

The bedroom door opened and closed. Soft footsteps approached the bed and I sat up. 'Who's there?'

'You're supposed to be asleep,' said Sam, husky voice little more than a whisper.

I sighed. 'I can't shut off my brain. I keep thinking about all the mistakes I made and how–'

'Shush.' Sam placed a finger over my mouth and then he gently pushed me down before he climbed into bed beside me. Then he pulled me against him, arms wrapped around me, my head resting on his chest.

'Go to sleep, Tyler.'

I closed my eyes, breathing in his fresh scent, comforted by the rise and fall of his chest.

Safe in Sam's arms, the questions and doubts melted away, the sound of his even breathing a lullaby that soothed me to sleep.

CHAPTER 31

Clouds billowed above the cemetery, dark and threaded with menace, a fitting send-off for a man who ruined so many lives.

Denise, Andrew's mother, leaned on my father's arm. Every now and then she would dab at her eyes with a neatly folded handkerchief, careful not to smudge her perfectly applied makeup. I was pleased to see her artfully styled hair being blown every which way and the veil attached to her perky hat whipping around in the wind.

She'd run out on Dad when Andrew was four, declaring motherhood was not for her, and had made little effort to see her son in the years since. Yet here she was, playing the grieving mother to an audience who knew it for a sham.

It was a pitiful audience at that. Sam and Chris had planned on attending, for moral support, but they'd both been called away by work. Rhonda, Connor and I were the only other people at the gravesite, apart from the celebrant Denise had paid to say a few words on Andrew's behalf. The celebrant's voice was stilted, no doubt aware of the true nature of the man whose virtues he was currently extolling.

The celebrant fell silent and took a step back so Dad and Denise could scoop up a handful of dirt and scatter it over Andrew's coffin. The celebrant invited the rest of us to do the same. I moved forward, tears in my eyes. Despite everything, Andrew had been my brother.

Denise blocked my way. 'Not you,' she said, briskly wiping dirt from her hand with her handkerchief. 'I don't know why you even bothered to come.'

'I'm sorry?'

'You should be sorry. You have no right to be here.'

Dad stepped up beside her, glaring at me. 'Why did you come? You're not part of this family. You're not my daughter anymore. I disowned you.'

Eyes stinging, I sucked in a breath. 'I... ah...'

I gazed over his shoulder, watching the celebrant as he retreated through the cemetery with unseemly haste. Not that I blamed him for getting as far away as possible from our family drama.

'I disowned both of you,' said Dad, shifting his glare to Rhonda, 'when I kicked you out of my house.'

Rhonda shot in front of me and poked Dad in the chest. 'You didn't kick me out, you miserable bastard. I left you, and it was the best day of my life.'

Dad's face went red and his shoulders stiffened. 'You are nothing without me, just a worthless female, useless.'

'Hey, Dad, steady on, you can't speak to Mum like that,' said Connor.

'Don't tell me what to do.' Dad rounded on Connor. 'I told you not to have anything more to do with either of them.'

'I am not going to wipe Mum and Tyler out of my life just because you're pissed at them.' Connor, expression serious, shook his head. 'I am never going to turn my back on Mum, and Tyler is the best sister a guy could have. She was willing to die, to save me. You're making a huge mistake shutting her out.'

'The only mistake I made was not getting rid of her after her mother died.' Dad whirled around, hate contorting his features, fists clenched as he loomed over me. 'You have been nothing but trouble from the day you were born. You killed your mother, and now Andrew is dead because of you. You've poisoned my wife's mind, turned Connor against me, and now you stand there–'

'That's it. I've had it with this crap.' I shoved Dad in the chest, making him stumble backwards.

'All my life, all I wanted was for you to accept me, be proud of me, treat me with respect. I'm done with that. I'm not wasting any more of my life worrying about what you think, or how to make you love me.' It felt good to finally say it, to break free from the mould Dad had cast for me, to be my own person regardless of what others thought. Liberating, intoxicating! I felt the best I had in ages.

Chest heaving, Dad pointed a shaking hand at me. 'You are evil.'

'Your daughter is less than perfect, but I wouldn't go that far.' The amused voice came from behind me and I spun around, gasping when dozens of Tr'lirians stepped out of the astral plane, Almorthanos in the lead.

He stalked towards me, eyes locked on mine, and I fought the urge to drop to my knees. In the Underworld the stench of Demania had emanated from him in sickening waves, but it seemed he'd left that behind with his old body. Now nothing detracted from the sheer presence of his soul. Dark, forceful, it called out to me, demanding my surrender.

He cast an eye over my frozen family, who were all down on one knee, their heads downcast. 'Oh dear, am I interrupting?' He waved a hand. 'Please, carry on. Listening to you people and your petty squabbles is the most entertainment I have had in decades.' He lifted one eyebrow. 'I can hold off on exacting my revenge while you lot rip shreds from each other.'

'Who the hell are you?' Dad pushed himself to his feet,

wheezing at the effort it took. His face was pale but determined as he puffed his chest out and thrust his shoulders back.

Almorthanos waved his hand and two of his people sprang forward to tackle Dad, twisting his arms behind his back and forcing him back to his knees.

Ignoring Dad's outraged yells, Almorthanos leaned close to murmur in my ear, 'I was going to slaughter your father first, as punishment for your defiance, but from what I just observed you might be grateful if I did.'

'Leave my father alone.' I glared at him; fists clenched.

'So you do still care for him, despite your words to the contrary.'

'What do you want, Almorthanos?'

'We'll get to that in a moment.' He grinned, exposing perfect teeth and a glittering smile. 'First, I'd like an explanation for how you managed to escape the Underworld and take over your cousin's body. Malia was most put out to discover you had escaped. She's quite taken with your young man and intends on creating her new dynasty with him.'

'That is never going to happen. Sam would never touch her.'

'He's not going to have a choice, and I'm sure she'll make it most pleasurable for him. He'll soon forget all about you, which is for the best as I have plans of my own.' He lifted his hand and stroked my cheek. 'It truly is remarkable how much you resemble my sister's original form. I didn't get the chance to appreciate it when you were in the Underworld. But to see you now; it warms my heart to know our daughters will share Malia's true face.'

'What?' I recoiled from him, vigorously shaking my head. 'That is never going to happen.'

'It will be as I wish. But first I have some business to take care of.' He looked over my shoulder, his expression hardening. 'Rallani,' he said, shaking his head, brown eyes cold, 'you were one of my favourites. I never dreamed you would betray me, your own flesh and blood, and side with Godden.'

Rhonda's head flung up, eyes wide, chest heaving. 'Malia left me no choice. She was going to kill my son.'

'Do you really believe his miserable life is worth more than mine?' Almorthanos straightened to his full height, words booming in the air. 'I am the head of Clan Davila. You should have been thankful we chose your son's body to be my vessel. Instead you betrayed me and for that you will die, along with your precious son.'

'No, please, not Connor.' Rhonda shot to her feet, fear etched on her face, and launched herself at Almorthanos. 'Kill me if you want, but let my son go.'

Almorthanos caught Rhonda and spun her around, hand gripping her throat. 'I have no mercy for traitors.' He shoved her away from him and she stumbled, dropping to her hands and knees.

He turned back to face me; his lips curled up in a smirk. 'You defied me, and conspired with my enemy.' He gave a nod and the Tr'lirians, black wings unfurled, surged forward and took hold of Connor, Rhonda and Denise, forcing them to their knees. 'As punishment you get to watch everyone you care about die.'

Dad was wrestled over to join the others as four Tr'lirians without wings marched over to stand in front of each member of my family, swords in hand, poised to do Almorthanos's bidding.

'Say goodbye to your loved ones, Tyler. From this moment on I will be your entire world.'

I instinctively reached for my necklace, ready to draw in as much aether as I could hold. My fingers found bare skin. My necklace was gone, destroyed when I'd set Almorthanos free. Without it I would never be able to stop him from killing my family.

He caught me around the waist, pulling me against his chest. I twisted so I faced him, one hand coming up to clutch at his neck.

Please let this work.

'Kill them and I'll reap your soul.' Voice as cold as I could make it, I glared up at him.

'You're not a reaper anymore. Grimm said your link to the Underworld was severed when you were brought back to life.' Despite the confidence in his words, I caught a hint of worry in his eyes.

'The necklace might be gone, but its power is inside me. How else do you think I escaped?' I didn't blink, hoping Grimm was wrong. Chris had no longer been a reaper when he got his new body but he had filled his soul quota, while I still had thousands of souls to reap. Surely I wouldn't be let off that easily?

I'd never wanted to be a reaper, but right then I wanted nothing more than to have the ability to rip Almorthanos's soul out of his body.

'You're bluffing.'

I sucked in a breath and closed my eyes, focusing on drawing his soul to me.

Nothing happened. I couldn't sense anything. He was right. I was no longer a reaper.

I sagged in his arms as he gave a low chuckle. 'Nice try,' he said.

No. It wasn't going to end like this. I wouldn't let it.

I drew on my anger and focused on the beat of my heart, demanding his soul answer me.

Heat welled in my body, burning through me and then exploding outwards, hitting Almorthanos. Light flared beneath my hand where I touched him and he roared in agony as his soul rose out of his chest. He collapsed to his knees, shuddering; the flimsy ribbon of light connecting his soul to his body the only thing keeping him alive.

I gasped as pain flared at the back on my neck and I could feel a trickle of liquid run down my back as one of the Tr'lirians pressed his sword into my flesh.

'Release his soul.'

Teeth gritted against the pain, I said, 'I'll release it when he promises to spare my family.'

For a long moment, no one moved; all was silent. Almorthanos groaned and dragged himself to his knees.

'Promise me you will not attempt to harm my family and I'll let you live.' My voice shook. It was getting harder to resist the call of his soul, my body quivering as increasing waves of pleasure swept over me. It teased me, seducing me with its promise of even greater pleasure to come. All I had to do was take Almorthanos's soul and I would be rewarded with mind-numbing ecstasy. His soul was so rich, so powerful; the desire to possess it so strong it smothered every other sense.

I could see his mouth moving but couldn't hear words, his expression growing ever more desperate as I didn't respond.

I dragged my mind away from his soul.

'Yes, damn you. I said yes. Release them,' he ordered his men, voice hoarse and shaking.

I looked behind me and saw his men had obeyed, though they wore uncertain looks as they stepped back.

'Get out of here, now.' I watched as Rhonda dragged Connor away, Dad and Denise swiftly overtaking them.

I turned back to Almorthanos, and it took every ounce of will I possessed to release his soul. My body protested as the pleasure from holding it dissipated. I ached, unfulfilled, struggling not to show it as he glared at me, the last vestiges of forbidden pleasure swept away by the rage burning in his eyes.

'You will regret this,' he said as his men encircled me, cutting off my retreat.

Hand shaking, I called on his soul again. It responded immediately and I drew it forth just enough to make him uncomfortable, not enough to let the lure of promised ecstasy sweep me away.

'Tell your men to back off or I'll finish what I started.'

Mouth screwed into a grimace; he ordered his men to follow my instructions.

The sound of an engine came from behind me and I risked a glance to see that Connor had pulled up as close as he could get to Andrew's plot, the back door of my Corolla open ready for me.

I faced Almorthanos once more, making sure his men were still keeping their distance. All the while his soul sang to me and I desperately wanted to keep going, to rip it out and feast on it. Before I knew what I was doing I had drawn it out of his body. It hung in the air between us, shining brightly, intoxicatingly beautiful, and he fell to his knees once more.

I braced myself as I released his soul, letting it snap back into his body. Before he could recover I sprinted to my car, diving into the backseat. Connor hit the accelerator as I slammed the door shut, heart thudding as I peered out the window to see if they were chasing us.

Almorthanos's men huddled around him, helping him to his feet, and I collapsed back into the seat.

Oh God.

I had come so close to killing him, and for what? False ecstasy that would have been followed by agony?

Body trembling, I dry retched as the horror of what I had almost done overwhelmed me.

'Tyler, are you okay?' Rhonda asked as Connor navigated my small car off the grass and into the car park.

I shook my head, not ready to speak, looking for any sign of Dad and Denise.

Rhonda saw me scanning the car park and gave a bitter laugh. 'Your father and wife number one took off the second you got us released. I'd have followed suit but Connor insisted we stick around to see if you needed rescuing. Not that there was anything either of us could have done, if it all went sour on you.'

'Mum, Tyler just saved our lives. Again. You could try being a little nicer to her.'

'It's because of her we needed saving in the first place. She's a trouble magnet, and I don't want you caught up in it.'

I smiled; the familiarity of Rhonda being mean to me kind of soothing. At least one part of my life was back to normal. I had no idea how to get the rest of my life to follow suit.

Rhonda's lament that I was a trouble magnet was proved right when we got back to Chris's penthouse and found two police officers waiting to speak to me.

This was not going to be good.

CHAPTER 32

The female officer gave me a cool smile. 'Miss Morgan, I'm Detective Sanders and this is Detective Johnson. We'd like to ask you a few questions about Emily Wilson.'

I struggled to keep my voice steady, glad I'd used a headband to hold my fringe back, not wanting such a blatant reminder this was not my body every time I caught sight of my reflection. 'Why? Is she okay?'

'That's what we're trying to determine. When was the last time you saw her?'

'Ah, that would have been Saturday morning. We went over to see my stepmother,' I waved a hand at Rhonda, 'and while we were there a friend of hers came by. She said she was going to be staying with them for a few days.'

'Do you happen to know their name or where they live?'

'She didn't say. I was talking to Rhonda when she left so I didn't see who picked her up.' I frowned, looking from one detective to the other. 'What's going on? Is Emily in trouble?'

'Her parents haven't heard from their daughter since Friday night, and she's not answering her phone or been in contact with any of her friends. Mr and Mrs Wilson thought she was staying with you and aren't aware she knew anyone else in Easton. Yet you're saying she did, but you don't know who?'

'I'm sorry. I wish I could be more help. All I know is it was a guy she was going to stay with, but other than that she didn't tell me anything.'

'And you didn't ask?'

'Look, I just met Emily. I really don't know anything about her. I certainly didn't feel it was my place to pry into her life.' I worked hard to maintain eye contact with Detective Sanders, well aware her partner's eyes never left my face.

'You let her stay with you for two nights, even though she was a complete stranger.'

'It was clear we were related, so of course I let her stay with me.'

'Clear, as in you could pass for twins?'

'Yes, but I'm two years older than Emily. From what her father told her about his life before he was adopted by the Wilsons, we had to be cousins.'

Sanders scribbled in her notebook and Johnson spoke for the first time. 'Did Emily take her belongings with her?'

'Ah, yeah, she did,' I said, thinking about the luggage I had stashed in my wardrobe, luggage that would have been coated in red paint when Talaom trashed the flat.

Detective Johnson's eyebrows raised. 'We went by your flat, looking for you, only to be told you had moved here while it was being renovated by the new owner.'

'New owner?'

Sanders snapped her notebook shut, no trace of a smile on her narrow face. 'The tradesman we spoke to said Chris Bradbury purchased the flat this morning and hired him to remodel it.'

'That's correct,' said Chris, from the front doorway. He tossed his keys on the coffee table and strode to my side, giving the detectives a bland smile. 'And I have offered Tyler the use of my home during the remodelling.'

He'd bought the flat. My stomach sank, not sure I liked the idea of having him as my landlord.

Johnson narrowed his eyes. 'From the expression on Miss Morgan's face, I'm guessing she wasn't aware you had purchased her home.'

'Yes, well, thanks for ruining my surprise.'

'My apologies.' His smile was far from sincere.

'Are we done here? I'd like to discuss the rest of my surprise with Tyler, before you ruin that too.'

'Just one more question,' he said. He turned away from Chris and faced me, one hand reaching into his jacket pocket. 'Can you explain why this was found in Logan Miller's car?' He held up a small evidence bag containing a bloodstained student ID card.

My ID card.

I swallowed heavily. 'I don't know, um, I'm not sure. We broke up over a week ago. I must have left it in his car, before then.'

'So you have no idea how it could have ended up in the boot of Miller's car, covered in his blood?'

'I do not know how it got there.' This was one question I could answer truthfully.

'And the knife, the one used to stab him to death. You wouldn't happen to know anything about that either, right, even though it was also found in the boot of your ex-boyfriend's car along with your student ID?'

Detective Johnson continued to talk but the pounding of my heart and a rushing sound in my head drowned out his words. I closed my eyes, sucked in a deep breath and held it for as long as I could. I opened my eyes and stared at him. 'I'm sorry, could you repeat that?'

His nostrils flared. 'We need you to come down to the station, and go over the statement Detective Lockwood took.' His top lip curled into a sneer. 'See if there's anything you left out.'

Chris gripped my elbow. 'Is that really necessary? Miss Morgan has just returned from her brother's funeral. She and her family need time to grieve.'

Johnson gave Chris a flat stare. 'Either she comes willingly, or we arrest her on suspicion of murder.' He switched his gaze to me. 'Your choice.'

I gulped down my panic. 'I'd like to speak to Detective Lockwood before I go anywhere with you.'

'I'm sure you would,' Sanders said with a smirk. 'He's already at the station, answering a few questions of his own.'

My heartbeat stuttered. From Sanders's attitude, I feared the questions Sam was answering were about his involvement with me. 'I'll get my bag.' I tried to move away but Chris's fingers dug painfully into my elbow.

'Tyler's not going anywhere without a lawyer,' he said, pulling me closer to him.

Sanders gave a sharklike grin. 'By all means, call your lawyer, Mr Bradbury. But they can meet her at the station because, make no mistake, Miss Morgan will be coming with us.'

Chris bristled up, but I pulled my arm out of his grasp and put a hand on his chest. 'It will be okay. I'll go with them and we'll get this sorted out,' I said, aware that would be easier said than done. This was what Talaom had planned, to implicate me in Logan's death, and I had no idea how I was going to get out of it. But refusing to go with the detectives, not cooperating with them, could make matters even worse for Sam.

Chris's expression said he hated to let the detectives take me, but he gave a reluctant nod as he pulled his phone out of his pocket. 'I'll be right behind you,' he said. 'Don't say anything until the lawyer and I get there.'

I nodded, not up to producing a smile, and turned to say goodbye to Connor and Rhonda.

'I'm coming with you,' said Connor, earning him a frown from Rhonda.

'Connor Morgan, right?' Detective Johnson tilted his head to one side. 'We have some questions for you too, about your car. Kind of interesting, don't you think, how we found it blown to bits not far from where Logan Miller's body was discovered.'

'If you're suggesting my son had anything to do with Logan's death–'

Johnson cut Rhonda off. 'I'm not suggesting anything, Mrs Morgan, merely pointing out yet another extremely unlucky event to befall a member of your family in the past week. Almost makes me think someone's got it in for you lot. Might be a good idea for all of you to come down to the station?'

Rhonda's expression soured, but she said nothing as we left the penthouse under police escort. I cast a backwards glance at Chris as we stepped into the elevator. He was deep in conversation with his lawyer and I hoped they were very good at their job. They would have to be to get us out of this mess.

Silence filled the elevator as we travelled to the ground floor. I kept my head up, determined not to act guilty in any way as the two detectives took up positions on either side of me for the walk to where their unmarked vehicle was parked. Sandwiched in between Connor and Rhonda in the back seat for the drive to the police station, my mind raced as I tried to think of answers to any questions they might ask me.

Nothing prepared me for the sight of Sam, sitting on the wrong side of the desk, as I was led into his office. He looked wrung out, hands resting on his thighs, a harried look in his eyes. He straightened up when I entered the room and gave me a weary smile.

A woman I didn't recognise sat in Sam's chair, and she did not look happy to see me. Sanders brushed past me to whisper in her ear and then stepped to one side. The woman behind the desk stood up, straightening her jacket, expression severe as she looked me up and down.

'Miss Morgan, I'm Superintendent Mills, and Detective Lockwood has assured me you will cooperate fully with our investigation into the murder of Logan Miller.' Her lips thinned, giving the impression she doubted anything Sam might have said about me.

'Is he correct? Are you willing to do whatever it takes to find out who killed Mr Miller? To see them brought to justice.'

I cleared my throat. 'Of course.'

'Then you won't mind undergoing fingerprint analysis to rule yourself out?'

Despite my best intentions, I knew my face paled. I could feel the blood draining away. I was in Emily's body, and Malia had been in it when Logan was murdered. She could have been the one to stab him.

'Hang on a sec,' said Connor, moving to my side. 'You can't do anything without her lawyer present.' He turned to me. 'Just wait until Chris gets here.'

Superintendent Mills frowned at Connor. 'Sound advice, Mr Morgan. Will the lawyer also be representing you? We want your fingerprints as well, to aid in the investigation into who blew up your car last night.'

'I don't know anything about that. My car was stolen,' said Connor.

'If that's the case, wouldn't you have reported it?'

'I was going to, after my brother's funeral, only this pair turned up first.' He pointed at Sanders and Johnson.

'But you have no objection to providing your fingerprints?'

'Sure, but I can't see how that's going to help. It's my car. My fingerprints are going to be all over it.'

'Once we have your prints, we can eliminate them and work on any others we find. So how about we get started with that?' Mills turned to Sanders. 'Why don't you and Detective Johnson take Mr Morgan and his mother and file the report for his stolen car.'

Before Connor could utter a protest, he and Rhonda were

hustled out of the room, and Mills indicated for me to take a seat next to Sam. I sat heavily, resisting the urge to reach over and grab his hand, not sure exactly how much Mills knew about our involvement.

She smiled at me, a smile without even a hint of warmth. 'Now then, how long do you think it will take for Mr Bradbury and your lawyer to arrive? I want to get this taken care of today. Detective Lockwood assures me you had no part in the murder of Mr Miller, but given your personal history that will not be enough to clear your name.'

'I… ah… I'm not sure how long they'll be.'

'We don't need to wait for them,' said Sam. He reached out and took hold of my hand, twining his fingers around mine and giving a reassuring squeeze. 'Tyler has nothing to hide. You can take her fingerprints now.'

'What?' I turned to Sam; eyes wide.

He faced me with a confident smile. 'You did not kill Miller, and your fingerprints will prove it.'

I met his steady gaze and took a deep breath. 'Okay. Let's do it.'

'Hold on just one minute,' said a new voice from the doorway. 'My client will not be submitting to any tests or answering any questions until after I have spoken with her.' An older man in a dark grey suit entered the office, with Chris a step behind him. 'I'll need a private room and time to talk to Miss Morgan.'

Sam squeezed my hand, giving a slight shake of his head. 'You don't need to involve a lawyer in this. You're innocent. Trust me.'

'Have you lost your mind, Lockwood? Of course she needs a lawyer. Innocent people get shafted every day,' said Chris.

Sam never took his eyes off me. 'It's up to you.'

I gave him a smile. 'Let's do it.'

With the lawyer spluttering out protests, and Chris glaring at Sam the whole time, we were led to a windowless room where a uniformed officer took my fingerprints. Then we were taken back to Sam's office to wait for the results. Sam held my hand throughout, and I took comfort in his calm demeanour. His complete confidence made it almost anti-climactic when Mills returned with a sour expression to announce my fingerprints did not match the ones on the murder weapon.

With Chris and the lawyer watching on, she grilled me about my relationship with Sam and I answered as truthfully as I could. Two hours later we were escorted out of the station, meeting up with Rhonda and Connor in the car park.

After the lawyer left I turned to Sam. 'How did you know my fingerprints wouldn't match? Malia could have killed Logan.'

'Nah, she's not the type to dirty her own hands.'

'She killed Emily.'

'That was to get revenge on you for making her give up your cousin's body. Besides, their plan was to implicate you. As your real body is still in the Underworld, there's no way the fingerprints would match.'

Chris grabbed Sam by the shirt front. 'What if you'd been wrong? Tyler could have been arrested for murder.'

Sam shook himself free. 'This was the fastest way to get her out of there. Now the police can get onto finding the real killer. I'm sure it was Talaom who killed Miller, so that puts Almorthanos directly in their sights.'

I hoped Sam was right. But even if the police did find evidence pointing to Almorthanos, how would they catch and keep him long enough to convict him? No, it was up to me to make sure he paid for every atrocity that had been performed in his name. I just wished I knew how.

CHAPTER 33

Back at the penthouse, with Chris furious at Sam, the atmosphere was not exactly conductive for team-work. Rhonda and Connor quickly fled, saying they needed to put in an insurance claim for his car, now they had an official police report. I let them go without protest, wishing I could afford the luxury of a time out. Instead, I gave Sam and Chris somewhere else to focus their anger.

'Almorthanos showed up at Andrew's funeral.'

Chris grabbed my shoulders. 'Are you okay? Why didn't you say something?'

I pulled free and put my hands up in a placating gesture. 'Things have been crazy since then. And I'm fine, although it could have been a total disaster.' I filled them in on most of what had happened. Almorthanos's assertion I was going to bear him daughters who looked like Malia was too creepy to even contemplate let alone to say out loud.

'Didn't Bradbury cease being a reaper once he was brought back to life?'

I shrugged, giving Sam a rueful smile. 'All reapers have a

quota. Chris had filled his, but it looks like I'll be reaping souls for a while yet.'

Chris stroked his chin. 'I've never heard of any reapers manifesting wings while in astral form. It has to be the necklace that allows you to do that.'

'But the necklace was destroyed, and I couldn't call on aether the way I could before. How can it have any effect on me now?'

'I don't know, but we need to find out before Almorthanos sends someone else after you. He doesn't sound like the type to give up,' said Sam.

'I know.' I rubbed my eyes, dreading the thought of what he would throw at me next.

A shiver swept over my body. 'I have to go,' I said as I strode over to the couch and lay down. 'Someone is dying.'

I placed a hand on the hollow of my throat and concentrated on the draw from my client, not sure it would work without the necklace. But my astral form slipped easily out of my body, wings unfurling behind me. Powerful strokes carried me up and through the ceiling of the penthouse. I flew over the river, heading for the north side of Easton.

Lost souls floated around me, forms indistinct in the light of day, their silent escort a grim reminder of the night I'd been called to reap Logan's soul. They kept pace with me as I drew close to the house I'd grown up in, moving behind me as I came to a stop in front of a dozen black winged Tr'lirians.

They weren't alone.

Draped in mist made up of nether, the Grim Reaper froze the air in the astral plane with his presence, a writhing chain of souls anchoring him to the Underworld. As I got closer he morphed into his human aspect, Jonathon Grimm, but was no less terrifying. His black eyes were cold, cheekbones as sharp as knives, and I could hear the screams of the souls he sucked dry to maintain his physical form.

I tore my eyes away from the tortured souls and risked a

glance at Dad's house, trying to hide my alarm at the wide open front door. From the pull of the dying soul, whoever I had been called for was hidden in the sea of Tr'lirians hovering behind him. I wanted to tear into them, wrest the soul from their grasp and blast Grimm out of the sky. But I couldn't, not yet.

'Where's my father?' I stifled a wince as the husk of a dead soul fell from the chain, disintegrating to nothing as it fell.

'You're too late. He's gone.'

My wings faltered and I dropped two feet before they steadied again. I forced myself to meet his cold gaze. 'You're lying, I'd know if he was dead.'

Thin lips curled into a smirk. 'Who said he was dead? He abandoned you. He and that ridiculous woman of his took the first plane out of here.'

Though relieved Dad and Denise were okay, I hadn't forgotten Malia's threat to kill everyone I cared about. Whose death had I been called to witness?

Grimm's glacial glare settled on my wings. 'Do you think masquerading as one of His kind will dissuade our master from punishing you?'

'He might be your master, but he will never be mine.' I forced a cool smile to my lips. 'I never thought I'd see the Grim Reaper reduced to a mere errand boy. But he no longer needs a right hand man now he's been reunited with Malia, and someone has to take Talaom's place, right?'

Grimm snarled and the nether supporting him in mid-air lashed out at me. My wings propelled me out of reach of the razor sharp tentacles while Grimm fought to regain control of his temper.

'Be careful what you say, reaper. I still own you.' He waved a hand and the Tr'lirians amassed behind him moved to the left. A young man dressed in shorts and a singlet, feet bare, dangled between two of them. His eyes were unfocused, blood obscuring his features, and he sagged in the grip of his captors.

'Threatening the people you care about did not have the desired effect,' said Grimm. 'So instead we'll kill random strangers on the hour, every hour. You won't know who they are, so you won't be able to protect, hide or save them.'

I shook my head. 'What do you want from me?'

'To see you suffer. To watch you drown yourself in guilt as you watch everyone around you die. You spurned our master, and He is determined to make you pay dearly for that mistake. Only when all hope is extinguished, when every breath you take is a misery, will He allow you to crawl to Him and beg to be forgiven.'

I closed my eyes, trying to block out the image of what my future would be like if I didn't find a way to stop Almorthanos. I should have killed him when I had the chance, at the cemetery. If I'd finished what I'd started, ripped his soul out of his body as soon as Connor and the others had fled, maybe that would have been the end of it.

Who was I kidding? Malia would never walk away if I killed her brother. She would raze Easton to the ground to get back at me. I would have to kill her as well; only then could I be assured no more innocent people would die. I pushed aside any doubt that I could follow through on my plan, and opened my eyes.

'Please, no more. You don't have to kill anyone else. I'll do whatever Almorthanos wants. Just let him go.' I waved a hand at the barely conscious young man. I hung my head, trying to look as meek as possible. Grimm had to believe I was well and truly cowed or I would never get close enough to Almorthanos and Malia to do what had to be done.

'Tyler, Tyler, Tyler.' He plastered on a fake smile. 'You must be punished, broken, before you are fit to kneel at His feet. Only when I am assured you no longer pose a threat to our master will you be allowed to grovel in His presence.'

He waved a hand and one of the Tr'lirians behind him moved

into position behind the unconscious man. 'And your breaking starts now.'

Before I could blink, the Tr'lirian rammed a sword into the young man's back, killing him instantly.

I cried out, stunned by the sudden violence, even as the compulsion to take his soul hit me. But Grimm was closer. He put his hands against the man's chest and pulled, drawing the soul out of the lifeless body.

The Tr'lirians let the empty body drop and I winced when it left the astral plane and hit the footpath with a stomach churning thud. Grimm raised the soul to his lips.

To hell with being meek. I would not sit back and watch him devour another innocent soul. Not when I could do something about it.

My wings propelled me forward and I stretched out a hand, desperate to touch the soul. My fingertips grazed it and I focused on its song.

The soul's light expanded and Grimm thrust a hand in front of his eyes to ward off the glare. The soul started to ascend, gaining speed as it began its journey towards rebirth. I wanted to do the same for the souls locked in the chain sustaining Grimm's physical form but with my client's soul released the draw of my physical body would pull me back to Chris's penthouse.

Nothing happened.

I could feel my body, and I would have no trouble finding my way to it with my eyes closed. But instead of being dragged back whether I was ready to go or not, I got the feeling I could stay in the astral plane for as long as I wanted. Not that I wanted to, with my present company.

Before I could flee, the Tr'lirians had formed a ring around Grimm and me.

Crap!

I could hear sirens getting closer by the second, but they wouldn't do me any good.

I had to go on the attack.

'Back off, now, or I'll rip the souls out of every last one of you.' I stared at each of the Tr'lirians in turn, ignoring Grimm for the moment.

'We're immortal, bitch. You can't touch us,' one of them said, though I noticed a few shared uncertain glances.

'I wouldn't be so sure about that. Wings or no wings, you all have a soul.' I held out my hands, palms up, and curled my fingers over as if I held two of their souls.

'I can take them and I can crush them just like that.' I clenched my hands into fists. 'And there's nothing you could do to stop me.'

'She's bluffing,' said Grimm. 'Not even I can take a Tr'lirian's soul if they still have their wings.' He turned to me, tendrils of nether creeping my way. 'I'm going to enjoy this.'

'Stay back. I'm warning you.' I pointed at Grimm.

'I don't have a soul, and I'm not using a mirror. So nothing is going to stop me from rending your soul into thousands of pieces. And this time there won't be any surprise resurrection.' His outstretched hands became skeletal as the Tr'lirians crowded in closer, giving me no avenue of escape.

I put my hands out to ward him off, and the nether lashed them aside. 'Wait, you said Almorthanos wants to punish me. He can't do that if I'm dead.'

He barked out a harsh laugh. 'Alive or dead, you will serve him, and every second of your service will be spent in the worst torment I can devise.'

The relish in his voice made me shudder. This was it. He was going to kill me and there was nothing I could do to stop him.

Unless…

I sent my awareness into his body, searching for the anchor point for the chain of souls he fed on to increase his psychic energy. I could feel them, hear their cries, my astral form vibrating as it responded to the depths of their torment as

Grimm wrung every last ounce of life out of them. The chain pulsed as dead souls flaked away and new ones were added to bolster his strength.

At the same time, Grimm wrapped skeletal fingers around my throat and pain tore through my astral form. Agony lanced through me and I could feel myself growing insubstantial, fading away as Grimm leached out my psychic energy.

I didn't try to fight him. I closed my eyes, stifling my screams as I followed the link between us.

There, just below his sternum, energy swirled. I forced my arms to move and latched on to Grimm and tried to wrench the chain away from him.

He snarled and tightened his grip on my throat as we wrestled for control of the souls he'd enslaved. He fought to pull in more of their power while I did everything I could to block his access. I didn't want to touch the power I could feel simmering through the chain, though it sang to me in an even more seductive tone than Almorthanos's soul had.

So much power. The ecstasy it promised set every inch of me quivering. But I refused to give in. To do so, to take the power these souls contained, would make me no better than Grimm. A monster.

Grimm's nether mist lashed out at me, razor tips cutting into my astral form, and I felt my consciousness wavering. I couldn't stop. If I gave in, if I released my hold on the end of the chain where it joined Grimm's body, I would be lost.

Dim shouts filled the air around me from the Tr'lirians unable to 'see' what was happening, but aware I was in a fight for my life with the Grim Reaper. He had morphed into his true form, no longer able to sustain the illusion of humanity. His cloak billowed around us, the edge cutting just as sharply as the mist.

I whimpered. I couldn't hold on. He was too strong, and my grip on the end of the chain weakened. Grimm let go of my neck to pry at my fingers, forcing me to let go. He smiled, a cruel smile that promised an eternity of pain.

I was going to die, for good this time.

Then, with the lightest of touches, a lost soul settled onto my right shoulder. It was immediately joined by a second on my right. I held out my arms and soon I was covered in lost souls, their flickering lights bolstering my spirits as I waited for Grimm to end it.

But he did nothing, a look of incomprehension on his face as he stared at the souls adorning my arms. More souls filled the air around me, forcing the Tr'lirians to retreat, creating a space where Grimm and I faced each other, each of us connected to souls but in vastly different ways.

Aether seeped into my astral form, freely given, replacing that which Grimm had torn out of me. Feeling stronger than I ever had, I reached out and touched the chain linking Grimm to the Underworld and it started to dissolve, freeing the souls trapped within it.

As each soul was released it joined the flock hovering around me and I smiled at the look of horror on Grimm's face as his form began to lose integrity.

'No. That's impossible. You can't... I'm the only one who can control them.'

'You don't control them. You use them. But I'm going to set them free.'

I started touching the souls nearest to me, their light a glorious affirmation as they were finally able to continue their journey towards rebirth.

Grimm was almost translucent now, nether swirling around him, trying to keep his form intact.

'No more souls are going to die to feed your filthy habit, Grimm. If you ever come back to the physical plane I will be waiting, and I will find a way to destroy you.'

Grimm's form was so indistinct I could barely make him out

at all, but there was no mistaking the hatred in his voice as he said, 'You will regret this, Tyler Morgan. I will see you pay for what you have done.' Then he was gone.

I kept my expression cold as I faced the Tr'lirians he left behind. 'If one more person dies on Almorthanos's orders then so does he, and you will all die alongside him. You saw what I'm capable of. Your immortality won't protect you.'

'You don't scare us,' said the one who had sneered at me before. 'You may have got the better of Grimm, but you are no match for our master.'

Damn. So much for my bluff.

They circled in closer, their wings buffeting me. But I did not have to face them alone. The lost souls swirled around me, forming a ring of aether, going faster and faster until I could no longer see the Tr'lirians. I could still hear them as they attempted to force their way through the ethereal barrier. Several minutes passed before cursing petered out and the souls slowed, many of them breaking away to float in the air in front of me.

The Tr'lirians were gone. With a smile of thanks I reached out to the soul closest to me, intending to send it and its companions on their way to rebirth, but it darted out of reach. The rest soon joined it and as a group they flew a short distance away and then stopped. One flew back, circling me twice before it joined the others.

I got the hint and flitted over to them. They took up positions around me, a silent glowing escort, as I spread my wings wide and headed back to my physical body.

They left as I slipped through the ceiling of the penthouse. After I reconnected with my body I sat up and looked over at Sam and Chris, who were seated side by side at the dining table, a laptop open in front of them.

My smile wobbled as I stood up and Sam shot to his feet. 'What's wrong?'

'Grimm was waiting for me with a whole bunch of

Almorthanos's Tr'lirians. You were right, before, when you said Almorthanos would never give up. We have to stop him, now, before more innocent people die.'

'It's already begun.' Sam gestured at the laptop, his expression bleak, and I sucked in a breath as Chris spun it around so I could see what was on the screen.

'Oh no.' I covered my mouth with one hand as I hurried to the table and watched the film clip that signalled the end of the world as I knew it.

CHAPTER 34

The footage was shaky, blurred, but there was no mistaking the terror on the faces of the people being marched into the largest pavilion at the Easton Showgrounds. Armed guards urged their captives along with hard shoves or by brandishing weapons. Men, women, children, they stumbled along, many crying, all of them casting fearful glances at the guards.

The screen went blank, remaining that way for a few seconds before words appeared; words that filled me with dread.

'He's going to kill them all if I don't hand myself in.'

Sam spun me around to face him. 'That is not happening. I lost you once. I am not standing by and watching you die a second time.'

I gazed into his hazel eyes, reading his determination to keep me alive. 'We can't stop him on our own. We need Cade and his men.'

He held me for a moment longer and then let go before scooping his keys up off the table. 'You and Bradbury should go out to Killian's compound. Talk to Cade, and tell him this has to end today.'

'What about you?'

'I've got to go down to the station, see if I can do anything to help on their end. I was just waiting for you to get back. They've called in the Special Emergency Response Team to help deal with the situation but with Tr'lirians involved that won't be enough.'

I clutched his arm. 'What? No. You can't leave. It's not safe.'

He just smiled and touched my cheek. 'Hey, how many times do I have to tell you, I'm not that easy to kill?'

'Malia doesn't want you dead. She wants you...' I couldn't say it.

'It doesn't matter what she wants. No way it is ever going to happen.'

I shook my head, sure that if he walked out the door I would never see him again, and not ready to say goodbye. 'Come with us to the compound. The cops suspended you. You don't owe them anything.'

'Tyler, you know I can't do that. This is my town, my job. I need to make sure SERT knows what they're dealing with. They're expecting terrorists, not armed assailants with wings who can zip in and out of the astral plane.'

I wrapped my arms around my middle, understanding his reasoning but still not ready to give in. 'Sam, please. If anything were to happen to you...' I swallowed heavily.

He cupped my cheek. Love shone in his eyes, and a promise I knew could never be fulfilled even if we did manage to take down Almorthanos. Not as long as I was in the wrong body. His head dipped and I averted my face so his lips brushed off my cheek.

'Be careful. If Malia gets her hands on you, she won't give you up a second time.'

His brow furrowed; Sam scanned my face.

I attempted a smile and lifted my chin. 'Meet us at the compound as soon as you can.'

For a long moment he just stared at me, eyes intent on mine, but finally he gave a nod and strode out of the apartment.

I sniffled, breathing ragged, and sidestepped Chris's attempt to hug me. 'We don't have time for this. We need to get to the compound.'

'Tyler, stop. What's wrong?'

I pointed at the laptop. 'You saw the film clip. You know what's wrong.'

His lips thinned. 'I meant what is wrong with you and Lockwood. For a woman who claims to be in love with him, you were doing a good job of avoiding him just then.'

I averted my eyes. 'It's nothing. Everything is fine. Can we please go?'

'The hell everything's fine.' He grabbed my arm. 'Tell me what's going on.'

I sighed. 'It's complicated. You wouldn't understand.'

'Try me.'

I gave another sigh. 'This isn't my body. It's Emily's.'

His eyes narrowed. 'It was Emily's body. Now it's yours.'

'I can't see it that way. It's different for you. You were dead for twenty-five years, and you didn't know the original Chris Bradbury. Emily was my cousin, and I'm the reason she's dead. I can't be in her body, kissing Sam. It's not right.'

His expression softened. 'I know it's hard. You just have to give it more time.'

I shook my head. 'No amount of time is going to make this feel right. I should be the one who is dead, not Emily. To have Sam touch me, knowing it is her body he's touching, it's obscene. I can't let that happen. I won't.'

'You can't think like that.' He took me by the shoulders and gazed deep into my eyes. 'You can have everything you ever wanted, even Lockwood,' he said with a grimace, 'if he truly is who you want to be with, but just don't give up. It will get better.'

I nodded, averting my eyes once again. I didn't want it to get better. I wanted it to stop. But that couldn't happen until after everyone I cared about was safe from Almorthanos and Malia.

I moved away from Chris and got out my phone. 'I'll call Connor and get him and Rhonda to meet us at the compound. We need to stick together.'

'Tyler?'

I finally looked at him, forcing a smile. 'Now is not the time. We have a war to win.'

He gave a slow nod, though I could tell from the stubborn set of his mouth he was not going to let this go. He remained silent for the drive out to Greenlakes. The front gate was guarded, and twice as many men as before patrolled the grounds. We were ushered into the main building without ceremony, and Killian waited for us in the same room as last time. He sat behind a large desk strewn with papers, a bandage wrapped around the top of his left arm and a large bruise decorating one side of his face. He stood up when he saw us, showing no sign his injuries pained him.

'If you have come to see if we are honouring our part of the deal, you can rest assured my men are keeping watch over your brother, his wretched mother, and your detective.'

The tightness in my chest eased and I let out a sigh. Sam wasn't alone.

I walked over to him. 'We came to help you fight Almorthanos. He needs to be stopped, now.'

'We will call upon you when we are in a position to move against him. We need time to regroup, heal, before we face our ancient enemy again.'

'We can't wait. He's taken hundreds of people hostage and he's going to kill them if I don't surrender to him before midnight tonight.'

Killian raised his eyebrows. 'A regrettable set of circumstances, certainly, but hardly our concern.'

I stared up at him, stunned he could be so callous. 'How can you say that? You promised me Cade would kill Almorthanos as soon as he was released from Demania, and it never happened. You let him get away, and if you don't help me do something about it innocent people are going to die.'

He glowered over me. 'Many of our people died that night, some of them while protecting your family. Don't you dare tell me this hostage situation is our fault.'

I put my hands up in a placating manner. 'I'm sorry, I know you lost people. I did too. Malia killed my cousin, just after I got her back.' My eyes stung and I rubbed at them to forestall tears.

'You reaped her soul. That's how this happened, isn't it?' He indicated the body I now inhabited. 'You took over her body, just like Malia did.' His lips thinned and his eyes bored into mine.

I dipped my head, breaking eye contact, guilt digging acid tipped nails into my stomach. 'It was an accident and I would give anything to go back, to stop this from happening,' I said. 'But I can't so I have to focus on what I can do, and that is making sure no one else dies because of me.'

He rubbed his chin, eyes narrowed. 'If you are so determined to save your fellow humans then perhaps you should turn yourself in. Your surrender could even prove to be useful. While Almorthanos is occupied with you, it would give us more time to prepare. Cade has returned to Angellin to rally the rest of our forces. When he gets back we will have the advantage of superior numbers and be able to pick a time and place of our choosing for the final battle.'

'Tyler surrendering will never be an option.' Chris strode forward and gripped the front of Killian's shirt. 'You hear me?'

'She might not have a choice,' Killian said, a smirk curving his lips. 'Not if she wants the hostages to live.'

Chris let Killian go and turned to me. 'Don't listen to him. There's still time for Lockwood and his buddies to save the day.'

I shook my head, knowing it was wishful thinking, and seeing from the desperation in Chris's eyes that he did too. To free the hostages, we needed Killian's help. If I couldn't convince him I would have no choice but to give Almorthanos what he wanted.

'The longer you wait the stronger Almorthanos will become,' I said. 'You've been stuck on this plane long enough to know there are many humans who will flock to join him. You need to move against him now, before he gets too strong.'

Killian shook his head. 'I will not move against him until I am ordered to do so by my clan leader. You can either sacrifice yourself to buy the freedom of the hostages or remain here until Cade is ready to lead our army and help us wipe out our enemy once and for all.'

I glared at Killian. 'I am not going to sit back and let them slaughter more innocent people. There has to be a way to stop him.'

'Good luck finding it.'

Angry words crowded my mouth but before I could let them out Rhonda and Connor were led into the room. I shook my head at them. 'It's no use. He won't help us.'

'Then it's time to leave town,' said Rhonda. 'We need to get as far away from Easton as possible.'

'I'm not leaving. Not while innocent people are in danger.'

Rhonda tossed her hair. 'Grow up, Tyler. People are always in danger. You don't owe those people anything. We need to save ourselves. Leave the fighting to Cade and the rest of his clan. If we're lucky they'll all kill each other and we can finally get our lives back.'

I glared at Rhonda. 'You can leave, but I'm staying.'

'Me too,' said Connor as he moved to my side.

Rhonda threw her hands in the air. 'You're going to get us all killed. Do you even have a plan?'

I sucked in a deep breath. 'No, but I have to do something.'

I headed for the door, with Rhonda and Connor at my back. When I reached the end of the hall I realised Chris wasn't with us. I walked back into the room and found him deep in conversation with Killian, both with their backs turned to me.

'Can it be done?' Chris's deep voice thrummed with hope.

'It is possible. I will have to converse with Cade. If he agrees, there will be a price.'

'Understood.'

'What's going on?' I asked.

Both men spun around. Before Killian could say anything, Chris strode towards me. 'It's nothing, a personal matter, one between me and my... father.' His mouth screwed up in a grimace.

I looked past him to where Killian stood watching us, a thoughtful expression on his rugged face. He gave me a slow nod and walked over to the desk and sat, seemingly dismissing us from his mind as he perused the papers scattered across it.

Chris took hold of my elbow, steering me out the door. 'We need to get hold of Lockwood, see what help the police will be in freeing those hostages.'

I let it drop for now, though surprised Chris was willing to call Cade his father. Not that he'd looked happy about naming him as such. But he was right, now was not the time to worry about family relationships.

As we walked down the hall my mobile phone rang, and I fished it out of my pocket. 'Sam?'

'SERT just radioed in; there's no one guarding the hostages. The Tr'lirians locked them in the pavilion and left.' Sam's voice was tight, troubled.

I stopped walking. 'Wait, no, that doesn't make sense. They must be watching them from the astral plane.'

'If they were, why would they let us free the hostages?'

'I don't know.' I rubbed my eyes, struggling to understand why Almorthanos would let the hostages go after all the effort to capture them, the video, and the ultimatum he'd sent me. 'Maybe something went wrong, and they had to leave.'

'The whole set up stinks. Are you still at the compound?'

'We were just about to leave.'

'Don't. It's the safest place you could be right now. I'll meet you there as soon as I can.'

'Okay,' I said, 'but don't take–'

A loud blast rocked the building and I fell to my knees, still clutching the phone to my ear. Shouts sounded in the distance quickly followed by another explosion.

'Tyler, what's wrong?' Sam asked, voice tight. 'What's happening?'

'They're here,' I said as black winged Tr'lirians flooded into the hall from every direction. One of the invaders ripped the phone out of my hand and dropped it on the ground, while another held a syringe that he jabbed in the side of my neck.

I dropped to the ground, dazed, drifting in and out of consciousness as I heard cries of pain from all around me. I fought to keep my eyes open, willing myself to stay awake, to protect Chris and the others. I couldn't hold back the darkness. It swept over me, and the last thing I heard was Sam calling my name.

$\mathcal{I}$ groaned, head pounding, thoughts sluggish as I struggled to open my eyes. They felt so heavy, as though they'd been clamped shut. I eventually opened them. Then I wished I hadn't.

Almorthanos loomed over me, satisfaction in his heavy lidded gaze. 'Ah, my sleeping beauty wakes.'

I struggled to move, to get away, fear spiking when I realised I lay on a bed, wrists and ankles tied to the corners. I twisted my body, pulling on the ropes, breath coming in gasps, barely registering the pain as the ropes bit into my skin.

'Shush, Tyler.' He caressed my cheek, deep brown eyes never leaving mine. 'Don't be frightened. I'm not going to hurt you. I'm going to make you mine, forever.'

I froze, staring up at him, horrified by the desire that lit his gaze. Never breaking eye contact, he sat beside me and I shuddered as wave after wave of his will poured into me, seeking to dominate, to mould me to a shape of his liking. I resisted, trying to turn aside, but his hands shifted to grip either side of my head, holding me immobile.

He lowered his head and pressed his lips to mine.

I clamped my mouth shut, and tried to pull my head away, but his will continued to batter at my defences even as his tongue forced its way between my lips. I was drowning, senses reeling, as he bombarded my body both physically and psychically. He was all I could feel, his desire, his overwhelming need to possess me as he plundered my mouth.

I sucked in air when he detangled his lips from mine.

'I own you,' he said.

'No.' I shook my head, marshalling my mental defences as I felt for the reaper inside me. This time I would not hesitate. I was going to rip out his soul and watch it burn. But I couldn't connect, couldn't feel that part of me anymore. My focus drifted, vision blurring as I failed again and again to summon my powers.

'What have you done to me?' I forced my eyes to stay open, using anger to keep the fog at bay.

'Just a little something to keep you relaxed. Make you more pliable. It wouldn't do to have you reap my soul while we're in the middle of getting acquainted. By the time I'm done, the drug will no longer be necessary, and you will have no thought but to serve me whenever and however I want.'

He captured my mouth again, his will pounding into me even more strongly than before. He lowered his body onto mine, settling between my thighs, his weight pushing me deeper into the mattress. Unable to escape, I acted on instinct.

I shut down, tuning out what was happening as I delved deeper into my consciousness, focusing on the beat of my heart and nothing else. My body went slack. Dimly, I felt Almorthanos shift off me. He gave me a shake but it was as if it was happening to someone else.

His will still slammed into me, but with no resistance, nothing to fight, it had little effect. All I could feel, all I could hear, was the beat of my heart as it gradually grew stronger, louder, drowning out everything else.

Minutes, hours, I have no idea how long it took before cruel fingers pried my eyes open, harsh light drilling into me. Tears formed as I fought to blink and was stopped from doing so. I wrenched my head free, coming back to myself, my immediate anxiety soothed when I realised I could still feel the steady rhythm of my heart, even if the sound of it no longer filled my ears.

I was on my side, relieved beyond measure to find I was no longer tied to the bed. I now lay on a hard surface, but that was all I had a chance to realise before someone kicked me in the stomach. Air whooshed out of my lungs and I curled into the foetal position to try to alleviate the pain.

'Leave her alone, you bastard.'

Sam's shout and the sound of a scuffle that followed it forced the last of my air to be expelled. What was he doing here? He was in town, at the showgrounds, when the Tr'lirians attacked the compound. He shouldn't be here.

Wheezing, cradling my stomach, I shuffled into a sitting position and looked for him.

Sam, a Tr'lirian holding him back, was part of a large group stationed in the middle of the compound's main room. Chris, Connor, Rhonda, Killian; they were all here, as well as many of the men and woman who had been patrolling the grounds. They were not going to be able to help me.

Two rings of black winged Tr'lirians surrounded them, one in the astral plane and one outside of it, cutting off the main route of escape for Killian and his men.

My eyes sought Sam's, still struggling to understand how he could be here. How any of this could be possible.

'The hostages were a diversion.' Weak, thready, my voice wavered as it all fell into place.

'And a fine one at that.' Almorthanos's smug voice came from behind me and I shifted around, still not willing to trust my legs on an attempt to stand.

He sat at Killian's desk, feet up on the blotter, dark eyes filled with derision. 'You ran straight to Godden, begging for help, and all I had to do was follow you.'

I wanted to close my eyes, to pretend none of this was happening and I hadn't led my enemies to Killian's compound. Instead I got to my feet and faced Almorthanos.

He swung his feet to the floor and stood. 'You and I will finish what we started later. Right now I need you to help me prepare the warmest of welcomes for Cade. I'm sure those I allowed to flee have made it to Angellin and informed him of the situation. He'll be winging his way here, but he's going to be too late.' He shifted his gaze to Killian. 'All he'll find will be bodies and my army ready to bury him alongside them.'

Almorthanos waved his hand and his men swarmed over the captives, plucking Sam, Chris, Connor and Rhonda out of the crowd, dragging them forward, forcing them to kneel in front of me. In a repeat of what happened at the cemetery, men took up positions behind them with swords held to their throats. Two others came to stand either side of me, their swords ready to plunge into my body if I made a wrong move.

I sucked in a breath, digging my nails into my palms to steady myself. Letting panic overtake me would help no one.

Before I could do anything, the double doors were flung open and Malia sauntered in, decked out in a flowing black gown made of a gossamer fabric that revealed more than it concealed. The v neckline dipped down almost to her waist while thigh-high slits exposed her legs with each step she took. She frowned as she took in the line of people kneeling on the ground in front of me.

'I gave specific orders Detective Lockwood was not to be harmed.' She glared at Almorthanos. 'I told you, he's mine.'

I'm sure my nails drew blood from my palms at the possessive tone of her voice. Sam would never be hers. I reached inside me, searching for the part that made me a reaper, hoping the drug I'd been given had worn off enough for me to reap hers and

Almorthanos's souls. Surrounded by the enemy, outnumbered, I knew I wouldn't live long after killing them, but the confusion might give Sam and the others a chance to get away.

'Relax, sister dear. Your man will not be harmed, as long as Tyler behaves herself.' He smiled at me. 'You will behave yourself, won't you, my love? You will do exactly what I ask of you, when I ask it, or those you hold most dear will be the ones to pay the price.'

'What do you want from me?' Warmth blossomed in my chest and I stamped down my relief at being able to access my power to reap, not wanting to give away my intentions.

'I want you to reap their souls.'

Eyes wide, breathing speeding up, I stared at him. 'No. Wait. You said Sam would be safe, and the others, if I did what you asked.'

'Not their souls. Theirs.' He pointed at Killian and his men. 'I want Cade to arrive and find his people dead at the hands of my pet reaper, their souls obliterated.'

My eyes found Killian. He stood tall and proud, despite the new bruises adorning his face. He hadn't given in without a fight; none of his people had. His steady gaze showed no sign of fear or defeat as he waited to see what I would do.

'Well, my love. Who dies today? Your friends or those you so foolishly put your trust in?'

I took several deep breaths, calming my nerves as I drew on my power, feeling it answer my call, filling every part of me. My heartbeat sounded loud in my ears, accompanied by a softer echo. It was an echo I recognised.

The necklace. It was destroyed when I'd freed Almorthanos from Demania, yet part of its power had remained with me, and I closed my eyes as I focused on its gentle beats. If I could merge with this last piece, add its power to mine, maybe I'd have a chance of saving them all.

A hard shove jolted me out of my trance and I stumbled, hissing as the point of a sword dug into my side.

'Now, Tyler, or they all die.'

Out of time, I put a hand on my chest, fingers splayed across my collarbone. I gave Killian a nod, hoping he understood what I was trying to tell him. He tipped his chin in response and I almost smiled.

I wanted to look over at Sam, to see his face one last time, but knew I would go to pieces if I did.

This was it. Time to make everything right. Time to join Emily.

CHAPTER 36

'Godden is here.'

The shout caused a flurry of movement.

Malia raced to Almorthanos's side, clinging to him as he barked orders. Dozens more black winged Tr'lirians flooded into the room, taking up defensive positions around their master and his sister, while others reinforced those watching Killian and his people.

I gasped, sagging in relief as Cade and a large contingent of white winged Tr'lirians appeared in the astral plane seconds before their forms became solid. Cade's eyes roamed around the room, shrewd and assessing.

'You're early, Godden. I was just about to have my pet reaper rip out the souls of your people.'

At Almorthanos's words, Cade's eyes met mine. He stared at me for a long moment, and then, surprisingly, gave a loud booming laugh. 'If you think this one would ever do your bidding, you are sadly mistaken. She's no one's pet, and from what I just observed I'd say it is your soul that is about to be reaped. Yours, and that treacherous bitch you call sister.'

Almorthanos frowned, and I felt the heavy weight of his gaze

238

as his will slammed into me with staggering force. I straightened my back and glared at him, fighting off the almost overwhelming urge to give in to his mental onslaught.

I dug deep into my senses, desperate to find the echo I'd heard earlier, searching for the necklace's heartbeat. There, softer than before, its beat stuttered, smothered by Almorthanos's will. The sound of it grew fainter and in desperation I wrapped my will around it. Hope buoyed when it began to beat louder, stronger, until it was almost a match for my own.

The urge to give in to Almorthanos's will faded and I was able to open my eyes and glare at him. 'As Cade said, I'm nobody's pet.'

Shock covered Almorthanos's features, to be quickly over-taken by rage. 'Then you are of no use to me and will die with the rest of them.'

'You have lost, Davila. It is time to end this.' Cade drew his sword and advanced on Almorthanos, not sparing a glance at those who barred his way. 'For the death of my sister and all those of Clan Godden that have died because of you, I will have justice.'

It was Almorthanos's turn to laugh, a mocking curve to his lips. 'Justice? There is no such thing, and you will never defeat me.'

'Look around. Your puny forces are no match for me and mine. Order your people to surrender and I will let them live. But you and your treacherous sister will die today, by my hand.'

Almorthanos continued to smile, and at his side Malia wore a cunning look. It didn't make sense. Cade was right, they were outnumbered. More white winged Tr'lirians appeared in the room and Almorthanos didn't even twitch. Something was wrong.

Almorthanos's smirk deepened. 'You forget, Tyler was not my only pet reaper and, unlike her, the rest will not hesitate to obey me.'

Before the rumble of his words faded, wind whipped through

the room, carrying with it dozens of dark reapers, their forms indistinct and yet no less menacing.

Almorthanos's voice boomed. 'I will tear your army to shreds and my reapers will feast on their souls. Once they have fed, every man, woman and child on this Earth, Tr'lirian or human, will be made to bow before me.' He gave a signal and his men drew swords. They advanced on Cade's men and the room filled with the clash of swords and shouts.

The reapers whirled in the air above the combatants, ripping out the souls of those without wings, heedless of the penalty they would now pay. There were so many of them, I could never hope to take them out. But I prepared to do what I could to even the odds. I called on aether, as I had on Mount Pilbeam, filling myself with it until every inch of my skin felt stretched and swollen. I prepared to discharge it, to take out Almorthanos and Malia.

But they were hidden behind a wall of reapers, their dark bodyguards forming a roiling blockade. I had no idea if my blast of aether would be strong enough to penetrate the barrier and reach those hidden behind it. I had to try.

Pain shot through my chest and I fell to my knees as my soul was wrenched from my body. Screaming, I latched on to it with both hands. When the immediate agony subsided enough for me to function I looked up to see a familiar face framed by a dark cloud.

Talaom.

The man who had killed me and sacrificed his own life so Almorthanos could have a new body, was now a reaper.

His hands reached for me, clutching my neck, and I felt a tug as he once again tried to take my soul. I scooted backwards, evading his grasping hands even as I sought to regain my scattered energy. Aether filled me and I moved to attack, but Talaom spun in the air and vanished in a swirling cloud of reapers, making it impossible to track him.

Conscious of the cries of pain and screams of agony coming

from all around me, of white feathers blowing in the swirling wind created by the reapers, I searched for Almorthanos. When I found him I readied to blast his soul to smithereens, but before I could do it he grabbed Sam, holding a knife to his throat.

I cried out and scrambled to my feet. A thin line of blood dripped down Sam's neck, staining his shirt as I ran towards them. Malia clutched her brother's arm.

'You're not to hurt him. I told you, he's mine,' she screeched.

Almorthanos barked out an order and one of his men jumped forward to grab hold of Malia and drag her back. She kicked out at the man holding her, but his long reach had him easily fending her off and he took no notice of the insults she hurled at him.

I ignored her, never taking my eyes off Almorthanos as I skidded to a halt in front of them.

'I will slit the good detective's throat, and then your family will die, along with Godden's cursed offspring.' He inclined his head to the left to where his men held Chris, Connor and Rhonda, swords still poised to end their lives.

The aether building inside me begged to be released, but it was not enough to take out both groups at once. To save Sam I would have to sacrifice Chris and the others. Malia stopped her screeching, going still as she eyed me, waiting to see what I would do.

One life or three.

I could not, would not, let Sam die.

I sent out a blast of aether that would obliterate Almorthanos's soul.

A swarm of dark reapers appeared in front of him, the aether slamming into them and shattering their souls into thousands of pieces. I flung up a hand to protect my eyes as the shards pelted me, readying another blast as soon as I could see again.

Almorthanos had disappeared, taking Sam with him.

In his place stood the Grim Reaper.

He raised his scythe, cloak billowing around his skeletal frame. 'Time to die, reaper.'

He swung the scythe at my head. I ducked, throwing my body to the left. I heard the whoosh as the curved blade sliced through the air beside me. I scrambled to my feet, dredging up as much aether as I could, knowing it was useless. I'd only been able to hold him off last time because the lost souls had helped me.

I threw what I could at him. He staggered, but quickly regained his balance and came after me again. My body trembled, exhaustion swamping me as I fought to remain standing. I would not cower before him. My hand shook as I pointed at him, ready to empty myself with one last blast.

Bright light flashed between us, blinding me. When I could see again he was on his knees, staring at the shimmering pool of light emitting from the soul that floated in the air between us.

Sarah.

She shone so brightly; her aura enhanced by the light of thousands of souls. At her command they reached out to form a ring around the Grim Reaper, trapping him. She turned to me.

'We can't hold him for long. You need to act fast if you are to free him.'

I shook my head. 'Free him? I don't understand.'

'You have to kill Jonathon Grimm; only then can the Grim Reaper be free.'

I rubbed at my temples. 'They're the same person. You can't kill the Grim Reaper. And how are you here? I thought you were trapped in the Underworld forever.'

'When you ripped out the anchor linking him to the souls he fed from you created a tear in the veil between the Underworld and this one. It allowed us to escape, but the nether is already mending it. You must kill Grimm before it closes or there'll never be another chance to release the Grim Reaper from Almorthanos's influence.'

His influence?

Could it be?

The Grim Reaper was a force of nature, elemental, and Chris had once told me he'd only gained sentience after prolonged contact with Almorthanos via the link between Demania and the Underworld. Was it more than that? Had thousands of years of being poisoned by Almorthanos's will created a whole new psyche, one that had taken over the Grim Reaper, perverting his nature?

'See what we see,' said Sarah. A thread of light stretched out from the shimmering mass around her and touched my face, gossamer fingers stroking my eyelids closed. When I opened them I looked at the Grim Reaper.

At first he didn't look any different, a terrifying, abnormally tall skeletal creature encased in a hooded cloak that made black look pale. Then I saw it; a seething pool of darkness in his solar plexus, oozing with menace. The longer I looked at it, the sicker I felt, just as I had when I'd been in the chasm housing the portal to Demania.

Almorthanos's taint. Like a cancerous growth, it was eating away at the Grim Reaper. How was I supposed to free him from something like that?

I looked to Sarah for guidance and the thread of light linking me to her shifted to my chest, thickening, flooding my body with aether.

'Are you ready?' Sarah asked.

'No,' I said, but gave a quick nod.

People were dying, the lure of their souls singing to me, calling for me to release them. If I couldn't do this, free the Grim Reaper, many more would die. I exhaled sharply and slipped out of my body, feeling the welcoming touch of the souls joined with Sarah as my wings unfurled and my astral form passed through their light and entered the circle.

The Grim Reaper, held in place by undulating ribbons of light, his nether mist kept at bay by a wall of souls, growled when he saw me. It was a low growl filled with such hatred my astral form shivered. I steeled myself for what I had to do.

I pushed aside the cloak, exposing the bones of his rib cage, and placed my hands on top of the darkness. At my touch it began to churn, throwing off a nauseating stench that set me dry retching, but I didn't let go. Instead I used the aether the souls were feeding me and poured it into the darkness, threading it through the pulsating mass.

My revulsion grew as the darkness fought the light's invasion. It felt alive beneath my hands, malignant, aware of what I was trying to do. Images bombarded me, of Sam with his throat slit, Chris with a sword sticking out of his chest, Rhonda cradling Connor's severed head. I whimpered as increasingly violent images played in front of my eyes, but instead of distracting me from my purpose they strengthened my resolve. Any one of those horrible images could come true if I didn't complete my task.

The flood of pictures stopped, and I saw the darkness weakening as the light overtook it. Bit by bit, the rest of the taint was washed away, leaving a shining ball of light in the Grim Reaper's core. I dropped my hands, and gazed under the hood covering his face, wondering if what the souls and I had done would be enough.

Light blazed in the eye sockets of his skeletal face as he stared back at me. He straightened, the ribbons of light holding him fading away as he lifted his scythe. He swiped the scythe in the air above my head and the clamour around us stilled instantly.

A rush of wind swept through the room and when I spun around I saw it was sweeping up all the dark reapers, many of them hissing as they struggled to break free. The wind was relentless, blowing fit to outshine a hurricane as it pulled them along in its wake, twisting and churning the reapers into a funnel shape. The Grim Reaper swung his scythe once more and the funnel of reapers shot through the roof, and were swiftly followed by the souls that had lent me their strength.

Sarah floated in front of me, a beautiful smile on her face, with the Grim Reaper an impassive statue at her side.

'You did it. I knew you could.' She embraced me, hugging me so tightly I would have been bruised if I wasn't in astral form. I hugged her back just as tightly.

When we finally let go of each other the Grim Reaper tapped his scythe on her shoulder and her smile grew even more beautiful as the light of her soul became incandescent. She was being sent on to rebirth, no longer doomed to an eternity trapped in the Underworld. I sobbed, my tears crashing to the floor as I said goodbye to my best friend for the very last time.

Once she was gone from sight the Grim Reaper inclined his head. Then he too faded away and the world crashed back into focus.

I returned to my body and stood, tears continuing to fall as I surveyed the broken and bloodied bodies that littered the room. So many dead, dozens more injured. It was unfathomable the amount of carnage spread out before me.

In the centre of it all stood Cade and Almorthanos, swords drawn, both of them staring at me, one with an expression of awe and the other one of hatred. That all changed in an instant as Almorthanos took advantage of his opponent's distraction to swing his sword, aiming for Cade's wings.

Cade spun lightly, his own sword knocking Almorthanos's aside and then continuing on to bury itself in his enemy's shoulder.

Almorthanos dropped his sword, a look of disbelief crossing his face as he looked at the gash the sword had opened, blood seeping from the wound. He sank to his knees, hand closing over the wound, grimacing in pain.

He looked up at Cade. 'I surrender. Spare me, and I swear to trouble you no more.'

Cade shook his head. 'No surrender, no mercy. Not for the

likes of you.' He swung his sword once more and this time it cut into Almorthanos's neck.

A shrill scream rent the air as Malia launched herself at Cade. He spun to face her, sword at the ready, and her scream cut off in a gurgle as she impaled herself on its point.

I had few precious seconds to comprehend what had just happened before the urge to reap their souls hit. I took several deep breaths, my entire body trembling as I stepped towards them. I averted my eyes from the ruin above Almorthanos's shoulders, concentrating my vision on his chest as I reached out and called his soul. It hovered in the air in front of me but I did not want to touch it, not yet.

Beside me, Cade had pulled his sword free of Malia's body and was lowering her to the floor beside her brother. Her breath came in slow gasps as her life leached out of her. I called forth her soul and she went mercifully still as it floated over to join her brother's. Only when they were together did I send them on their way.

A collective sigh filled the room and, duty done, I turned to search those still standing for a familiar face.

My knees buckled when I saw him.

CHAPTER 37

'Sam.'

I shook all over, relief making me dizzy. I wanted to run to him but wasn't sure my legs would hold me up.

He smiled and my paralysis fled. I flew across the room and skidded to a halt just in front of him. My eyes and hands coursed over his body, searching for injuries, an explanation for the dark blood that coated the front of his shirt.

'Are you hurt? Oh my God, is this your blood?' My breathing sped up as my hands dived under his shirt.

'Hey, it's okay.' He took my hands in his, staring deep into my eyes. 'I'm fine. We're all fine.'

He inclined his head to the left and I looked to where Connor was helping Rhonda to her feet. Other than a few scrapes and looking wild around the eyes, they both appeared to be uninjured.

I frowned. 'Where's Chris?'

'Talking to Cade and Killian.'

I looked behind me and saw Chris deep in conversation with both men, his body tense. He looked over at me, a resigned smile lighting his face. He looked back to Cade and nodded once before striding over to join us.

Around the room, a group of Cade's men were herding those of the enemy that had survived the clash into the middle. Many of them were injured and had to be helped by their brethren, all of them avoiding looking at their slain leader and his sister. When they were all together Cade approached them, sword still dripping with Almorthanos and Malia's blood.

'Hear me, Davilian scum. Relinquish your wings and remain on this plane for the rest of your mortal existence or die here and now. But for those who choose to live, if any of you takes up arms against a member of Clan Godden after this day I will hunt every one of you down and Davila will be no more. What say you?'

Mutters arose from the group facing him but it wasn't really a choice. One by one they pledged to obey Cade's commands, and those about to give up their immortality were sent to wait near Killian.

I winced to think of them having to stand still while their wings were torn from their backs.

'I can't watch this,' I said, turning to Sam. 'Can we leave?'

I wanted to spend a few moments with Sam and the others, time untainted by death and destruction, before I said goodbye. Those I loved were now safe, there was no reason to linger, and it was time for Emily's parents to bury their daughter. I would return to the Underworld, complete my duty as reaper, and one day, I hoped, the Grim Reaper would grant me the release of rebirth.

Sam gave my shoulders a squeeze. 'I'm not too keen on sticking around either.'

'We can't go yet,' said Chris. 'We need to wait a little longer.'

I exhaled slowly and shook my head. 'I can't do this, Chris.'

He gave me a gentle smile. 'It will be fine, I promise. I'll take you to another room.'

I gave in with a sigh and soon we were all seated in a cosy lounge on the other side of the house. Still not far enough away to silence the screams completely, but with the door closed, it was dampened enough that the tight band around my chest eased.

'Hey,' said Sam, brow furrowed as he kneeled in front of me, my hands clasped in his. 'It's going to be okay. It's over. Almorthanos and his crazy sister are dead, and whatever you did to the Grim Reaper seemed to do the trick.'

'What did you do?' Connor asked. 'All we could see was a big ball of light surrounding the two of you.'

I shrugged. 'I killed Jonathan Grimm. Well, the essence of him, and that returned the Grim Reaper to his natural state.' I explained how he'd been infected by Almorthanos's presence, warping his purpose. 'Now he's back to being an impartial harbinger of death.'

Rhonda's eyes widened. 'So does that mean you're off the hook? You were tricked into being a reaper. You deserve a chance at a normal life.'

I shook my head. 'I'm still a reaper.' I could feel it, deep inside me, a gentle urge to ease the suffering of the dying. 'But I don't mind. Someone has to do it. Why not me?'

'I guess having a reaper for a girlfriend won't be so bad.' Sam wore a crooked smile. 'You can give me the heads up on any homicides, right? Help me catch the bad guys.'

Here it was. Time to come clean.

'I won't be able to do that, Sam.' Tears filled my eyes. 'I won't be here.'

'Where are you going to be?' His eyes narrowed and he released my hands and stood. 'Tyler, what are you planning?'

'She plans on dying. Or so she thinks,' said Chris, coming to stand shoulder to shoulder with Sam. 'But I've got a better idea.'

'Will someone tell me what the hell is going on?' Sam looked over at Chris, back rigid.

'Tyler refuses to accept she has a right to live, because the body her soul currently inhabits isn't the one she was born with. She's planning on skipping out, letting Emily's body die and remaining in astral form until she's filled her soul quota.' He fixed me with a hard blue stare. 'That is your plan, right?'

I stood, hating to see the dawning pain in Sam's eyes, but refusing to shy away from this. 'I can't live in this body. I won't. I love you, Sam, more than I ever thought possible to love someone, but I can't live a lie. This is not my body and I would destroy myself with hate and guilt if I were to stay in it.'

Sam's jaw clenched and he shook his head. 'I'm not ready to lose you. Not by a long shot.'

'You don't have to. I hope,' said a new voice.

Killian entered the room carrying a body wrapped in a heavy sheet. 'If Chris is right, Tyler can have her old body back.'

'What?' My head spun as I looked from Chris and back to the wrapped body in Killian's arms. My body. Tiny electric shocks ran through me as I stared at it, throat working hard to produce saliva as I remembered the condition it had been in when I'd left it.

Broken, charred, disfigured.

Hope warred with fear inside me. Could this really work?

'It's worth a try,' said Chris, answering my unspoken thought. 'You were planning on skipping out on us anyway. What have you got to lose?'

Hands shaking, trembling all over, I sat back in the chair.

Sam resumed his position in front of me. 'Bradbury's right. You've got nothing to lose and everything to gain.'

I smiled at him and caressed his cheeks with both hands, wiping away the tears that he shed unashamedly. I nodded once. Without taking my eyes off his, I slipped out of Emily's body for the last time.

The energy that had been coursing through my physical body with the nearness of my remains hit me tenfold now I was in astral form. My silver wings shimmered with it. I gasped, back arching as I hovered in the air.

Gradually the sensation subsided enough for me to be able to move and carefully manoeuvre myself until I hovered directly above my shrouded remains. I reached out and touched it just below the head, closing my eyes as I waited to be drawn back into my body.

Power thrummed through me and I cried out as the whirlwind swept me along, slamming me back into my body. I screamed, heels drumming the carpet as the pain of my injuries tore through me. Endless torment followed as every limb felt as if it was being shredded, skin tearing, blood gushing from the wounds. Then a wave of pure light washed over me, bringing peace in its wake.

I tried to open my eyes, blinking in confusion when they were barred by cloth.

Hands touched me, gently peeling back the sheet to clear my face and I looked into Sam's beautiful eyes.

His tears wet my cheeks when he leaned in and pressed a gentle kiss to my forehead.

'Oh my God, it really worked!' I heard Rhonda gasp. I turned my head and saw she was also crying, the back of one hand pressed to her mouth. Connor stood beside her, half holding her up, cheeks also wet.

My eyes found Chris. He wasn't crying. He looked pleased, though sad, and at first I couldn't understand why. Then it hit me.

He'd given me a second chance, allowing me to live my life... with Sam.

Sam unwound the sheet and helped me stand, wrapping his arm around my waist and holding me close. Together we faced Chris.

'Thank you,' I said. 'This means everything to me.' I wanted to go to him, hug him, but was scared it would only make things worse. He was hurting, and I wasn't the only one to see it.

'Bradbury... Chris. You did good,' said Sam, his hold on me tightening. I got the feeling it would be a long time coming before he would let go of me, and I didn't mind one bit.

'What now?' Connor asked, wiping at his eyes.

I smiled at him, amazed at how easily it came despite the tears filling my eyes. 'Now we take Emily home.'

Cade and Killian could sort out the mess here at the compound, but my cousin deserved better. So did her parents. They would finally be able to say goodbye to their beloved daughter. I would forever miss Emily's bubbly spirit, and regret the part I had played in her death, but knowing she had been given a chance to live again eased the pain somewhat.

As for me, I was still a reaper.

With the size of my soul quota that wouldn't change for a long time to come, maybe not even in this lifetime, but I truly didn't mind. I had a job to do, and I would take pride in easing the passing of those who died, ushering them on to their next life.

Everyone deserved a second chance.

Even me.

ACKNOWLEDGMENTS

Writing Winged Reaper and getting it published, and now republished, has been a roller coaster of a ride, and it would never have happened without the support of my family and friends.

Hugs and kisses to Mum, Grant and my beautiful children, for always being my number one support team. I am also grateful to Donna, Jennifer and Jael, who have assured me that no matter what I write, it is going to be an awesome read. A writer can never have enough people who believe in them so strongly.

Sue-Ellen Pashley is not only a fabulous writer, she is a wonderful friend who is always ready to beta read for me and gives valuable insight that helps my stories shine. Kris Sheather went above and beyond to find Winged Reaper a home, while Helen Goltz once again has let Tyler spread her wings three years later. You ladies rock!

I also would like to give a shout out to my fellow Year of the Edit Online participants for helping me recraft the opening. Your assistance was invaluable.

Finally, thank you to all the readers who have embraced Tyler and have been eagerly waiting to find out what happens to her next. Thanks for sticking with me.

ABOUT THE AUTHOR

Shelley Russell Nolan is an avid reader who began writing her own stories at sixteen. Her first completed manuscript featured brain eating aliens and a butt kicking teenage heroine. Since then she has spent her time creating fantasy worlds where death is only the beginning and even freaks can fall in love.

The first two books in her debut adult urban fantasy series, *Lost Reaper* and *Winged Reaper*, were published by Atlas Productions in 2016, with *Silver Reaper* published in 2017 to complete the series. 2018 saw the release of her *Arcane Awakenings Novella Series*, and Odyssey Books will be publishing the first book in a new post-apocalyptic series in 2019.

Born in New Zealand, moving to Australia with her family when she was seven, Shelley currently lives in Central Queensland, Australia, with her husband and two young children. They share their home with two wrecking ball kitties, a deformed budgerigar and two dogs that are fairly normal as dogs go.

Shelley loves to hear from her readers so feel free to contact her on Facebook or leave a review on Amazon or Goodreads or on her website - shelleyrussellnolan.com